This was not a period that Vorselus ever desired to recollect. The unimaginable terror of that hideous night, when creatures of the ultimate darkness stalked abroad! He must forevermore flinch from the ghastliness of the memory. These were the true children of the primordial Rhexellites, the most debased and despised specimens that still crept through burrows and caverns beneath the lands smiled upon by the Gods. Down there they festered, as he could testify in astounding numbers. He doubted not that they had been released or liberated in some fashion, for their murderous appearance at that juncture could not, he later reasoned, be the work of happenstance. Fast it occurred, terribly fast: the irruption from the keep, then the temple, and from the common folk's quarter, from which some of the less polluted subjects of dead Gorgras ran for their lives, accompanied by those Peoki—stationed only that afternoon among the little cubic houses—who were sober enough to seek safety. Came a torrent of mindless bestiality! Naked they clawed toward the men, with hairless, corpse-white bodies, lean and hungry looking, with repulsive spidery limbs sporting curved claws on the wiry fingers of their misshapen paws. Below their low-domed pates gleamed monstrous eyes, big as saucers, glared faces of pitiless hate with noseless nostrils, mere holes in those evil masks, and the filthy red mouths filled with long needle-like fangs.

Wonder and terror await when you commence *The Journey through the Black Book.*

THE JOURNEY THROUGH THE BLACK BOOK

By Jeffery Scott Sims

Published by Dyrezan Press
Copyright © 2022 by Jeffery Scott Sims
ISBN: 978-0-9899322-5-7

Chapters

I. VORCHEK'S PERUSAL

So Vorchek read the book, and as he did so a strange feverishness overcame him, a sensation of perspiring, tingling, tormenting anticipation that threatened to master his reason and make of him a willing tool of the book's power. That it possessed a power unearthly he doubted not, for much had been written with authority concerning the ancient tome, much more dubiously whispered by knowing confidants, and from his perusal of the first page that volume breathed an aura of peculiar wisdom arcane and uncanny. The author, Vorchek admitted, had known of what he wrote, had acquired expertise in matters wonderful and dire, had used his knowledge and experience to peer into and explore the hitherto unlighted halls of the most frightful and marvelous mysteries that mankind ever imagined.

But three months before, on a typical morning at the small Phoenix college where he precariously retained a post, had Professor Anton Vorchek received the package. His secretary of sorts, Theresa Delaney, a charming, lovely young girl with a high fashion sense and a cavalier attitude, had breezed into his office, a forsaken cubbyhole littered with papers and heaped with books; barged in unannounced as always to carelessly deposit with a crash atop his cluttered desk the hefty oblong wrapped in brown paper. "This just came," she said, with a slightly hurt air in her pretty voice suggesting that she had undergone wearisome, heroic endeavors to bring him a dreadful burden. She threw herself down into the other reclining chair, propped her feet on the desk (dislodging a cascading sheaf of anthropological treatise with her sleek boots as she did so), smoothed her striking red dress, lit a cigarette and sighed. "It's for you," she added.

"I surmised that," said Vorchek. "Good morning, Miss Delaney." He spoke in a well-modulated, precise, somewhat accented voice harboring elements of the Old World, elements illuminated by much else about and around him. He was a mature man, a little past the prime, with old-fashioned habits, formal attire rather out of place these days in a college setting, a strong hawk face partly concealed by

1

a short, manicured beard, his dark hair tending to iron-gray at the temples. His small office reeked of the old and the dusty and the aroma of pipe tobacco. Out of place he might be in his world, yet in this den it was Theresa, with her self-absorbed youth and her callow indifference and her bold colors, who incongruously stood out.

Vorchek put aside his handful of notes, fastidiously adjusted his quiet tie and took possession of the package. "Can this be," he mused, "that for which I have been waiting?" He clipped the binding string and tape with scissors, then sliced through the crackling layers. With this delicate task carefully performed he reached within and drew out the contents.

"Oh," Theresa groaned, "it's another old book." This it was, rather like numerous others she had seen in his hands or stocked in his ever swelling collection, but from the professor's delicate handling even she could deduce that this must be something special. As Theresa had absolutely nothing better to do at the moment, she chose to devote her casual attention to the unveiled object, and to her companion's comments.

"Not just another," he informed her eagerly, without taking his eyes from the thing. He fumbled in a suit pocket for his thick spectacles, donned them. "This, my dear, is something unique, a true prize for any scholar, a magnificent acquisition for one such as myself, who dabbles in the weirder aspects of reality. For years I have been constrained, by the cruel ravages of time and the crueler limitations imposed by time-honored secrecy, to read mere scraps of this work, fragments of chapters buried in archives and tattered pages hidden away within other documents, tantalizing bits and pieces stumbled upon by chance or rumor. Now at last I have, to further my studies, a major surviving portion, intact throughout, of the fabled *Black Book* of Jacob Bleek."

Theresa snorted, almost a laugh. To Vorchek's horror she reached out and tapped the volume with a booted toe, saying, "It's not even the whole thing? What a rip-off. Still, Professor, it looks heap plenty as it is." Indeed, it was a very big book, perhaps ten by fourteen inches, thick, massive as she knew, bound in dense, crumbling leather.

"It is plenty," Vorchek replied, jerking it away from her questing foot, "in fact, the culmination of a life's dream. This book constitutes the Holy Grail of what are called the occult sciences, the ultimate work of practical magic, the most valued, the most feared of its kind. Now I own it by right."

"How did you get it?"

Vorchek shifted uncomfortably in his seat, laid down the book, shot her a covert glance. "That is neither here nor there," he said uneasily. "I became aware of its existence, I negotiated with the possessor, we agreed to terms. Those were dear enough, I reckon. So, it is mine, to have and to hold, to use as I see fit. I expect much from the mighty mind of Bleek."

Theresa shrugged. "Who is he, anyway?"

"One of the foremost scholars of human history," declared the professor. "A mere man, he, who lived long ago in dark times, yet a man with an unbounded brain and a quenchless thirst for knowledge. He sought all the wisdom and power of the Gods—so it has been written by both worshipful acolytes and envious detractors—devoting the majority of an exceedingly long life to acquiring knowledge from everywhere in the world and throughout the ages. Think of him, if you will, as an early scientist of great repute. His contemporaries called him a sorcerer."

"Sounds like bunk, Professor," Theresa sniffed, "more stupid than scary, if you ask me."

"I did not," Vorchek huffed. "I tell you, Miss Delaney, that Bleek's work opens doors unto vistas unseen by the common herd. That has ever generated fear among fools. Unlike so much of the popular rubbish peddled under the heading of the occult, the *Black Book* is the genuine article. There are too many scholarly accounts attesting to its awesome utility. Perhaps, I grant you, that I still harbor doubts—as an honest researcher I must—but I shall act immediately to confirm or deny the averred possibilities."

He rose, placed his hand solemnly on the book. "First I must read all, read and analyze, calculate and cross-check the data received. Now I study. Therefore, my dear, at this time you may get out, go away, leave me alone until I call for you again."

With a wry grin Theresa got up lazily, saying, "Standard procedure. Have fun, Professor."

And for three months Professor Anton Vorchek read the book of Jacob Bleek, expending almost every waking minute in obsessive, squint-eyed perusal. His relations with the college were such that his normal work-load made few demands on his time, a routine largely determined by himself. During this period he skimped on teaching to the extent compatible with continued employment. He read, took notes, compared those to previous notes derived from other sources, followed up minor references in the ancient text with rounds of delving into archives of curious lore. As he sojourned with the book

3

he learned, became convinced that it did indeed offer incredible insights into the nature of the universe, revealing frightful secrets only guessed at by others, providing intellectual mechanisms for manipulating that mysterious knowledge, methods often abhorred and shunned by later, lesser commentators.

Unquestionably Bleek had been a practical wizard, his potent mind dedicated to unlocking those secrets underlying conventional nature and using them to uncover even more, the mysteries beyond the mysteries. Much of the text consisted of long series of spells, complex formulae which acted to release the magical potential underlying the drab material world and focus the unleashed power toward obtaining concrete ends. These ends seemed typically odd, often morbid, occasionally insane, yet in the final analysis the intent was ever to seek knowledge, and through knowledge, power. The antique author wrote little of himself, but what Vorchek deduced of the man from his interests led the earnest reader to believe that Bleek had been cold, determined, possibly dangerous. Truly he sought to make of himself a god, to wrest every last secret from the vast cosmos and make the whole eternal structure serve him.

Bleek, in his day, plumbed the farthest gulfs of matter and light and entity, tore aside the veils that shield men from the warped realities of distant space and time. He claimed to step across the planes of existence into other dimensions, exploring worlds within worlds, emerging at designated locations, where ever they might lie in the natural continuum. So too he outlined, in amazing detail, the methodology by which he had broken the bitter bonds of time, smashing those cruel barriers that had imprisoned man since the dawn of humanity. He frankly wrote of astounding journeys into the sweeping epochs of past and future, beholding with alien eyes the great deeds in life of the long dead, observing with crystalline curiosity the bold endeavors of the marvelous races still to come in centuries and millennia yet unwritten by nature.

This aspect of Bleek's hoary research, the recurrent theme of unlimited travel through time, most excited Professor Vorchek. It spoke not only to his magnificent intellect, but to his deepest desires. All his life, as he trudged the grayish annual road allotted to him by biology and fate, he had yearned to break free of that high-walled path, to embark upon exotic and fanciful detours into other ages. The future, to be sure, tantalized him with its infinite possibilities— and did not Bleek hint, more than hint, at those dramatic glories in the countless ages to come?—yet Vorchek, the anthropologist at heart, the sifter of yellowed documents, the fondler of broken implements and discolored bones, craved most of all the lore of the past, the once living worlds of yesteryear, the familiar minds of the great thinkers who had gone before, the welcoming hands of the olden heroes now but dust. He wished to visit those worlds, to travel those lands, to greet as an equal those mighty men of past renown. Bleek claimed to know how to do this, claimed to have often done it; indeed, stated that the majority of his elder knowledge had been gained in such a manner.

According to Jacob Bleek, the man of science who lived in an age when there was no science, time was no more than a kind of thin but opaque film that overlay the cosmic buildings blocks of matter and energy. As that worthy poetically phrased it,

> All our days in their ranks be but a shroud
> So light, though darkly obscuring the source
> Of destiny over firma and force
> Yet dispersed as easily as a cloud.

Having stated the proposition, he went on to argue for the methods best utilized to smash the barriers of time. He described, with uncanny conviction, the means of raising and speaking with the dead or those still unborn, brusquely stating that these techniques, popular among his lesser associates, were unfortunately limited, to be disregarded by the adventurous pioneer of magical acumen. Bleek favored, indeed devoted an entire massive chapter to, the amazing method of casting oneself into far ages, of entering those worlds and dwelling as a natural inhabitant.

He included a formula, an intricate composition of polysyllabic intonations seemingly disconnected from anything like human speech, which in coordination with peculiar elements and the focusing of freakishly arcane power could propel a man through time, landing him in his temporal destination "both spirit and corpus." This formula smacked more of artistic expression than the bedrock grounding in reason that Vorchek preferred, although he noted with a little thrill of glee that its textual substance incorporated surprisingly advanced mathematical equations, in forms that heavy research indicated were much more than uneducated strings of random numbers or concepts. The math, as it happened, some of which appeared to transcend the efforts of the professor's contemporaries, convinced him that the time travel spell (for such it must be deemed, despite the odd sound of that phrase) was meant as a serious key to unlocking the door to eternity.

Bleek could be maddeningly imprecise at times, however. Though he delineated the spell with absolute clarity, laying out a perfect catalogue of the necessary materials and readily identifying the source of power that would energize words and substance, the actual physical and mental consequences of stepping from one time plane to another eluded the greedy reader. Bleek wrote with grandiloquence of the boons bestowed, airily referring to his own voyages, only with frustrating lapses of detail, sufficiently so that Vorchek suspected lacunae in the text. That unnerved him, left him unsettled when he most needed certainty; only the craving to partake of such an expedition drove him on to read, to study, to plan.

Professor Vorchek concluded, as he felt he must, that fate or the Gods (of whom Bleek wrote with commingled reverence and boldness) had ordained that this book come to him, and that the secret of time travel be laid out before his eager eyes. Did not Bleek state that only one power source could fuel the spell? Did he not identify it as none other than the Cross of Xenophor, that archaic talisman fashioned—so wrote the earliest known practitioners of sorcery in Egypt and Sumer—before the dawn of recorded history, fabricated, so it had been intimated through the centuries, by the omnipotent and omniscient mind of Great Xenophor, Lord of All Things, the Creator and the Destroyer; the God over all the Gods, real or imagined, praised or feared? Was not Professor Anton Vorchek, of this place and this time on Earth, the sole possessor of the Cross?

Yes, indeed. Call it fate, call it predestination, call it the coincidence rendering all others trivial and meaningless, but he possessed the Cross, had acquired it through furtive means (as had the book come to him), the result of prior research into the occult. Of course he had heard of the Cross, knew what could be known of its history since the reigns of the pharaohs and the Caesars, was aware of certain insidious claims made for it, and when unusual opportunity had dropped it into his lap, he had run with the prize. Having gotten it he hoarded it, a proud owner, pleased as Punch, scarcely knowing what to make of the thing. Now he knew. Somehow all the steps of his life had led him to this moment.

As it had been written, so it would be done. The hypothesis must be put to the test; trial must be made. Vorchek would undertake his grand journey into the unknown, through the pages of the *Black Book* of Jacob Bleek. Having decided that, there remained for him only the choosing of a destination. Where should he go in time? For purposes of the test, any time would do; the spell granted him ability to soar into past and future with equal agility. He reckoned that only the past would serve. That suited his inclinations, while feeding his scientific requirements. Travel into the future would plunge him into realms of total mystery, eras perhaps incomprehensible to a man of his time, and as a scholar he feared most of all the problematic results of incomprehension. He could not discern, from Bleek's writings, whether he could carry away with him any tangible effects of such a journey. Might he doubt himself in retrospect, surmise his wild future progression a dream, an inner vision only, a vision untestable? The past accorded him equal delights, and more chance of testability. He could enter the recent past, for example, seek facts unknown to him prior to the trip, check them for accuracy upon his return. That would certainly prove the case, yet too tame a scheme, though, to tempt him. Better, he reasoned, to explore an historical epoch of renown, one in which he excelled, where *in situ* discoveries could be made, their legitimacy corroborated by research after his return.

That should do it—that the best way, logic assured him—but still it was not enough. If he must accept the hazard, then Vorchek demanded benefits commensurate with the risk. Bleek wrote of lost worlds of the past, great kingdoms and peoples thriving before history as presently understood by conventional historians. If the professor dared hurl himself through the years, then he must grant himself the promise of great tidings, knowledge of worth far beyond that available to his fellows. He wished to see with his waking, material eyes those fabulous realms whose descriptions sounded like the raving fancies of a madman.

Most of all Professor Vorchek wanted to accomplish a journey to the legendary city of Dyrezan. Could he believe that it had ever existed? No authoritative history mentioned the place, nor even hinted at its reality. Antique scholars recorded rumors of it, as of a land already so old and forgotten that it had largely faded from the collective memory of man. Self-proclaimed wizards and alchemists of a later period wrote of it as myth, that kingdom of the dawn where magic once ruled, wielded surely by a mighty race of magicians who in their heyday lorded over the Earth. Jacob Bleek wrote smugly of his calls on those giants of mind and power. Could Vorchek follow Bleek's lead? If he could go there, learn of its ways, pinpoint its geographical location, then on his return he could definitely helm an archeological mission to the site, find the objective proofs he would ultimately require.

During those three months of closeted study in his college office Vorchek pondered, inwardly debated, at last resolved. Came a day when he stood in that same office and outlined his proposition to his seated audience, an audience of two: Theresa Delaney, his annoyingly diffident but loyal assistant, and his current finest graduate student, a dedicated young gentleman and budding scholar named Philip Matthews. Vorchek had introduced the two, saying, "Mr. Matthews knows of my work, the esoteric subjects that I pursue, the curious terrain I have staked out as my specialty. He approves, expresses the desire to know more. He hopes for, I take it, what is termed the 'inside track.' I am amenable. I need such an associate now." Philip, a tall, slender, well muscled and agreeable youth, laughed disarmingly, said, "I want in on the ground floor of something big. The professor talks a good game, if he can deliver. I'm willing to find out for myself."

Vorchek succinctly laid out his scientific agenda: "I undertake, by utilizing the wisdom contained within this book of Jacob Bleek, to carry out an experiment involving a journey through time, into the incredibly remote past. With his calculations as my guide I will venture to the mythical city of Dyrezan, there to observe and record the reputed splendors and wonders of that land and epoch. I intend a safe return to this our age, taking then the professional steps necessary to verify what has gone before. With evidence, with proofs, I will have not only enjoyed a fantastic adventure, but will have formally rewritten the history of the human race as currently known. That, you must admit, would constitute a grand achievement.

"I must have companions. There may be work to be done on the other side which I might not be able to see through myself. Miss Delaney, my devoted associate and friend, is ever reliable, and if I may say so a good sport to boot. Of course I invite her to join me in the crowning event of my career." (Theresa rolled her eyes at Philip, but smiled and said, "Thank you, Professor. It's an honor.") "Mr. Matthews, your strength and your keen mind may both serve me." (Philip nodded, staring blankly, said, "I'll do my best.") "It goes without elaboration, surely, that also I need witnesses, others who may experience as do I, so there can be no possibility of concluding that all to transpire be merely subjective vision. We shall cross over together, live together, observe together, record together, as a unified team. That is the right way. Three is the proper number. Three we

8

shall be, shoulder to shoulder throughout."

Necessarily Vorchek had prepared them before-time with snippets of information and suggestive speculation, so that only the details of what he told them now were fresh. Still, what he presented at this juncture stunned them both. When he finished his summary of intentions, they hesitated long before responding.

Then Philip leaped up, forcing a chuckle as he ran strong fingers nervously through his wiry black hair, blurted, "I'm with you, sir, but . . . it's not possible. You're pulling my leg. It can't be. Things like this just don't happen."

Theresa laughed out loud, with a toss of her long blonde hair, ran a long, lacquered nail down her nose as she replied to his outburst, "You wouldn't say that if you knew the professor as well as I do. When he says something, he means it, and the stranger it sounds, the more serious he is. If anybody can make it happen, bub, then he can. I guess this is the real deal. Count me in, Professor. As for you, Phil, make up your mind. For better or for worse, it's a straight offer."

II. THE EXPERIMENT OF THE BLACK BOOK

They came together again on the designated day at the house of Vorchek. That was an old structure, a former ranch house, a tired survival from the age of the pioneers, a wooden, two-story peaked affair with a wide porch, lots of windows, and a deep basement of crumbling red brick. It sat atop a lonely, barren hill far out of town, approachable only by a poorly maintained gravel road, surrounded only by desert scrub. Here, when not at the college, Anton Vorchek spent most of his time, for he had created within a milieu pleasing to himself, a world filled with past things, old-fashioned furnishings jostling with the bizarre objects in his scattered collection of ancient or prehistoric oddities drawn from years of research exploits. Here he maintained his study, awash with papers and books, in the old breakfast room, by the creaky circular staircase ascending to the bedrooms upstairs. In the old living room, a big space, he kept the bulk—though scarcely all—of his personal library, row on row of crammed shelves masking the walls, each volume meticulously catalogued, each one dedicated to matters scientific, historic, unplaceable or downright peculiar. On the Victorian mantle over the disused fireplace two ugly Bantu ju-ju dolls hemmed in another rank of texts dealing with obscure subjects, several of which Vorchek had taken down for the task at hand. A nearby flight of stairs, with a new rubber-sealed door guarding against the ever-present desert dust, descended into the basement, Vorchek's sanctum, his private laboratory. Here he carried out his real work. There were more books, plenty of metal file cabinets for papers, shelves holding tools and electrical instruments and stoppered bottles of useful chemicals. Cheap wooden or aluminum tables covered with cheap plastic sheets bore items of recent interest to him, such as the shards of an unpleasantly stained Anasazi clay pot chased with morbid reliefs and bearing faint traces of a script that he fully intended to decipher one of these days, after the present business.

The trio sat in the small den, the only area on the first floor given over to comfort, sipping hot tea following their light meal, passing around rumpled documents as Vorchek expounded. He puffed at his pipe between pronouncements and advice, worse for wear after a long night and early morning of last minute reading, still well dressed as for goodly company, his tie still remarkably straight. Theresa Delaney, still looking the glamour queen in a black, silky outfit (she supported her expensive tastes from the proceeds of a generous trust fund established by parents now dead), sat in the antique, cushioned rocker lazily smoking yet another cigarette while lazily petting the professor's cat, a sleek black, wise-eyed feline named Claudia. The girl intermittently listened to her mentor while she rocked, but she had heard it all before, in excruciating detail, had stayed the previous night to help him with equipment, had heard much of it then, too. Vorchek spoke now mainly for Philip Matthews, looking especially scruffy after a bad, tumultuous rest, who already knew quite enough, required more chiefly to be genuinely convinced, even at this late stage, that his companions were absolutely serious about what they proposed to do.

Vorchek said, "We invoke entirely legitimate, if poorly understood, powers, which we style magic, though there is no suggestion of sleight of hand or legerdemain. These forces are real, as actual as the chemical energy derived from a lump of coal or the atomic variety fired from nuclear fusion. Think of it that way, Mr. Matthews, and you may grasp the principle of magic, even if it be not truly akin to those forces we now take for granted. Our fathers were equally amazed by the powers we have come to consider

10

commonplace.

"Magic is a wholly unique force in that, stemming as it does from another plane of being, it cannot be activated simply by heat or pressure. Magic is drawn into our realm by the focused operation of mind; it utilizes the spark of mental energy to bring it forth, to fuel action. Two mechanisms accomplish this: the generation of unearthly vibrations which, properly fostered, approximate those radiated from the unseen barriers that divide our world from the mystic lands of the other plane, that dimension or universe, if you will; and the employment of special objects and materials that have become, by whatever fashion, imbued with properties inherent in that world beyond. This marinade of the strange could be the result, for example, of learned sorcery, or of lucky intrusions of arcane force into our world from that other.

"So you see, there is reason underlying our work, an internal logic which, if proven valid, will yield the results we seek. We create the necessary vibratory agency via the chanting of the spell imparted to us by Jacob Bleek in this his book. No mumbo-jumbo there, but the cunning grouping of syllables and phrases torn from a tongue ancient and unknown to us, the mythic language of the Rhexellites, whose shadowy civilization, legend claims, perished before ever homo *sapiens* walked this planet. Their vocal apparatus, I deduce from the structure of the spell, bore scant similarity to ours, but we can, as Miss Delaney would say, 'wing it.' Bleek writes that he did so, to majestic effect. You have memorized those apparently meaningless words, that we may chant them in unison. Then there is the object, the vessel of cosmic power which we must employ: the eon-shunned Cross of Xenophor, a thing with mass and physical properties residing within our universe yet, say reports of old, not of our universe. Cultic rumors describe Xenophor as the God of ultimate evil, the mad destroyer, the bemused lunatic lurking behind the sordid screen of reality; also they call Him the First Cause, the Creator of All Things, to whom all wise men must bow. Do not query me, for I merely convey the fruits of legendry. Suffice to say that the Cross is steeped in weird energies (I have scanned it with my home-made devices, garnered discordant but uniquely provocative readings), and it should serve its purpose, if all else be true.

"I have told you much of the Cross. Here it is." The professor rose, stepped to a cabinet, extracted from a drawer the subject of his speech, held it determinedly forth as if to repel a vampire. Truly the Cross of Xenophor was a beautiful item, a hefty chunk of metal,

11

gleaming gold, with a longer column and a shorter row of twinkling green gems inlaid, pure, clear emeralds that flashed and beckoned in the soft lamp light. Their ovoid shapes suggested green gimlet eyes, knowing, thoughtful, inscrutable. Unintelligible markings obscurely reminiscent of script finely incised its exposed surfaces. Vorchek turned it toward him, regarded it with steadfast reverence, muttered, "I wish I could read those words."

Somewhat later, as Vorchek busied himself below ground, while they waited for the chosen moment, Philip said to Theresa, "I've got to tell you, I don't believe a word of it. It sounds crazy. It has to be crazy. I've been hearing what his colleagues say about the old man. They call him a nutter. They say he's come up with useful ideas during his sane phases, but when he's running after his latest obsession his brain shuts down and he isn't worth two cents. I'm starting to get it now. They know him too well. He talks a good game, but nothing can come of this rot. I'm surprised you can't see through him."

Theresa said haughtily, "Just you wait. The professor has shown me things that would blow your brains out your ears. He's not toying with us, nor is he round the bend. He doesn't know what's going to happen. This is a test. We'll play it his way, by the rules—whatever they are, in a case like this—and find out. Win or lose, the professor will learn something, which is all it takes to satisfy him."

"Not for me, not for long. I can't be his fool. If nothing happens, I'll laugh in his face."

Philip did not laugh that night. Something did happen.

The hour approached, the minute, when according to the centuried pen of Jacob Bleek the rites must be exercised. Vorchek had timed it with artful precision, according to the alignment of stars in the heavens, a simple procedure with those clear desert skies, though he had been prepared to estimate by astronomical instruments. At fifteen minutes past eleven that evening the three descended into the basement laboratory, assumed their stations seated about a table from which its regular debris had been swept. On that table now reposed the *Black Book*, laid before Vorchek, flat and open to the critical page of magic formula; two copied sheets before the young people on which their leader had painstakingly transcribed the clumsy mouthfuls of sound; and the Cross of Xenophor, lying in the center of the table, its head almost touching the top of the book, its jewels appearing to smolder in the light of the single bright bulb directly overhead in that otherwise dark room.

12

The light etched chiaroscuro portraits of faces in harsh brilliance and deep shadow: Professor Anton Vorchek rapt, his eyes narrowed behind reading glasses, calmly stroking his beard; Theresa Delaney across and to the left, pensive, her small, perfect features wrinkled in frown, her small, delicate hands holding down her copy; Philip Matthews at a wide remove to her right, his boyishly handsome face tight and blank, his arms folded as if to ward off a chill that was not evident that evening at that place.

Vorchek said, "I shall recite the first passage on my own. Attend to my pacing, the timbre and pitch. Then I shall begin again. The second time, you join in, matching my chanting precisely. This time all of our practice must count. Do not miss a beat, nor stumble, not once, until we complete the spell."

Vorchek commenced. He intoned those first words of the spell, eleven seconds of them, difficult, cracked sounds with which his tongue struggled. He paused, nervously massaged his left temple with stiff fingers, then began in earnest. As he spoke Theresa and Philip joined in, the mouthfuls of inhuman noise flowing together into one low, even drone. The weird syllables spun into the dry, warm air, muddled echoes dripping from the four brick walls. The olden words conveyed no explicit information, certainly none evident to a speaker of English, but they hummed and thrummed, weaving chains of exotic auditory vibrations about the three. Sounds merely, yet they induced tingles of the nerves and itching of the flesh. Eyes watered as lips framed themselves around the elements of the spell.

And as the lengthy chant progressed something more happened. The Cross of Xenophor awakened to unholy life. Initially the seven emeralds flamed as from internal fire, mounting in intensity to a green blaze painful to see. Motes of fierce light scintillated from them, captive green stars flaring and vanishing on the instant. Then the bright gold, the body of the Cross, began to glow of itself. Its strengthening radiance seemed to reach out aggressively to smother and dim the homely electric bulb. That source steadily dimmed, suddenly went out, leaving the activated Cross as the sole illumination. It beamed into three faces, making them ghastly.

They concluded the spell. The Cross continued to shine. Vorchek bowed his head, muttered to himself a fresh mantra, very different from what had gone before, reciting in the archaic speech of Jacob Bleek the coordinates, as laid down and formulated by that reputed wizard, in time and space of the mythical realm of millennial-dead Dyrezan. Not reference points to which an historian

13

or geographer could relate, these designations were murky terms of arcana, devised by a master weaver of spells, guaranteed to work despite ignorance of the concepts. The professor read them from the book, his index finger tracing slashing paths across the page. That completed, he placed his hands with fingers splayed on the table framing the dread volume, and he said, still as if chanting, over and over again the curious word, "Dyrezan, Dyrezan, Dyrezan . . ."

The light of the Cross flashed once, such that the trio rocked back in their chairs. Subsequently the object maintained its constant glow with, however, an alteration in the properties of its radiance. It plainly revealed the experimenters and the central portion of the table about the thing, but the remainder of the room fell into shadow; no, more than shadow, for that outward gloom composed itself into absolute blackness, as if the room, perhaps the world, had been annihilated and devoured by utter darkness. That was an awful moment. Theresa crouched lower in her chair. Philip squirmed and made to speak, but Vorchek hushed him with a savage gesture.

Shapes teemed in the inky blackness beyond the circle of sickly glare. Something moved there, amorphous forms of still greater darkness, shapes incomprehensible, impossible to define or intellectually grasp. There were many of them, too many of them, a host, a multitude of that which, lacking substance, possessed existence; bodiless movement. They crowded close.

"My God!" Philip hissed through clenched teeth. Vorchek shook his head, pointed to the Cross, whispered, "Be careful, boy. Be sure of your God, if you must invoke Him." Theresa twisted round desperately with a choking sound. The girl shuddered, cried out between breathless gasps, "I won't stand it if they touch me."

And the light of the Cross ceased. There was no vision, nor sound, nor sense of touch. Professor Vorchek felt himself alone in measureless immensity, an infinity of nothingness that encompassed himself. Mind he had, a mind that furiously worked and probed and sought, but there was nothing, even in himself. He was not, although he thought, awareness suspended, dangling over universal void. There was simply nothing out there, while he lacked any iota of self to claw against the endless night.

Nothing, nothing; yet he was watched. What dregs of persona he retained grew aware of another, hopelessly beyond his ken though horribly close at hand, an entity that observed and studied him with callous dispassion. It was there, but where? He felt its eyes on him, gazing intently upon his wisp of being, staring from all directions

14

simultaneously as with an infinite number of eyes. It was everywhere at once, or it was the everywhere, the soul of the vast emptiness into which he helplessly sank. The mind of Vorchek shrieked, thrashed in an attempt to understand, fled from the brink of understanding.

Images invaded his mind, pictures projected onto the screen of his thoughts. The absolute blackness receded, revealing forms that, despite their utter strangeness, he could just barely comprehend. Orbs of light flashed past and through him, exploding suns and burning worlds. Eerie tendrils of glowing gas seeped through starry darkness. Filaments of flickering light swung across immense spaces to enfold him. He felt himself sailing back into and throughout the material universe. In his current state he dared not hazard a guess as to where he had been, what realm of perfect mystery he had entered and departed.

The scene changed abruptly. He saw himself, a fleeting glimpse, in familiar surroundings, and when that scene winked out he saw another vision, the portrayal of another man, a stranger to him, an unrecognized personage in past trappings, perhaps those of Elizabethan England. That image vanished, to be replaced by another, of medieval form this time, and then came another stranger wrapped in a toga amidst marble halls, then a bronzed, skirted man with piercing eyes framed by grandiose monuments, and more, many more, men spied in curious garb within indefinable settings. Vorchek did not know them, nor know why he should see them now, flipping through their brief presentations as through the pictures in a magazine.

Another shift, again without warning, gave onto a close view of a planet, perhaps as seen from orbit, a world which he identified as Earth despite alterations, not all of them minor, of the land masses. The image blurred, transformed into a sensation of lazy floating or drifting through air, high among the clouds, revealing scapes of icy mountains, sheer-walled gorges, trackless expanses of trees, endless plains. Occasionally he observed—so quickly that his grasp of the matter arrived after the image had fled—hints of human presence: a long, straight road bisecting a great forest, huddles of farm plots, tell-tale shadows cast by high, angular structures.

An enormous wall of rugged, bare peaks loomed before him. Titanic were those mountains, rising a good two miles or more above the surrounding plateau. He flew onward, toward them, still without sense of self save awareness, passed between the two tallest peaks, craggy masses of giant granite boulders and shattered splinters of rock, a wasteland of stony debris. Amidst the natural rubble he spotted signs of human presence, evidenced by little cubic buildings of basalt perched high on ridges overlooking the plain. He swept past, over the range, and had he possessed materiality he would have gasped at the sight which swam before him.

Coming over the mountain wall he found himself entering an astounding bowl-shaped valley of incredible dimensions, a huge depression sunk within the ring of that sere range which he had seen only a part of before. There was something, he thought, oddly unnatural about those mountains and the valley, a notion which struck him forcibly before he took in aught else. The mountain ring, viewed from within, was perfectly circular, the valley far below in the depths perfectly round. The lower inner slopes of the mountains and the valley, quite unlike the regions outside, teemed with fruitfulness and life. It was a green place, that great valley, well watered by streams and copious lakes, an inviting patchwork of verdant woods and fecund fields. Just the scale of it all astonished the mind of Vorchek. A small nation could fit inside the beautiful territory confined within the high rocky ring.

All this impressed, but it was not the green and living valley, that suspiciously artificial valley within the mountain ring arranged as if by cunning, that stunned thought. Above the valley, above his apparent position in the sky and somewhat beyond even the highest peaks, loomed an object startling to behold, something that should not, could not be there. A dark ovoid hovered there among the clouds, a gigantic solid mass miles across, motionless above the center of the valley, hanging up there among the scurrying clouds. Without volition, but inflamed by desire, Vorchek approached it. He passed through a screen of fleecy fog, moving upward through shrouding grayness, emerged on the other side level with the object that intrigued him so. Imagination unrestrained could not have prepared him for the discovery that dawned.

It was a city, a city in the sky. Vorchek cried out at the glorious vista, a cry of joy and wonder emanating from mind untrammeled. From the dark, featureless underbelly which he had observed from afar rose the glittering towers, spires, citadels and ramparts of a great metropolis. White were its buildings, structures broodingly Cyclopean or impossibly fragile; gold and silver or dazzlingly multi-colored were its minarets and arches. Gray and forbidding were the massive walls enclosing the whole.

Vorchek soared into the confines of the city, speeding over a lattice-work of avenues. He thought he detected movement on those streets. They ran mainly in nice geometrical configurations, forming squares and rectangles about masses of structure, in other places radiating from hubs like the spokes of a wheel. That layout of road inevitably focused on truly great edifices, striking monuments or splendid fairy palaces. He noted briefly sectors of the city given over to tangles of narrow lanes, regions where the architecture appeared relatively less awesome. So, too, did some paths twist and turn picturesquely through areas of open woods and green lawns minutely splashed with vivid color, or around regularly shaped bodies of crystal water.

Then Vorchek hurtled toward the floor or ground of the city. He lost the bird's eye view, saw one large building of white stone and glass rushing to meet him. At the moment when he could expect a crash the scene grew dark, and he lost finally all awareness of the mysterious visions which had amazed him since the time—long ago, was it?—that he sat at the laboratory table reciting with his colleagues the spell from the *Black Book* of Jacob Bleek. Once more nothingness enveloped him.

Until he woke up.

III. THE WORLD OF VORSELUS

Vorselus, wizard of Dyrezan, woke from a troubled slumber to a new day, one which he fully expected to plague him abominably. That his rest should be disordered he little doubted, not in these perilous times. There loomed before him this morning the audience at the court of King Skyrax, Lord of Dyrezan and Emperor of the civilized world, where big matters were afoot, where the great nobles and best magicians of the sky-flung city, including many of the Grand Council, would congregate to confer with their sovereign on the business of state policy, a subject as intricate and difficult, he imagined, as the sorcery he practiced. These were trying times, the moment an awkward one, what with some of the finest mages and nobles departed from the city, those remaining behind a querulous and, perhaps, a discontented lot.

There was all that, and the King's inescapable command that he,

17

Vorselus, should involve himself in these disagreeable affairs. What meant politics to him? Vorselus liked to think of himself as the sorcerer's sorcerer, a scholar dedicated to his work, a single-minded student of obscure and curious knowledge, especially that dealing with magical lore, the engine of mighty Dyrezan's past and eternal glory. Since his receding youth Vorselus had pondered, to the exclusion of all else, the arcane arts, learning constituting his only ambition, leaving it to others to act as mundane earth-shakers. Now, for reasons he could not conceive, they desired to draw him into their wildly spinning and personally precarious orbit.

Troubles enough to be sure, and he would have groused at those anyway, but he suspected there was much more to tax him now. Into sleep had come visions, dreams hateful and hostile, or so he tentatively deduced. They could not be the conventional, casually false dreams, not in this room protected by spells which shielded his mind from meaningless trivia. Indeed, his secret charms should defend him in this chamber from any outward manifestation, and yet something had happened.

And it happened again, now:

He came to groggy awareness, climbing up from a deep well of intense sleep, enfolded in pleasing softness. Eyes closed, he knew that darkness surrounded him, which seemed normal and right, and yet he knew that it should not have, for had he not been involved in activity of a sort, concentration and mental effort that had taxed his resources? He opened his eyes. The darkness was there, and he wished it gone that he might see and understand how he came to be in repose. And then the darkness went, for at the thought—as if because of the thought—a globe of misty candescence blazed into soft light, illuminating the familiar room about him. Familiar, yes, oddly so, yet unexpected, for there had been another room, very different from this one. This was a luxurious chamber, of fair size, the walls faced in striated marble, from which hung colorful tapestries representing scenes of exotic pageantry. It contained ornate furniture of ebony and ivory, mahogany and gold, and the truly enormous bed on which he lay covered in delightfully cool dyed silks, his head resting on mounded, airy pillows. This was his room, sure enough, one he knew so well from long acquaintance, yet nettlesome mosquitoes of doubt pestered his brain. It was not meet that he should so readily recognize this place.

He sat up in the bed, began to step down, froze in sudden terror. Part of his mind screamed that nothing was right, that all this represented danger, the lurking of unknown perils. Where were his companions: the girl, rather important to him, the boy, probably useful? Should not they be close at hand? Had they deserted him? Possibly he still drowsed, but for the life of him he could not recall their names. That was not a good sign. The strangeness of his location troubled him more. It should have happened differently, that which was meant to be. There was the book, and the initiation of the journey, and he would go somewhere. Instead of a coming, however, he feared a becoming. Who was he? At that he screamed silently again, for in a flash of despair he realized that the experiment had gone grotesquely wrong. He had indeed succeeded in his journey, only the vital fabric of his consciousness was being subsumed into the specter of the other...

Vorselus rose, shook himself, willed the bright globe to dim slightly to a suitable level. Now what, by the Gods, was that all about? This was his room, as ever, nothing different, nothing out of place. He must get a grip. He would not be assailed by foolish doubts; who was he to fear, to question his own reality? He knew who he was: Vorselus, a respected and learned mage of great Dyrezan, the city of the sky, seat of empire and the heart of the world. A giant among giants was Vorselus, a sorcerer in a kingdom of sorcerers, versed in arts magical, less powerful than some maybe, better than most certainly. This was his room, in his manor, in his city, lording over his world. He did not fear. He bowed to no man save to revered Skyrax, King of Dyrezan and Emperor of the civilized domains, and that worthy surely loved him and embraced his counsel, as would be proven this day.

"I am Vorselus," he said, and his voice was deep and cultured, decisive. He turned to the mirror, the wall mirror standing upright in its silver frame adorned with artistically rendered faces of alarming mythical monsters, beheld himself dressed in his sleeping shift: a tall man, lean but hard, with a strong, bearded face, his brown hair elegantly graying at the temples. He saw the face predicted, so why did aspects of that visage cause a return of those insane doubts? The beard seemed rather longer than it should, the hair lighter, the ears unnaturally pointed. Did he entirely own that face? "I am Vorselus," he said again, and this time even the enunciation of his name fostered reservations.

He laughed grumpily. Lest he forget who he was, Vorselus, clever and well-appointed magician that he be, kept a full household about him catering to his comfort. Forthwith he turned, yanked the bell-pull by the bed. Elsewhere in the house chimes tinkled. Footsteps pounded on the floor without his door. A knock came. "Enter," he said. The slave obeyed.

As should he. Vorselus owned several slaves, captives of the sporadic wars against barbarians or those minor kingdoms of the outlands whose wise men knew not the power of great magic. Being his property, they lived to serve. This fellow was no different, in fact obeyed with singular alacrity, for he was Ling-das, seized at birth from the lowly Tamalcar bands of the icy north, since an early age the personal servant of his master. The still young Ling-das, as a reward for faithful performance, held an exalted position among his unfortunate peers, receiving better room and board in return for managing the manor's inconsequential necessities: material concerns, the tiresome chores of buying, cataloguing, and apportioning the goods required to maintain the estate and its tenants. Vorselus, who had a good head for all save crass business, relied on his man for everything. Also, Ling-das was privy to all his affairs.

"You called, my lord," said Ling-das with a formal bow. His master testily replied, "Indeed I did. Dress me." "As you say and will," muttered Ling-das, already busy at the drawers of the cabinets flanking the mirror. He was short, heavy-set, with long, lank sandy hair and a rounded, good-humored countenance. In an instant he produced undergarments, hose and sandals, the long, thick robe of white with the red descending stripes that indicated a wizard of importance. Street attire this was, which made sense, as Vorselus realized then, for duty called this day, and he would be going about shortly. He remembered that now, again, wondered why he had forgotten. He went forth soon on an uncommon errand.

Ling-das recited in singsong as he labored, ticking off a mental list of observations, news and rumors. "The city floats quiet this morning. Garok, Kardowan's man, sounded off in a tavern last night, bragged of special honors in store for his lord. I have this from Tellio, cousin of the serving wench who heard the boast. One of Albragon's henchman was present, seemed to agree without agreeing, as I hear it. Your name by him was mentioned, with delicate regard for your standing at court. That may be a blessing, whatever comes. It is spoken aloud in the streets by many that the King's favorites, Nantrech and Morca, are forever lost to us, that tidings of their deaths pass by word of mouth. That is odd, for no official source—"

"What, precisely," cut in Vorselus, holdings his arms high as the robe flowed down over him, "was said of me?"

"Albragon's lackey—Mase, a cutthroat, I swear—averred that Vorselus is an honest man, devoted to the stability of the empire and the house of Skyrax. He said that was plainly a reasonable stance for one such as yourself. He went on to say that the people of Dyrezan may count on your reason, more likely your caution. Garok, in a rather sneering manner, declared that such would be true wisdom in the days to come. His statement hushed the discussion."

Vorselus felt ludicrously pleased that his chief slave showed easy cognizance of his master's existence and persona. He hoped that settled the weird flutters toying with his contentment. The details of what Ling-das recounted to him, however, caused extreme aggravation. No wonder he was out of sorts. He, preferring a quiet life of esoteric research, had been lately drawn into the tedious machinations of the highest orders, men who generally preferred to scramble for honors and notoriety among themselves. He wanted nothing more than to retire to his library for the day, there to further work on that blasted spell of dematerialization, which refused to come right. He had thought up some unique twists that demanded elaboration before he could dream of a trial. This day, though, real work must wait. He, Vorselus (that one, nobody else), must this day be presented at court, of all places, that he might propound on incomprehensible questions of policy. Only a command from the King could have sucked him into that whirlpool.

"Enough," he said abruptly. "I come down immediately to break fast. See to it." Ling-das scurried away to manage the preparation of the meal. Vorselus tidied himself, descended the simple stairs to the next lower, the ground floor. Rather would he ascend to the third and highest, where he kept his offices, his books, his chamber of experimentation. Instead he must eat and depart. It promised to be a dreary day.

The modest dining hall lay prepared this day, as most days, for him alone. A dozen servants, plucked from half a dozen foreign lands, buzzed like bees to make easy his breakfasting. He sat at table, chewed fresh brown bread sopped in golden olive oil, nibbled at pink melons from the fields of Calaspia, imbibed wine from select valley vineyards. A quartet of musical slaves strummed a soothing tune for his indifferent enjoyment. The food sank heavy in his stomach. A thought sprang to mind of the injustice of his owning these people, the violation of nature it represented; then he choked on a mouthful, wondering from where had that ridiculous notion arisen.

21

Domination and servitude were universal norms! So sour was his countenance that no one dared speak to him until Ling-das reappeared to breezily relay a message from a court courier, reminding him that the great ones expected him at the third hour.

"It must be done," snapped Vorselus. "Gather my papers, whatever else I may require. I will be ready before time. Tell him I come presently, send him on his way."

And so, in short order, with much grumbling over trifles and curt words directed without cause against his people, Vorselus went forth into Dyrezan. This day Vorselus dispensed with his carriage and horses, preferring to walk his way across the city to his destination. Not typical behavior, nor could he explain it (indeed, he strove not to think of it, choosing to account the meaningless change of habit to sheer whim), deciding off-hand that he needed the exercise. He had the time, and the stroll would do him good, satisfy his body and allow him to restore order his mind. So he walked the familiar avenues.

Only this day it was not the essence of familiar that filled him. Instead, the wonder of it all forcibly struck him, this city of Dyrezan with its magic marvels and fantastic works. It all pleased him, entertained every step of the way, like a visit to a strange and appealing new land. From his courtyard Vorselus passed into the Street of the Golden Wing, fronted by the fine houses of his neighbors, colleagues mostly, decent dwellings of varied styles where they lived and studiously labored. No other masters of households were about this early; if awake, they were probably at their breakfasts or books. Only the servants were active yet, and those few were far from busy. They hailed him respectfully until he passed out of the little flagged lane into the big thoroughfare.

This was the Avenue of Azamodeus, dedicated to that shadowy deity of the Seventh Plane, and a fitting tribute to His terrible majesty. Many citizens and slaves rode or walked in the wide road of broad granite paving. Here the homes were grander, more widely spaced, surrounded by private parks or forbidding walls. Temples, too, abounded, most of them in this sector also the private constructions of the important men who held sway in these parts. Vorselus, turning right toward the heart of the city, passed shortly on his left the formidable abode, a veritable castle, belonging to the great Lord Albragon. A great lord indeed, he, distant kinsman of the King, his family line involved in political affairs since time immemorial. A grand fellow, a large man with large tastes, Albragon dwelt serenely and secretively behind those high black walls of onyx, shielded from prying eyes by his huge staff and famed desire for privacy, a trait strongly enforced against the unwelcome despite his public standing and frequent appearance at court. Rumors swirled about the man, mainly relating to matters lewd or politely unmentionable. Who knew? His own kind deemed him a wise and industrious magician, ever practicing in the service of the empire.

With time to spare, Vorselus detoured into the Sacred Gardens, that artful floral wonderland of woods and flowering perennials that girdled the heart of Dyrezan, its ponds and streams fed by sweet water pumped from vast cisterns within the city's substructure. He wandered the winding paths by the central River Tethe, lonely at present, marveled at these replicas of nature and the little marble havens of the Gods, marveled that he should marvel, for they were so familiar to him.

Passing beyond the belt of greenery, he entered the grandiose complex at the city center, the focus of all the world. Here towered the greatest temples, the palaces of state, the administration buildings from which were conceived and dictated the laws of the empire. These roads already teemed with traffic, the wide lanes leading in watched by posts of imperial guardsmen in their showy armor, every man armed with wholly utilitarian pikes, swords, and shields. Along the way he passed one of those somber, cubic, antique temples dedicated to the most high Xenophor, beneath which throbbed the gargantuan magical engines that sustained the existence of Dyrezan in the skyey void. Through five hundred generations they had strained against base nature to uphold this city above all others. So long as Xenophor willed it, might they never fail!

He entered the Plaza of Kings, and across that great space he beheld the Palace of Skyrax, where the House of Skyrax had lorded regally since the inception of the city, since the dawn of time as common history would have it. Of white marble, with green-veined columns, flanked by spires of gleaming gold and twinkling crystal, the palace rose in a series of stacked levels, ringed by flights of marble steps, up to the main edifice where King Skyrax lived and— when the notion diverted him—governed.

Vorselus wended his way through the thronging plaza crowd of gawkers and hawkers, loungers and petitioners, mounted the interminable steps to the portico of the entrance hall. There soldiers of the Guard closed about him, brusquely demanded his business. They would have behaved thus to any visitor, he reasoned, but he knew also that few here knew him by sight, so he guessed they took

23

especial care. Suspicious characters were unlikely to survive the climb of the steps.

"The mage Vorselus," he announced, waving his seal ring, "commanded to audience with the King." An officer consulted a scroll, nodded formally. "You are expected," said he; "follow me." And with that Vorselus entered the forbidden precincts of the palace.

Each corridor, each chamber passed revealed fresh splendor, but having arrived Vorselus had no time for sight-seeing. He was ushered hurriedly into the Hall of Receival, where across the platinum paving he saw the golden throne vacant on its dais, with a noisy crowd filling the big room between. He recognized many of them: the Elders of the Council, the high priests of the most important Gods, the wise men and the nobles of Dyrezan.

No sooner had he entered than one of their number broke free of the teeming, murmuring humanity present to greet him. Vorselus expanded with pride, amazed that one so great as Lord Kardowan himself should stoop to acknowledge him. That genius of the mystic arts approached boldly, a surprisingly little man in physique, a giant of stature in all that counted. He stared with black, piercing eyes under his high forehead and bald dome, outstretched his arms making wings of his black and yellow sorcerer's robe to say, "Salutations, Vorselus. I see that all our best men are here today. It is as I advised. When critical decisions must be made, no man of substance should be left out. Surely you have considered the choices. How do you vote amongst us?"

"None of that," cried Malfador, Chief Elder of the Grand Council. The portly old wizard, cloaked in gray, took Kardowan by the arm, sought to pull him away. "There will be no grandstanding. Each man shall vote his conscience this day." Kardowan haughtily shook him off, whispered something with a frown. Malfador backed away with a grimace of anger, showing yellowed teeth.

Stout Albragon intervened, regal Albragon, a big man with a bushy moustache, draped in barbarous finery. He too flashed teeth, a large grin that seemed to demand friendship of all the world. Said he, "Come, we are all as one today, in meaning the very best for the King, long may he live, and Dyrezan, long may it soar. I appreciate the eagerness of my fellow magician Kardowan, greatest among us, who always means well and does better. I know that he and the council are hand in glove. Good Vorselus knows that without being told."

Malfador stalked away, Kardowan and Albragon moved on with

24

more cheer. Vorselus, seeking to occupy himself while he must wait, toured the high walls of the chamber admiring the brilliantly colored and cleverly executed frescoes and murals which depicted the near eternal sweep of Dyrezanian history, from the dim days of the Founding to the current King's coronation a decade ago. While enjoying himself this way he was again accosted, this time from a very different source.

"It's a lot of noise over nothing," said the elfin girl at his elbow. She was no less than Princess Lora, daughter of the King and his only child. For a motherless girl who had seen scarcely fourteen summers she acted remarkably self-assured, an air which came gratis with her position, Vorselus guessed. Truly she seemed more amused than awed by the gathering.

"You can't really do anything today, can you?" she asked, her small, pale features brightened by her little grin. "Oh, I've heard all about it. I know what you're up to, some of you anyway, and I just can't believe you think you're going to get away with it. You daren't act without Nantrech and Morca—that's impossible—and they wouldn't have it if they were here, so what's the point? Besides, Kardowan will play a dirty game if you give him the chance. My father can't be that big a fool."

Such talk made Vorselus distinctly uncomfortable, and it relieved him when the royal daughter flitted on her way to disturb someone else. He knew very well what she meant, understood the ramifications of this day's vote. Lately he had thought of little else, and now the morning's odd distractions receded from mind to bare the situation to him.

Kardowan craved power. There was no getting around that troublesome fact. He wished to be the mailed fist behind the throne, for the obvious reasons perhaps, possibly for others less clear or welcome. He deemed this his moment of culmination. Vorselus was more than casually aware that many of the great lords supported the fellow; Kardowan had assiduously cultivated their favor in recent months, most of all that of Albragon, who might be dissatisfied himself with the status quo and his place in the imperial scheme. Kardowan the dangerous sorcerer, Albragon of royal blood, so many others hungry for advancement; it was a tricky moment.

Ordinarily it should not have been. Who was greater, more learned and respected than the famous Lord Nantrech? Wizard and scholar, keen explorer and author of a shelf of books on his thrilling adventures in remote and entertaining lands, Nantrech had so pleased

25

the King with his stories and discoveries as to guarantee himself special regard beyond that of his kindred worthies. What of Lord Morca, a man who for magical acumen and ferocity in battle knew no peer? Captain of the Royal Guard, superlative leader of men, his merest whims on matters of security were law unto the King. While they lived and habitually strove for greatness—for themselves and for the House of Skyrax—what man, nay, what combination, dared oppose them?

But they were gone, far away to the east beyond the distant eastern sea, between them helming that blasted military expedition into the unknown lands where, so legend told, mysterious kingdoms of old once held sway, and where rumor bragged that treasure and tribute were to be had. With the inquisitive Lord Nantrech in nominal command of the expedition, and the fiery Lord Morca in actual charge of military operations, they had marched out the year before with a thousand picked troops and a team of savants to explore, to conquer, to increase (if that be possible) the glory that was Dyrezan.

No one had heard from them in months. Without their advice, said the gossips, the King grew restive, doubted the soundness of his decrees, became concerned over the wavering course of imperial affairs. He had by him the Grand Council, of course, Malfador and his aged crew, good men and loyal, but maybe too accustomed to obedience, more apt to agree than to recommend after their interminable debates. Skyrax, no doubt, his favor unemployed, had begun to wander in his affections, to reach out for new companions to enrich his days, and fresh minds to direct his unchecked power into useful channels.

Kardowan nominated himself, alone, to replace that missing duo of great ones. Skyrax entertained the notion, yet sought advice on the choice of advisor. The vote could not bind him—there was no suggestion of that from any quarter, not even Kardowan—but the King was (what the generous way to put this?) impressionable, easily turned. Suffice to say that the vote mattered, could readily lead to real consequences.

Skyrax made his entrance. An illusory eagle flickered into the air above the shiny throne, beaming a soft golden light, the apparition accompanied by the braying of horns. The eagle faded and then the King swept in from behind the curtains to stand by his seat. All present stood riveted to attention, crying in unison, "Hail Skyrax, of the House of Skyrax, Master of Dyrezan, its citizens, its subjects all.

26

Hail Skyrax!" He took his seat, a slight man, slender, thin-haired, watery-eyed, wrapped in a thick robe of dark blue as against a chill that none else could feel. Malfador mounted the dais, faced the audience at the King's right. Princess Lora dropped herself onto the dais steps below and far to the left of her father.

Malfador solemnly intoned, "The King condescends to ask speech of us. Hear Him." He nodded to the King, who returned the nod and said haltingly in a high-pitched, plaintive voice, "The business of the empire has taken from me my closest counselors. When I will see them again, no one can tell me. This situation bothers me exceedingly. Perhaps it should be resolved, for the time being. Noble Kardowan offers himself as my temporary support. Should I lean on him? I will attend to your opinions."

Malfador spoke first, as was his due. "Nothing critical presses," said he. "In the absence of controversies or perceived dangers, I see no reason—"

Interrupted the King loudly, with strident insistence, "There is much to do, and decisions weigh heavy and painful on the throne. I will not have my life all care and wear. I will be jolly when I can. Who shall ease my burden?"

"The Council—"

"Azamodeus take the Council! Give me one good man, with whom I may easily treat."

At that the attendees exploded into consecutive speech, beginning with Albragon, who suavely bawled, "My Lord, take the greatest among us as your helpmate! Choose wisdom, learning, and loyalty." Continued the relay—which seemed to Vorselus to smack of orchestration—with one speaker after another who readily identified himself as a staunch supporter of Kardowan. They praised him to the most elevated circles of Xenophor, referring to his keen insights and magical abilities in the most obsequious terms. Said they, "Allow Kardowan to humble himself in your service!"

There were other voices, advocating caution or stasis, but they sounded weak and uninspired by comparison. They did not charge Kardowan with any wrong doing, preferring rather to hint at difficulties and complications to come. Vorselus saw the problem. The man owned no overt faults; he was cold and hard and frightfully self-important, and it was said—idle chatter!—that he desired more than life could honestly grant him. What counted such mild recriminations, if the King wanted him? It did appear that Skyrax bent in that direction.

27

"What say you, Vorselus?" asked a feminine voice in his ear. It was Lora, who had slipped from her place to speak with him, leaning close to be heard above the heated din. He replied, "Do not tabulate the value of my opinion. I have no personal stake in this." Said she, "Then I may count your opinion the wisest, if earnest."

On impulse Vorselus raised his hand to be heard. The sudden silence unnerved him. Assailed by the stern regard of many eyes, he said, "There be no necessity for haste. Let us agree today to consider, to converse intelligently and at leisure, without rancor, among ourselves. Lest we forget, this gathering is called because our best, brilliant Nantrech and steadfast Morca, are absent. It pains me to convene without their sagacious voices. Send a delegation to them, apprising them of what we do. Let us tarry amiably for their response. Their wisdom should be heard, lest we unknowingly falter."

There came outbursts of agreement, a vigorous storm of protest. The tempest roared, "If they were here, or in communication with us, action would be unnecessary. We must act, for they are gone an age, long dead for all we know. Shall we wait until their shades address us?"

Much more followed. Tempers flamed, opposing groupings formed in the hall. At last Skyrax, wearied of the tumult, called the vote. That took no time at all. The issue decided by the present body, the King gratefully, with an air of weariness, accepted the proffered advice. Kardowan won; not handily, but he carried the day, and he mounted the dais to stand at the right hand of the King, driving Malfador below him. Kardowan made a conciliatory speech. Afterward, with the King's blessing, the crowd dispersed.

Descending to the plaza, eager to be home, Vorselus encountered Garok, Kardowan's beefy, sour-faced retainer, leader of his personal bodyguard. Through his thick beard he grunted, "It's the quiet man who lasts longest. You ought to remember from now on when to hold your tongue. You came down on the wrong side today. Don't make that mistake again. Go back to your books, wizard, and forget what's too hot for you. Do that, and you won't make enemies."

IV. A GIFT FROM THE PRINCESS

That afternoon Kardowan's ascendancy was cried about the city as a happy circumstance for the people of Dyrezan. The public news, carried in by servants, reached the ears of Vorselus, who received it with a shrug, for it told nothing but the result, somewhat embellished, of what was styled the "election," and the King's acceptance of same. Vorselus chose rather to ruminate on the unpleasant warning which had followed, one calculated to fire his ire instead of reducing him to acquiescence. Really, he cared little for such nonsense (let the big boys knock their heads together if they would), but it galled that they treated him with contempt. It must be so, for why else did they imagine him prey to induced fears? Surely he was entitled to more respect than that.

It got worse. That evening a fellow appeared at his door, a slave, a lackey who gave out neither his name nor his house's name, yet who insisted that Vorselus sign a collective proclamation heralding as a boon Kardowan's victory. In a fit of pique Vorselus had the man cast out, hotly denouncing him, his secretive master, and all those who would disturb his routine. The slave scurried into the night, scowling furiously.

Next morning came a considerably more welcome visitation. Ling-das intruded on his breakfast to declare, "A gift from court, master, awaits you in the hall. It is accompanied by this scroll."

"Read it to me."

Ling-das recited happily, "'Sealed by the hand of Skyrax: It is my intent to thank all who contributed to the joyous outcome of yesterday's crucial event. I note your contribution. Furthermore, my darling daughter Lora confides that you acknowledged her as an equal, heard thoughtfully her views, found it meet to agree with them. In return for this gentle kindness she asks me to make a special gift to you in her name. This I do, out of my regard for her. Lately she received a present from my subjects in far Astara, one which I deem not wholly suitable for a girl of her age, though entirely fitting otherwise for a princess of Dyrezan. This item, therefore, I pass on to you. Enjoy it as you will.' Below is the imperial seal, with the mark of Skyrax."

Said Vorselus, "Quite magnanimous of him, under the circumstances, for he ignored my counsel. Still, a spoiled daughter's pleas do soften the heart. This news, at least, cheers me beyond mere gratitude. Bring in the gift."

Ling-das bowed with a curious smile, exited the room, remained absent for an unusual interval. When he again appeared he came with company, leading by the hand a striking young girl dressed from head to toe in sheer and revealing foreign finery. "Your gift from the Princess," announced Ling-das, who then fled the room without waiting for dismissal, his features contorted with the makings of a laugh.

Vorselus studiously observed the girl. Young, but not too young—he thought of her as "ripe"—with jet-black hair powdered in gold dust like a dome of starry night framing her face. Those eyes were a startling blue, that face soft and sultry, the epitome of the classic Astaran look, from a land famed for the beauty of its women. And she was beautiful; she was astonishing, radiant; effervescently appealing; a shock to the system of a dedicated bachelor like Vorselus. He had never seen anything like her. Behold female perfection! A coarse sack could not have hidden those fulsome curves, yet she was attired to accentuate every plane and fold of her creamy skin. She was an image of all delight, a human treasure, though possibly not, he supposed, a proper plaything for a child princess.

For some minutes Vorselus did not speak, while he strove to muster words suitable to the moment. At length, better composed, he asked crisply, "Your name?" She replied (in a voice like musical strings and warm honey), "Teresia, my master." "Your place of birth?" "Vincalnac, my master, in the kingdom of Astara." "Your station?" "Slave to Vorselus the mage, formerly to Baron Hamage of Vincalnac, granted to Princess Lora, who offers me to Vorselus with the consent of mighty Skyrax." "Your function?" "Dancing girl, master, trained by the priestesses who serve the temple of the Goddess Yolaine."

Said Vorselus, "That deity is unfamiliar to me. Some barbaric goddess, I take it?"

"If you will have it so."

Ling-das reappeared. "The courier still waits, master," he informed, "so he may carry your thanks to the Princess without delay."

"Indeed? Why the hurry? Send him on his way, passing with him my boundless gratitude to Princess Lora and my Lord her esteemed father."

To the other servants within hearing Vorselus said, "Feed her, take her to the main hall. There," he said to her, "You will dance for me."

30

And in soon time she did.

The magician reclined on his sofa in that ornate room, watching the girl spin and twirl about the furnishings through her presentation of flesh and form while she sang in a language he did not know. Words were unnecessary, however, for he derived the desired gratification from the inherently erotic nature of the dance. Teresia was surely all she claimed to be. There was in her sleek motions that which fired the heart of a mage who normally considered himself above such things. He mused aloud, "I am delighted. Fancy them thinking so well of me. No gift could please me better. It was an odd choice for the outlanders to grant to a young girl. These Astarans must be a hedonistic lot, such as to put my people to shame."

"If you will have it so," replied Teresia, as if he had spoken to her. She came near, pirouetted, swept across his front in trailing lace, pranced behind him. He craned his neck to follow her. She shook from a sleeve an object which dropped into her palm, then drove it close to his face. Vorselus saw the metallic flash of the blade.

He shrank back, tumbling to the floor in the process. Only that accident saved him, for the girl made to strike home with the dagger, and the point stabbed air rather than palpitating heart just by a hair's breadth. She scrambled right over the sofa after him, landing on her knees above him, ready for another dive. Vorselus cried out, rolled, leaped to his feet as she darted forward.

He thrust out a hand, the fingers like splayed spikes, screaming, "One more step and you die, your bones boiled within you!" With his next breath he would have recited the words of death— unprepared, would they have acted in time?—but the girl froze in place. Vorselus grinned evilly. Barbarians rightly dreaded the magic of Dyrezan.

He hissed, "Drop the knife, now." Teresia sagged, shrugged, obeyed. "Sit down," he demanded, "where you are, on the floor." When she had once more obeyed him, sinking into a limp crouch, he kicked away the dagger, then asked, "Have you any idea of the penalty for attacking your master? Before I visit it upon you, you will speak." Teresia sat mute, hopelessly shaking her head. "So be it!" he cried. "Wild beasts shall rend you."

Tears gushed. "Don't kill me," she pleaded.

"Why should I not? There are slaves aplenty."

"I do not strike for myself," she replied.

He snorted. "Rubbish. You hate servitude, a natural sentiment,

31

one which beckons you to murder."

She shook her head again, her dark locks flying. "I will tell you all, and what I tell will prove worth knowing."

Vorselus considered this statement, doubted, wondered. He rang the bell. Ling-das showed himself. His master said, "Take her to the library. Watch her; she is dangerous. Keep her until I join you."

Vorselus went forth. The germ of an idea had occurred to him, one which he scarcely dared dwell upon until he made inquiries. These he set in motion immediately, sending his own man to the royal palace to offer renewed thanks for the gift, and to ask after particulars of its history. Well within the span of two hours an answer came, short but to the point, asking him, in effect, "What was he talking about?" There had been no present made by the Princess nor anyone officially connected with her. It was as Vorselus feared.

The news left him in a daze. Late events, for reasons not quite clear, had wrapped him in a tight cocoon of danger. He must find out at once the cause of his peril. Deciding this, he repaired upstairs to his den of mysteries, his magical chamber, where he stored his arcane materials, his elixirs and potions, his scrolls of power and charmed amulets. He chose one of the latter, one possessing mild but effective properties when employed against the defenseless. He took himself to the library, dismissed Ling-das, confronted the girl..

"Be seated. I shall question you," he said, thrusting at her the silvery amulet fashioned in the form of a circled adder, its swollen eyes globes of moonstone. She accepted it meekly. "Hold it between your clasped palms. Do not lie to me, do not evade. I will know if you do."

"I will speak only truth."

"I think that statement accurate, whether you will it or no." Vorselus stood over her, arms akimbo, glaring down at his captive. "Firstly, Teresia—that is your name?—is the history of your early background, as told by you to me, an honest rendition?"

"It is."

"So be it. How came you to Dyrezan?"

Teresia cringed, lowered her eyes. "My people sold me into the household of Lord Albragon."

Vorselus snickered unsympathetically. "Indeed? I know the gentleman, somewhat—the convivial sort, eh?—and gossips tell tales. If I may credit half what I have heard, life for a pretty girl within his walls would be hectic, some would say entertaining."

"Certainly the one," she replied hotly, "definitely not the other.

32

The man is a degenerate beast."

"You speak of a lord of Dyrezan. I do not approve."

"I speak truth."

"So you do," Vorselus agreed, being in a position to know. When she spoke he watched her hands. "Albragon kept you busy for his pleasure, did he? He bequeaths a unique education. It is also of no importance. Did he send you to me?"

"No."

"Expand on that statement, girl, lest you anger me. How did you come to me from him?"

"I did not. Last night, without any warning, he gave me to another. At his order I was conveyed to another house."

"Whose house?" queried Vorselus.

"I don't know." On the last syllable she screamed, dropped the amulet.

"Pick it up," commanded Vorselus.

"It burns!"

"Only when you lie or skirt the truth," he explained. "Pick it up, and do not drop it again, or I will punish you." The amulet was steeped in a modest spell, one easily circumvented by the learned, but the girl's ignorance rendered her helpless. She could not commit falsehood without his knowing it. "Very good. Where were you taken?"

"To a big house down the street from the castle of Lord Albragon."

"You try me. Where?"

"I don't know the master." She squealed in pain again, but this time held onto the offending amulet out of fear. Vorselus had experimented with its effects, knew its potency. He admired her stamina. After several deep breaths she resumed. "Therein dwells," she gasped, "Lord Kardowan."

Vorselus almost reeled from the shock. Through great strength of will he concealed his weakness. Thus she delivered truthfully unto him the answer he most dreaded, the one calculated to inspire extremes of terror. While suppressing the surmise, he had guessed rightly. He did not understand the fact as yet, but he accepted the sense of it, an evil variety of sense. He asked, "What did Kardowan require of you?"

Now the story tumbled out quickly. That lord had offered her release from the repellent delights of Albragon's lair, and her absolute freedom as well, in return for undertaking the mission proposed by

33

him. She would be sent under cover of fraudulent bona fides to the domicile of a bad man, a conniving enemy of the state, and there she would insinuate herself into his presence, and having achieved that she would strike at the first opportunity. She would be honored for the assassination, her life and liberty secured for her fealty to the King and the people of Dyrezan.

And Vorselus was that vicious criminal doomed to death! Kardowan had arranged his murder in this curious fashion, obviously (there could be no other reason) because of the brief speech made by Vorselus, running counter to the mighty sorcerer's ambitions, at the King's council. It was his only link to the man.

The girl babbled on, her speech slipping at whiles into curious jargon. "I figured it was a crock," said she, "but the choice wasn't mine, and he offered me plenty. I'd die if I refused, die if I failed, die if I admitted anything to anyone. On the other hand, I got freedom and escape from Albragon's torture. See it any way you like, but it was an easy decision for me. Well, I blew it, and now I'm going to get it."

The wizard sat down heavily across from her, responded listlessly, "It looks very bad for you." The gears of his mind creaked round slowly, attempting to gain purchase of the discordant data sliding through them. The broad outlines of the nastiness ordained came to him clearly, but naught else. "Why me?" he cried.

Began Teresia, "Look, I'm really sorry about all this--"

"Shut up," he said. The curt words silenced the girl, inflamed his brain. Why him, indeed? Why would Kardowan attempt to kill him? The fellow could not imagine Vorselus a serious threat. Quite the contrary, he wholly divorced himself from those political machinations that might antagonize a grandee, that one or any other. He was a safe commodity, loyal but disinterested, ever willing to let affairs take their course so long as events allowed him to live as he pleased. What difference adhered in this situation?

He asked, "Did they—Kardowan or his men—explain why you must do this?"

The girl shrugged, shook her head. Vorselus rose. They had not; she knew nothing more. They would destroy him, without any human link in the murderous chain comprehending the matter. It was a murky, miserable, aggravating business.

At a ring Ling-das came running, appearing so quickly that he must have waited close by throughout the interview. "Any trouble?" he asked, with genuine concern. He eyed the prisoner hatefully.

"No," said his master. "She has told me what she can. Girl, give me that amulet. Ling-das, take her away. Lock her below, securely. I will ponder her fate."

"She is to die, of course," said Ling-das. "I will arrange it, quietly, if that is your way."

"Hold her until you receive further instructions." The eyes of both slaves flashed in surprise. Vorselus started to leave, then turned back to the girl, thrust the silver charm again into her hands. He locked eyes with hers, his face inches from her own. "One thing more," he demanded harshly. "When did you arrive in Dyrezan?"

Teresia quailed, sputtered, "My people gifted me during the feast of Tamatron, on the third moon." Vorselus grunted, "Not very long, then. Have you been out and about in the city?" "Until last night I remained trapped in Albragon's castle." "Have you ever seen me before?" "Never, master." She sounded scared, looked wonderingly as he snatched away the amulet.

"That is all. Ling-das, take her. I go." He stalked from the room, overcome by pangs of fear and baffled fury. He took himself to his magical chamber high in the house, there to sit and ponder.

Much needs be done. He had not the slightest idea what to do, but he must do it, and soon. He had to learn what was going on, how it applied to him, why it required his earthly removal. He knew a little already, perhaps suspected more. A cold, merciless logic underlay the attempt on his life. If that were his only concern!

Yet there was more. The slave Teresia must die—the fate decreed to all slaves who raised their hands against citizens—only he hesitated to issue the routine order. He held back, when giving voice to her doom should come without effort, because a little voice within (was it that same interior voice that had nagged him since yesterday morning?) begged him to spare the girl. It was madness, yet he deigned not to act. Only lunacy could explain this, or the haunting familiarity of the girl's face. He knew her, from somewhere or somewhen. He mocked himself for a fool, but Vorselus knew that he had been waiting for this girl to appear.

V. SINISTER MACHINATIONS

On the following day Vorselus learned much, surmised a deal, speculated about more. In addition, he went increasingly in fear for his life.

That morning, feeling piqued by his peculiar predicament—so beneath a wizard of his stature—sudden anger seized him, and he descended enraged and alone into the rough stone chambers of the lowest level where the female slave lay sealed in her living tomb, and he unlocked the iron door and threw it open, thrusting a torch within and crying harshly to her, "Girl, you perish this hour. I shall rid myself of one complication, at least."

Teresia screamed and threw herself to the floor, groveling, and with her face pressed to the dusty stones pleaded, "No, Master, I beg you, do not slay me. What I did I did without heart, only under compulsion, and had I known it was you who was to die, nothing could have raised my hand against you."

"What means this?"

She dared raise her head from the dust. "Master, at the moment I saw you, I knew we had met in an earlier year of my life, that I was somehow bound to you by duty and by love. In a flash I knew this, yet my poor understanding failed me at first."

Strange fever seethed unchecked once more in the brain of Vorselus. Was it for this that he had come to her? Nevertheless he scoffed at her claim. "Never have I left this city in my life. You have only just arrived. In what year, slave, did we meet?"

Teresia lowered one white cheek to the floor, replied dully, "I don't know. When I look back on that, I see darkness. It is like a hole in my existence. I know of it only because the hole is there."

Vorselus said, "Girl, rise." She did so, warily. He said, "My heart is a great mountain, and be sure that your feeble pleas cannot move it. Nevertheless, I too am aware of the connection between us. I sensed it immediately, and as a result of that your dire action surprised me more."

"Mercy," she whimpered.

"You are not to die," announced Vorselus. As Teresia beamed a relieved smile he frowned, adding hastily, "Do not forget henceforth that you are my property. Obey me always. Now, you must eat. Ascend before me. Afterward, we will converse at length."

Upstairs Ling-das risked remarking, "Master, I dread the consequences of your forbearance." Snapped Vorselus, "What is it to you?" His servant replied, "My health and well-being resides in your house. All at once there's too much weirdness here for your safety, therefore for mine. That worries me."

Vorselus relaxed, sighed. "Then we think alike, faithful Ling-das. You please me, as ever. I trust that you need not fear. For reasons beyond the obvious this girl is important to me. I will study her. What news in the city?"

"Wheeling and dealing in high places, nothing that I can figure. I detect the widespread assumption that you're supposed to be dead already. The source and the meaning eludes me at present. With your leave, I will go about again, hear what is said, discreetly question."

"You have leave."

Later Vorselus commenced a very different interrogation of the girl. This time he led her into his most secret place, the inner sanctum of his magical chamber, and there, surrounded by the leering visages of frightful gods chiseled and painted on the circular basalt ceiling and walls, he placed his subject on an unadorned oaken stool at the exact center-point of the smooth basalt floor, and he drew with treated blood a series of bright crimson circles and more angular geometric forms about her, and cautioning her to silence he stepped away to a slab of stone counter where he had arranged a number of arcane items. From porcelain jugs and bottles of colored glass he spread around his markings doses of fine, scintillating dusts and luminescent droplets of liquids. Returning to the counter, he removed from a dark slot beneath a hoary book, which he opened, and with his back to the girl he commenced to read.

Vorselus recited the Eighth Incantation of Toliman, conceived by that ancient worthy of a former age, which reveals as through a diary the incidence and arcs of the subject's life. It was not a truth spell per se—unlike the amulet, it did not peer into the brain's recesses seeking hidden thoughts lurking behind corners—rather a broad-brush mechanism for establishing identity, allowing a clever mage to view random facets of another's life. Against an undefended mind it was a marvelously effective tool.

The spell finished, he intoned decisively Toliman's word of power, a secret wrested, legend averred, from that brilliant mind on the rack before his ignominious death. Vorselus cast into the air a powder of commingled rare earths and finely ground, dried human tissues stolen for fee from the sepulcher of a dark southern sorcerer. As the powder wafted into the circled zone it flared and smoked. Vorselus experienced visions.

The first revealed episode disagreed with him. He watched, as a bystander, Teresia foolishly lunging at him with the knife. He blinked, to behold the girl in the gaudy, dimly lit seraglio of Albragon, and what he glimpsed in that scene so sickened him that he exclaimed out of disgust, an outburst sufficiently expressive that the living, present Teresia understood, and he heard her gasp in pitiful embarrassment. He did not see her, however, for the past images dominated his senses. He saw her standing sullen on the block at Vincalnac, saw her dancing in a temple decorated with polished skulls and illuminated by open flames in massy iron braziers, saw a little girl receiving curious instruction from grim-faced beldames in black. All this he saw, then a swaddled babe, yet the scattered, backward running chronicle did not cease there.

The images grew dark. Through that screen of blackness he vaguely saw his subject squirming on her stool. A fresh vision showed her, as an adult, hurtling headlong through a void. No, not her; a similar girl, certainly, most akin, but with differences of feature, long golden hair flying. Focus, though, he maintained, as if on the same human entity; an identity of spirit. It was she. That was Teresia, he realized, in another incarnation. There she sat at table in a strange room of crude, barbaric construction, sat in gloom with two others. One of them was himself! No, neither was that he, but a familiar stranger, like a long lost brother. Vorselus felt he knew the man. He had seen that one before; in a dream?

There the images stopped abruptly. Beyond that point in time— whenever it was—lay true mystery. Vorselus tried to decipher what he beheld at the last. That was magic being stirred, magic onto which the instructions of Toliman had latched, a peek into another time vouchsafed to a magical adventurer.

Vorselus leaned against the counter, shook his head to clear it. The slave girl sat before him expectantly. He asked thickly, "How much do you remember of that other time?"

Her eyes widened. "I know nothing, Master, of mysterious times and places. I am prey to ghosts of memories, which assail and torment because my ignorance of them feels unnatural. I believe I should know, but I don't. That's the truth."

"You are not the master-mind," Vorselus mused. "Even then— past or present?—you were choked by lack of insight. One knew more in those days, before your current life. Was that myself? Is that where and when you consorted with me?"

Teresia shrugged helplessly. "It must be, for there isn't another

38

explanation. As you say, we've never crossed paths in this world."

"Quite so. There is still another, a third spirit, for whom we must account. He was present at the last, ere you were reborn. Do you know of whom I speak?"

"I don't."

Vorselus frowned. As he logically reconstructed the situation, Teresia had been awakened to these former associations solely by sight of him in the flesh. Careful questioning elicited responses which confirmed this impression. She thought of a vague duo, knowing nothing of a third member of a spiritual trio because she had not yet confronted him. The wizard muttered, "He is out there somewhere, though."

He clapped his hands, said briskly, "That is all. Knowledge accrues, though the meaning dances out of reach. My dear, do not fear me. Regardless of recent unpleasantness, you are not my enemy—of that I am convinced—nor am I yours. I ask you to join my household of your free will, to live here happily and in peace, to serve me and to work with me. We can learn together. There may be joy in that for you."

Teresia acceded to his request with delight. There was much more to this matter that Vorselus was eager to pursue, and it was with keen regret that he forbore. At this delicate juncture present matters of life and death loomed larger.

Ling-das reported back that afternoon. "I hear it this way," he began. "Lord Kardowan plans a big move. His henchmen strain at the leash, awaiting orders that they already expect. Their lord's goal is consolidation of his new-found power, to such an extent that it can't be contested by his colleagues, either those remaining in the city or the real big boys off with the army. The late tale of their demise blows in the wind, without convincing evidence. The story, I imagine, is intended to mislead. When that bunch returns, if they ever do, Lord Kardowan wishes to be so secure that he can raise the entire strength of Dyrezan against them."

Exclaimed Vorselus, "And the first step in this grand reckoning is my murder? Ling-das, you tell me nothing. This is foolishness. I ask you why I am at risk."

"Lord Kardowan will not move against his chief enemies," Ling-das declared with assurance, "until he has the King under his thumb, nor until those enemies are divided and weakened. He begins his campaign in a small way, testing the waters, you might say, in order to discover how much he may get away with, and how soon. You opposed him, to a minor degree, which recommended you as the target for his initial test. He thought to crush you easily, sweep you from the stage of life without complications, affording him the opportunity to covertly establish his supremacy without courting danger to himself. Fence-sitters might jump his way if they saw you go down without retribution."

"It is monstrous," muttered Vorselus. "If what you say is true, then I have no choice but to strike back. The specter of a duel with Kardowan, however, chills my blood. I cannot stand up to him alone. I require allies, yet who will stand with me? I have led an insular life; I dangle too far from the inner webs of power, must beg for favors from those who could aid me. Why would they? These rumors are sketchy, innuendo without definite substance. I am convinced that Kardowan holds the knife at my throat, but lacking proof I hesitate to invoke the authorities."

Ling-das coolly observed, "Lord Kardowan is well on the way to controlling those authorities. Don't trust them."

Vorselus brooded, his features shadowed by uncertainty. "I must brew more magic," he said at last, "that I may see more clearly. This I should have done at the start, only the oddities of these recent days distracted me. Yes, let me peer through present gloom, that I may know the menace surrounding me."

So the mage took again to his secret chamber, and consulted his ancient tomes, and delved into their arcane lore, and plucked forth from their pages another spell, one associated with a series of charms that promised to give him sight of things not beheld by his mundane eyes. This formulation, styled the Deliverance of Tanaster from the famed wizard who once employed it to rescue himself from vengeful enemies, was prized for its ability to cast the senses into forbidden places where the invoker dare not tread.

More stirring of noxious solution, the application of heated ointments that reeked of corpse stench, the crushing of a venomous multi-legged thing drawn from an ebony box, the spattering of its steaming ichor into a brick pool of musty chemicals, and Vorselus whispered the words, motioning with forefingers and thumbs on the cadence of the syllables. The mixture eddied, grew dark, puffed stinging vapors into the noisome air. The conjurer coughed and blinked, spat acidic condensation from his lips. The potion frothed vigorously. He gazed intently into the silver-framed rhomboid mirror standing opposite him beyond the steaming liquid.

Said Vorselus, "Show me the house of Kardowan." An image

shimmered in that mirror, a view of the well-known edifice of the great sorcerer. "Show me the master of the house," Vorselus commanded of the magical force. The image faded to darkness. Obviously the great one was absent from his domicile. "Show me his dark chamber," he said, referring to Kardowan's special place of conjuration. Again, nothing happened. Vorselus rapped fist on brick out of frustration, kissed the smarting knuckles. He had foreseen this problem.

He was not the only wizard of Dyrezan familiar with this spell. Indeed, it was considered a classic of its kind, and all of his colleagues—surely those of any note—must live in awareness that it could be employed against them. This was not the concern that it might seem, for magic was a difficult business, requiring intense mental effort and the expenditure of valuable materials. The Deliverance of Tanaster would not, normally, be utilized without valid cause. Privacy, on the whole, remained safe.

What, though, of those with something to hide? The mage who needed to operate in the shadows might choose to employ safeguards, defenses against the prying incantation. A great magician could effectively seal limited chunks of geography from probing eyes. Kardowan, make no mistake about it, was one of those greats. Perhaps at all times, definitely this one, concealment was a primary goal.

So Vorselus' enemy protected his secrets. The house of Kardowan lay off limits to magical investigation. Nothing could be learned there.

Possibly he was not at home. That important man might be spending much of his time at court since his ascension. Was there any chance that the palace of Skyrax could be assailed from afar, ethereally broken into for viewing? Just the thought gave Vorselus fits of trembling, lest his action be found out, but he was desperate, reckless from fear. He turned the charms toward Skyrax's inviolate citadel.

He garnered nothing from the attempt. Of course the palace was shielded by the court warlocks, esteemed and redoubtable conjurers. He gave over that endeavor, wracked his brain, thought of something else. Kardowan may have covered himself and his property; what of his men? Vorselus turned to the lesser, that he might learn of the greater.

He sought the current location of Garok, Kardowan's chief man at arms, a burly brute well recompensed for his services, a likely

41

participant in nefarious schemes. Scanning possible hang-outs, Vorselus found him at board at an inn on the fringe of the government quarter, eating heartily and drinking copiously with three other ruffians in a shadowy corner. The wizard watched them long without gain, hearing only lowly talk and crude jokes, until suddenly Garok grunted through his furry beard:

"It misfired, that's all. Our lord learned everything through his spells. The girl choked, betrayed everything, spilled what she knew. The quarry knows our lord is after him. The boss won't waste any more time on him; he's after bigger game, and wants this little fish hooked immediately. He's being reeled in now. It's all arranged. Before the sun sets, he'll be finished. Once he's lured in, you play your parts as ordered. You got your pay, and there'll be more when it comes off. Believe me, this is only the beginning."

That was all of unique importance. Inconsequential chatter continued for well-nigh an hour, until Vorselus broke the distant connection and wound down the spell. The magic broth calmed, the mirror darkened. He left the chamber, retiring to his library to think.

They had been discussing him. The references to the girl, the quarry, the action that failed, these he readily understood as pertaining to him. Kardowan knew all; how, but by employing, with considerably more success, the selfsame spell that Vorselus had used? He should have guessed that. He was being watched by them, even as they plotted against him.

Another strike against his life was in the offing. It could come at any time. The situation simply terrified him. He strove to think of a way out. As he agonized Ling-das intruded, bearing startling news. No less a worthy than the eminent Lord Albragon was at his door, requesting audience on a matter of critical importance to Vorselus. Reported the loyal servant, "The lord begs that you receive him without delay, master, for your life hangs in the balance, and he desires to offer you his aid."

VI. THE FLIGHT FROM DYREZAN

Every slave of the household was instantly summoned to await bidding. Vorselus went to the door himself. He cried, "Enter, noble Albragon, and grace my house." The big man, soft, corpulent, genteelly smiling, strode heavily in massive boots into the foyer, his immense bulk wrapped in expensive, varicolored silks, his fat fingers festooned with gaudy rings. He said, "My retainers wait without." Vorselus clapped his hands, barked, "Ling-das, see to their needs. Feed them, offer amusement. All else, attend Lord Albragon." That personage jovially muttered, "You honor me, sir."

Vorselus practically stumbled over himself lavishing praise and, through his human tools, comfort to this important and renowned fellow. Some time passed before Albragon, sprawling easily at table with wine cup in hand, got to the point. Fingering his moustache he said:

"Rumors thicken about you, friend Vorselus. I trust that I may call you friend? Though we have had few dealings, I have long known you for an upright citizen, and a magician deserving praise. Your accomplishments, while quiet, are exemplary. Perhaps that is what has pulled you into an orbit of difficulty.

"I hear that you have run afoul of our colleague, the Lord Kardowan. Disconcerting at any time, positively dangerous now, for he, as you surely know, holds the ear at present of the most glorious Skyrax, your king and mine. It is bruited that Kardowan whispers slanders in that royal ear, seeks to eradicate your good standing, if not more. Are you aware of what I say, or does this come as news to you?"

"Painfully aware," cried Vorselus. "Of a sudden, I feel myself enclosed by malice. One attempt on my life has been made. Another, I know for fact, is in the works. I am to die this day. It is Kardowan who pulls the strings, solely because I spoke against him at the conclave. As if others did not! He desires my corpse to make an example to them."

"We cannot allow that," said Albragon. "It would not be just."

"Your statement salves my fears. And yet—" Vorselus hesitated. He poured another drink for his guest, emptying the bottle, called for another. "And yet, common talk has it that you are thick with Kardowan. Is not he your friend and associate?"

"I am every fine wizard's friend," purred Albragon. "As a relation, however indirect, of the royal house, I take pains to work with any

43

man who finds favor with the King. That is my duty. It will continue to be so. However, I demand justice in our public affairs. That is the hallmark of Dyrezan's greatness."

"Hear, hear!" exclaimed Vorselus. "No more would I ask. So, my lord, why come you here?"

Albragon grinned, leaned forward, paused to glance at the attending slaves. His host took the hint, dismissed them. Albragon went on, in a low voice, "I have arranged for you a private audience with the King. Princess Lora, who likes you, helped me manage it. Our benevolent ruler will see you on the instant."

Vorselus sprang to his feet, cried, "Oh, happy day! Gladly will I plead my case. But, good sir, I know not what dangers lurk beyond these walls. I feel myself all but a prisoner."

"I came to you personally," said Albragon, "that I might banish such terrors. For your safety you must travel in secret to the palace, with the genuine protection that I can offer. My carriage waits parked in the street. It will convey you covertly. I ride with you myself as guarantor of your healthy arrival. My men will see you into the halls of the palace, where the Princess—kindly nurtured child!—will lead you by the hand to her father. In her presence, no one will dare strike at you."

Vorselus nodded nervously, rapped his fingers on the table top, saying, "That settles it. We go at your pleasure."

"It pleases me to set forth now." Albragon rose, bowed, shook the hand thrust at him. "It brings me joy to be of service to you in a dark hour."

Vorselus hastily retired to prepare himself. Scarcely was he gone from the lord's ingratiating presence, however, than nagging doubts plucked at his mind. It was good of Albragon to intervene on his behalf, yet the man's reputation was so equivocal—why not be blunt within his own mind—so unsavory, that his sudden appearance called forth cruel questions which insisted on insinuating themselves into the equation. Vorselus admitted that he had never liked the man, whose character was bandied about with ribaldry in the meanest dives. He wished that a better patron had arisen to stand by him.

He would take, however, what he could get. Still, there hovered that threat, indicated by Garok, hanging over him this day. Life was too chancy to take chances. Before he rejoined Albragon he carried out a certain task, then called to him Ling-das and Teresia. In his formal robes, this he said to them:

"I go to the palace, there, hopefully, to repair my circumstances.

This man promises the cooperation of the Princess, who is benign and gracious, not wont to lend herself to skullduggery. That cheers me.

"Nevertheless, until this business be resolved, I walk in the shadows. Anything may happen. I fear for myself, and for my people. Ling-das, I charge you with the safety of my household, until I return. If you do not hear from me again this day, throw yourself on the mercy of the Princess Lora, and the court, Malfador and the Council, everybody or anybody who stands for decency. I would not have you, faithful one, suffer due to my misfortunes. Also, look to my books and materials arcane. Let no unfriendly hands seize upon them. Already, before I called you, I shrouded my secret chamber in magical snares and webs of defense. No one can get in there, without my leave, save at the risk of his life and soul.

"Especially, my servant, see to the health and well-being of this one. Teresia is important to me, for reasons which I must still grasp. Her coming means more than it appears."

Ling-das replied, "All will be done, though surely you will rejoice with us ere nightfall."

Vorselus clasped the fellow on the shoulders. "That is all, Ling-das. You may go." At his signal Teresia remained.

The wizard said, "Strange girl, I would be more easy in mind were it not for you. Your intrusion into my life is a factor for which I cannot account. Something more goes on here, something that only you and I dimly perceive, and perhaps one other, whom I know not. As your master I tell you to coordinate your actions with Ling-das, who is wise and accomplished beyond his station. If there be protection for you, he can provide.

"Now, I tell you more, as the professor." The girl's eyes widened and she gasped. Vorselus nodded. "You know that odd term, my dear? I learned it during your magical interrogation. It rings the bell? It is a man. Your fate means much to him."

Teresia said, "You are the professor."

"I am not," cried Vorselus. "Do not mistake me. I am who I am, and all I will ever be in this life. What has been, or what will be in far epochs, is senseless mystery which I tell you cannot influence the present. That must be true . . . and yet, at times, when I speak to you, I imagine that someone else—someone almost present—speaks through me. You are aware?"

"I am."

"Reason as you will. I feel an inordinate duty toward you, girl sent

45

to strike me down. I realize that action was the haphazard chance of life. Truly, I count you as a friend, though I could not explain that to another man living in my circle. Watch yourself, and perhaps in time you will be restored, to where ever you belong.

"There is no more time. Go to Ling-das." Vorselus marched downstairs to where Albragon waited with an impatient scowl, announced that he was ready. "Take me to the Princess," he said.

He entered the massy, thickly curtained carriage with its master, and surrounded by a screen of armed outriders they clacked down the street and into the broad avenue. Within, cloaked in the artificial twilight that smothered the westering sun, Albragon gave him a small leather purse, saying, "This contains papers which may interest the King when you show them to him. Hold them among your robes until he requests the contents." Vorselus accepted the package.

The four horses, under the steady hand of the driving slave, whisked them shortly into the great plaza about which rose the grand monuments of Dyrezan, stopping before the palace steps. Albragon stepped down first, surveyed the populous square with feigned casualness, then beckoned to his guest. Vorselus emerged, was escorted by a ring of henchmen up the steps and into the hall, where the guards bowed to Albragon and stood aside. "This way," commanded the great man, pointing away from the main corridor lighted by many lamps. "It is best that you travel a circuitous route. Princess Lora, choosing to favor me her kinsman, waits for you beyond. No one, not even I, am privy to what you two will discuss. Enter the passage, turn left, proceed to the purple doors on the right, enter therein and speak your piece. She will guide you from there."

Vorselus followed these directions alone through narrow corridors unpeopled, nor illuminated save by infrequent torches at the junctures of corners. Clutching the purse he turned, passed briskly to a set of double doors painted purple and ornamented with images of silver crowns, pushed through into the chamber. Within all was bright with lamp light. Three swordsmen stood waiting before the lamps, their faces darkened in shadow but plainly visible. They were not royal guards. They wore no uniforms, save that of private livery. One was Garok, Kardowan's man. "What means this?" cried Vorselus. "I come for audience with the court."

"You will have that," informed a voice, "at your trial, should you live so long." From an alcove stepped Kardowan himself, wreathed in the dignity of his official gray robes. He continued, "Vorselus, citizen of Dyrezan, I arrest you for treason against the royal family,

46

for the intended crime of assassination. Your scheme has failed. You go no further this day."

"I waste no words on you," Vorselus said warmly. "Your lies will not avail. Albragon knows I am here, and why."

"He does indeed," sneered the great mage. "I owe him a debt of thanks for his loyalty to me."

Vorselus blanched, cursing himself for a fool. He should have known. "So even the device of the Princess is again a blind? Your accusation is idiotic, Kardowan. It will not stand."

"So? Mase, the purse." A grinning, unshaven henchmen reached out, yanked the article from his grasp. Mase handed it to his lord, who opened it. Kardowan extracted, not revealing documents, but two very different items: one thing resembling some kind of malevolent charm—its basis a sort of large, desiccated spider—and a short but razor sharp, unhandled blade. He chuckled evilly, saying, "This is how my colleague will tell it: you begged him to arrange secret audience with the King, claiming information that must be imparted to the ear of Skyrax. He obliged, trusting you at your word, as we wizards are wont to do." Kardowan laughed. "Little did Albragon realize, he will sadly aver, that reckless ambition could drive you to such enormities."

"They will not believe it!" Vorselus shouted.

"The King will," came the gloating reply. "My testimony will convince. As for others, they will be paralyzed until I am rid of you. Your fate will quiet them, until I am ready for my next move. Men, at him!"

The three brutes in the instant drew their short swords and closed with him. A few paces, three thrusts of steel, and it was over; such, at least, was their intention. It did not come off so easily. For two days now Vorselus had been practicing, rote reciting to himself spells of self-defense. When he left his house he carried with him, not only the pernicious gift from Albragon, but a wallet containing his own substances, lovingly prepared for emergencies. He thrust his fingers into the open container, felt slimy ooze, crawling things. Something bit his finger; a good sign. Vorselus shrieked, "Azamodeus!" and a formless dark passed across the man, that Mase, directly before him, and coalesced into a shape repellent beyond sane description. The fellow screamed, crashed back against the far wall, as if hurled by a mighty arm. He sagged to the floor, limp, his head lolling on his neck at an alarming angle.

The other two assassins danced back, turning every which way,

47

dreading magical opponents. Kardowan barked a command, waved them aside, snickered with spiteful delight. "Stand ready," he said to them, then, "So, Vorselus, you are not quite the simpleton you pretend. That is good. I crave a little sport. Dare you pit your talents against mine?"

"Surely," he shot back, with more confidence than he felt. "You are the traitor. Death must be your punishment." And he thundered again the horrid word, "Azamodeus!" and loosed that baleful force from beyond the spheres on a keener foe. The shadow reappeared, that abhorrently shaped travesty of animate shadow, and it closed on Kardowan like a coiling snake. That mage thrust out his arms wide, fingers splayed, growled a rapid series of words like curses. The menacing shade dissipated on the instant.

"What you know," he said, "I know, and much more. A clever trick, that, one I learned in youth, half-forgotten with the years. Azamodeus—he of the seventh level—is an old friend of mine. We go back far together. I have sent him away on a minor errand. Now, Vorselus, meet another of my many acquaintances." Kardowan pulled forth from his full sleeve an object akin to a slender, spiky branch, willowy and flexible. He held it in firm, still hands, yet Vorselus detected hints of subtle motion in the thing. Yes, it squirmed—it writhed—at a word from Kardowan it sprang!

"Belanine!" he roared, and the thing metamorphosed into something else, of greater size and awful aspect: a skinny tree that crowded the low ceiling, with a ropy trunk rising from fat supporting roots and many thin branches fringed with scarlet leaves and dark crimson thorns, all twisting and lashing with frantic motion. The vegetable claws whipped toward their victim.

Vorselus screamed in abject terror at this horror, the fruit or eidolon of Belanine, a hideous entity unknown to him; pawed witlessly at the branches, felt the flesh skinned from the back of his hand; staggered, went down, tumbled to the rear. Solely by chance he fell through the purple doors into the corridor.

"Do not let him escape!" yelled Kardowan to his men, who had instinctively drawn close to him at sight of the fearsome being. Stung by the fury in his voice, they scrambled to comply, hollering and brandishing their swords, but the uninviting bulk of the monster blocked them, and while they endeavored to edge around it the leafy beast drew itself up on its thick roots and lurched forward, determined to reach its prey. The thing slashed wildly at Garok as he attempted to squeeze past, sending him reeling back with mutilated

48

face.

"Belanine!" Kardowan thundered again. He made passes in the air with his deft fingers. The deadly tree paused. Vorselus was not there.

He was running for his life down the dim passage, turning, breaking into the main corridor, hurtling across the hall and through the palace doors into the outer air. The sun feebly lanced through gathering dark clouds, the result of great magic in play, onto the steps and the plaza, where startled guardsmen turned as the wild-eyed mage dashed by. Vorselus was halfway across the square before Kardowan emerged, and from the top of the steps bellowed, "Hold him, stop the traitor! Kill Vorselus at once!"

Precious seconds passed before the guards, collecting themselves, took up the pursuit. Vorselus meanwhile had vanished from the square.

He kept running until his breath wheezed from him painfully as from lungs full of gravel. Safe for the moment, he had nowhere to go. It was not arrest that he dreaded, but peremptory murder. Evidence to support his fears quickly surfaced. Now creeping down an alley, he spied palace soldiers stampeding along the adjacent thoroughfare, their weapons unsheathed. He heard his name mentioned in a rough, unflattering manner, the uncouth words laden with threat. High in the cloud-mottled sky, among the tower-tops, a black orb rose wobbling, stabilized in the air, began to spout harsh statements in the coldly confident voice of Kardowan. "To all citizens of Dyrezan," it said, "to all who love their King, seek and slay the traitorous Vorselus, who would shed the blood of beloved Skyrax. Destroy him on sight!"

The fugitive darted into a concealing mass of wagon traffic, dashed across the Avenue of Kings, staggered into the green park, where he collapsed, utterly spent, behind the dense flowering bushes by the banks of the idyllic Tethe, beneath a steep mound graced by the winged statue of the minor hawk-faced goddess Perellvias. There, temporarily shielded from unwelcome attention, he panted himself gradually into a state approximating normality.

His situation was grave; nay, it was horrific. He dare not show himself, nor flee home, where enemies must already wait. Any attempt to contact the authorities would land him in the merciless clutches of Kardowan. Cut off from his most potent sources of magic, he had largely expended what he brought with him. He was no fighter. Vorselus was helpless, effectively friendless, in the midst of this great city his cherished home.

What, then, to do? Lying down and dying was not an option. He must escape, reach a place of safety. That qualification, however, ruled out every locale in Dyrezan. Flee the city—unspeakable notion—men might suffer exile from Dyrezan, but they did not voluntarily leave. It would serve no purpose. The civilization to which he belonged was a Dyrezanian world, and beyond its broad compass there was naught but barbarism and wilderness. There was nowhere for a condemned man to run.

It was an insane idea, anyway. Dyrezan was not like other cities, where he could hope to sneak out of the gate and flee stupidly and blindly into the countryside. Dyrezan sailed the skies, hovering far above its subject peoples of the great valley and the lands beyond. There was, he knew, a way down—the very magic that sustained the city high over the firmament provided the means—but never in his whole life had he seriously considered making use of it.

His enemies knew that as well as he did. It occurred to him that this absolute conviction worked in his favor. They would not expect him to run. They might not be prepared for that unlikely—nay, that preposterous—eventuality. If he evaded their net now, they might not think to cast it farther, at least until he had, for the time being, made good his escape.

The thoughts focused, the ideas crystallized. Getting out was conceivably possible; to where, then? Vorselus rose, brushed himself off, offered a prayer (it could not hurt) to watching Perellvias, set out along the green bank for the Celestial Gate, that terminal at the city's edge which connected Dyrezan with the subservient world of the terrestrials. He kept out of sight as best he could, ducking behind dense growths when passersby came his way. Overhead, at intervals, the authoritative voice of Kardowan urged his fellow citizens to the unusual liberty of murder.

There was somewhere he could run, a crazy chance, one that chilled him with the enormity of its dangers, yet still a chance. He slunk out of the park, slipped through the tangled lanes of an old neighborhood of the lower orders. He was far from his own district. No soldiers, as yet, prowled these streets, and the many pedestrians ignored him. He traversed a block of padlocked limestone warehouses, emerging from behind a decorative granite wall onto the avenue which led shortly to the guarded gate.

All these terrible events had been made possible due to the absence of Dyrezan's best men, those great ones off with the army exploring and, presumably, conquering somewhere in the remote and little known east. There were Nantrech and Morca with their troops and a team of stellar minds. If he could reach them—lay his case before them—perhaps they would respond with something other than a quick sentence of death. Good men, reasonable men, men without fear; if he must beg for mercy, let it be to them. Nonchalantly he approached the gate. Too many guards watched him, idly at present. They did not appear on alert. Their commander, to judge from his gilded and crested helmet, detached himself, put himself forward without apparent menace.

"Good day to you, sir," said the man with proper deference. Vorselus supposed he looked presentable enough, appropriately sorcerial. The soldier asked, "How may I please you?"

Said Vorselus, "I descend to the valley this day. My slaves—incompetent fools!—fail me. I must attend to this farcical business in the villages myself."

"Indeed? That is a shame. I would not have a worthy citizen troubled on my watch. Tell me your business, fine sir, and I will detail one of my men."

Vorselus cursed to himself this untimely compassion. He said sternly, "That cannot be, much though I appreciate the generous offer. No loyal son of Dyrezan may leave his post at this time, unless he is ordered away. Have you not heard? A fugitive, an enemy of the King, lurks in the city. You may be called at a moment's notice to join the hunt. Skyrax may have need of all your pikes and swords."

"That is well said." The fellow stared down the road at the glimmering towers rising in the distance. "I have heard something of troubles. I await orders."

"Then I shall pass. You must hold your post until word come."

"This way, sir." The man graciously escorted him through the olive marble gate, with its beauteous frescoes studded with the idealized eyes of mighty Xenophor, into the terminal. Obviously the truth of the situation had not crossed his mind. Why should it? That truth was wholly impossible.

Vorselus had never seen the interior before, but he knew of it by report. It was a spacious chamber, a cavern lined in bright metals, some precious, others obscure, formulations of alloys enhanced by mysterious charms that still amazed as they had in the time of the first Skyrax eternities ago. There were strange machines, composed of those metals and glass and weirdly glowing crystal, in banks along the near walls. Minor mages, men trained to function without understanding, manned these massy devices.

One called with a slight bow, saying, "Enter and make ready." Vorselus proceeded to the center of the room, stood within a rail of gold set into the polished bronze floor. It was a big space, one capable of holding a full company, or much merchandise. Through this room came all the visitors and all the goods that entered Dyrezan.

The man said, "We commence." Several hands moved in unison, pushed or depressed levers. From many lips rose a softly muttered chant. The machines throbbed. The inlaid crystals gushed their glows with greater potency. The high ceiling, so dark before, flickered with crackling tendrils of snapping blue light. An acrid odor assailed the nose of Vorselus.

Sourceless mist enfolded him. The chamber, its occupants at the machines along the wall, vanished from view. Vorselus' stomach lurched oddly as he felt the floor drop from beneath his feet. So it seemed; what he knew was that he no longer stood on solid surface, but hung, as it were, in a sightless void.

He deemed it a repulsive way to travel, being accustomed to solidity, even if it were that of a city hanging in air miles above the earth. That was normal and natural, the reality of his entire life. This creepy weightlessness unsettled him.

That it did for all of five seconds. As quickly as he plagued himself with ignorant forebodings Vorselus felt firm ground beneath his feet. He could see the floor now, precisely as before. The mist cleared in a moment, not dissipating, just gone. It was, he saw, a very similar floor, but not the same at all. He was in another softly lighted room, also spacious and lofty, also with its machines and serving wizards, but much less impressive. This one was purely functional.

Huge doors were drawn open from the outside by indifferent soldiers. Sunlight flooded in, making the traveler wince. Came the cry, "You may depart, sir, when ready."

Vorselus paced to the exit and emerged into the sun. Someone said to him with consideration, "Is there no one, sir, to meet you?" The wizard shrugged, passed by, strode a ways and turned to gaze upon what he left behind. It was a large, weathered bronze dome, rising from grubby earth, furnished with a handful of lounging soldiers who eyed him with some puzzlement but no keen interest. A wooden stockade—a mere wall of wooden posts set into sparsely grassy soil—encompassed all. Already, with so short a time separating him from the city, he found himself in primitive, alien territory. He looked up into the sky, seeking something, spied it instantly. Far above, level with scudding puffs of cloud, he beheld with an ache of longing the oddly tiny black mote that was Dyrezan.

He collected himself. "I go not far," he said vaguely to whoever had spoken. "My people await nearby. I shall walk."

The commander of the lower terminal nodded, although he seemed to greatly wonder at this. "As you say," he replied, but there was that in his voice which struck Vorselus as worrisome. He did not know how to act, chose to be gone on the instant. With an anxious gesture and queasy stomach he turned and made for the open stockade gate.

He departed through the opening in the stockade, turned one last time as two soldiers drew the gate shut. Vorselus saw their commander hurrying toward the dome before the door shut. Whatever his error, he knew that spelled trouble. The mage proceeded at a faster clip. Before him stretched a new and strange world, a land unknown.

VII. AMONG THE TERRESTRIALS

A brisk walk down a dirt road from the lower terminal, covering distance sufficient to shield him from the view of its guardians, placed Vorselus on a slight rise from which he could fairly survey his daunting surroundings. This he saw:

In every direction stretched about him a distant but still titanic ring of craggy mountains and cliffs of lifeless rock hiding the horizon. Above him hung the blue heavens framed by those spiky peaks, with the curious, disturbingly remote dark spot of Dyrezan hanging as if suspended by unseen wires. Far away Dyrezan was, yet as Vorselus knew appearing to the eye, from this angle, so much smaller than it should due to the vast magical energies upholding it, cosmic forces that actually warped or diffracted the space beneath and made the city seem at a vaster distance still. Within the circumference of the mountains lay the Valley of the Gods, from which Dyrezan sprang in olden times; an insular world of fields, woods, and streams, strewn with copious evidences of human presence. He glimpsed the taller spires of far off villages, beheld manifold signs of intensive agriculture amongst the farms and pastures. The road upon which he trod connected to others, all primitive lanes winding about the fence-enclosed areas.

Vorselus had known that this world of the sacred valley existed, that it fed and supplied the glorious city of the sky, but he had never seen it or its like before, and its nature and extent disconcerted him. It was a very big place, although he knew it to be merely a tiny corner of a gigantic world. Also he knew there were exits through the mountain ring, passes through which the caravans rolled and the armies marched, but at present he knew nothing of their location. If he were to reach Nantrech's army—a conceit that now smote his reason as absurd and insane—he must make for the east. Toward the east, then, unless hard reality argued otherwise.

Vorselus clumped down the road, feeling suddenly weary. He carried no food, little money, few resources, and it had already been a busy and taxing day. Try as he might, his attempts to calculate the magnitude of the journey before him failed utterly. He must take it one tired step at a time.

The road turned into a little wood, emerging on the other side by a weedy creek leaping with fish. Across a slender foot-bridge stood a gate in a decrepit post fence, beyond that a peaked-roof cottage amidst ripe fields of grain. Vorselus decided that the cottage was quaint. Never in his life had he called anything quaint, but the term belonged in his vernacular, and he guessed this was it. A ragged, dirty man, burned brown by sun, came around the house, made briskly for him, while a woman and children peeped from the doorway.

The man bowed, addressed him with reference. "Welcome, sir, to my land, the domicile of Sragan, who speaks. This be a rare honor. Hail you truly from the Sky City?"

"Indeed I do," replied Vorselus, who presumed that his clothing told that tale. "Just now have I descended from among the clouds."

"You can't have business with me," exclaimed Sragan. "I'm only a simple farmer. I've done nothing."

"I bear no fearful tidings," the wizard assured him. "I pass by, embarked on a pilgrimage which will carry my feet far beyond this bountiful valley and your charming home. I would go east, into distant lands, once I have made my way through the mountains."

"Out there?" the farmer cried. "Into the wild lands, traveling alone? It must be a needful quest."

It was not Vorselus' desire to answer questions, but to ask them.

He said so, pleasantly, but with snap in his voice. "Bless me with food and drink, good Sragan, and then tell me of the eastern road from the valley, and I will be on my way."

Sragan defined hospitality in word and deed. In a minute Vorselus sat at table, replenishing himself before the family, who dared not sit with him until he insisted. Then they sat mute until Vorselus sparked conversation. At his prompting they burst into a babble of curiosity. Said the wife, "The great ones come and go, but they never stop here." Asked a young boy with hands already roughened by labor, "Do you really make magic to fly from the sky?" Queried a younger girl with a mop of hair in her bright eyes, "Then why does he have to walk like regular people?" The head of the household put a stop to this prattle, giving Vorselus his chance to ply a few pertinent questions.

"To leave the valley and go east," explained Sragan, "you must travel south-east. From here keep to the right forks, which will lead you to the villages of Thraster, Ibicune, and Forian. From the last the main road carries you into the mountains and over the pass. Farther than that I can't say. In youth I served with the army, and a great conquest that was, but our march led north and west. I have climbed to the pass you seek, and gazed over the bare plains beyond, but I can't speak to more. It is only from report and common sense that I tell you the road goes on. Wonderful goods sometimes reach the valley from that direction; so, there must be a road."

Little more could Sragan tell, however Vorselus pressed his host. Yes, the army of Nantrech had marched away into the unknown through that pass. No, he couldn't say how far they had gone; to the ends of the earth, maybe? Although sated by his repast, Vorselus felt a sickish hollowness in his stomach.

He derived grateful cheer, however, from Sragan's offer of a room for the night. How foolish not to have requested it? He would have to think of these necessities in the future. While they dined and chatted, afternoon had given way to evening. Vorselus did not have his inviting home waiting for him, no coterie of devoted servants to care for him. All that was forever lost, unless he should win through to allies and redeem himself.

He accepted the offer. He slept in a cramped room (he owned bigger closets, and this the best in the cottage at that, vacated by the master and his wife for their guest's maximum comfort), in a small bed (two normally slept in that bed, and were those pillows stuffed with straw?), among rustic luxuries that scarcely rose to the level of meager essentials as he understood it, yet slumber quickly drowned his consciousness. He slept hard, but intervals of dream assailed, dreams of menace and fear, dreams of three strangers whom he thought he remembered, fleeting characters like dream persons recalled from earlier dreams. It distressed that he should be one of them.

He woke at dawn, to find the family of Sragan up before, ready to feed him again and see to his needs as they could. Outside, drizzle fell from an overcast sky. Vorselus felt cold and feckless. But he ate, and life surged within him, and Sragan volunteered food for the journey, which Vorselus would fain accept, save that he carried no pack. So Sragan gave him one—a dingy, stained thing that strapped to the shoulders—filling it with bread and dates and a skin of spring water before seeing his guest off at the gate. Said Vorselus in parting, "Should the Gods grant that I ever pass this way again, your kindness shall be rewarded many times over."

The light rain had stopped. The skies cleared. Vorselus tramped like a slave carrying the burdens of others down the muddy road, past other farms, crossing creeks, resting under trees when he desired shade. He nibbled at his rations, simple food that temporarily satisfied without sating. He entered villages, drew stares, went on without speaking. For the time being he required no further information. In this wise he spent the next three days, until he reached, in the lee of the majestic mountains, the village of Forian.

During his trek across this proprietary granary of Dyrezan he made do with the food provided by Sragan, stopping only for water and shelter. His identification as a wizard of the Sky City assured him basic courtesies—perhaps they imagined him a lord, to boot—but he dared not demand, nor was he quick to ask, lest he be refused and trouble follow. He wished to escape from the valley without drawing dangerous attention. In Forian it came.

It all came from his doing of a good deed there. Forian was a decent sized town, with clustered habitations, a few worthy of remark, some shops, and rather squalid temples all of wood and thatch. Hard on his entrance that morning into the gravelly streets he heard a commotion ahead, and from between two cottages sprang a running man, wild of aspect and demeanor, naked and muscular, with wide eyes and lank, greasy hair streaming behind. He dashed straight at Vorselus, shouted something unintelligible, swiped at him with a clubbed fist, dodged sideways when the mage stumbled and fell. Other folk appeared, hard men rushing forward. "Watch out," they cried. "He's crazy!"

The pursuers surrounded their prey, a ring of brawny muscle and threatening farming implements. Two paused to help Vorselus to his feet. One said, "That's Lanso, the lunatic. He's been stricken by demons all his life. Usually harmless, but he got out by himself, got confused, I guess, went berserk. If we can avoid killing him we'll have to chain him up."

Vorselus said, "Inherent madness? I have heard of this thing. It is, I take it, an ailment of the mind's tissues."

"As you say, sir, I'm sure," replied the other. The notion fascinated Vorselus. Dementia, the disease of the brain, did not exist in Dyrezan, where potent remedies were easily conjured. So elementary was the cure that even slaves were routinely treated and healed. Vorselus, although he had never indulged in the technique, was aware of the simple treatment, and felt quite up to rudimentary doctoring.

"Stand back," he demanded of the enclosing throng. Lanso stood wary, arms outstretched, fingers childishly splayed, glancing this way and that like a trapped animal. He pleaded for mercy, the words sloppy, incoherently vocalized. Vorselus approached. Concerned muttering wafted from the group. They dubiously made way. The mage locked eyes with Lanso. The abysmal creature tried to look away, could not. Yes, that much worked. The weak mind was hostage to the slightest exertion of magical will. Vorselus said, "Lanso, look at me. Look into my eyes. See the light within. Feel its fire entering your mind." Lanso stood motionless, his eyes vacant, his large unshaven jaw slack. "Come to me, Lanso, through the shrouding mists, awaken and emerge. Sense, and understand, experience clearly what is around you. Feel and understand." Vorselus focused his innate powers, those fundamentals of the arcane bred through countless generations into the bones of the sorcerers of Dyrezan, projecting that sublime strength into the mind of his patient.

A vague humanity flooded into that blank face. In his posture, his demeanor, Lanso all at once partook less of the grotesque, more of the healthy man puzzled by untoward circumstances. He stared thoughtfully at the hostile faces around him, looked down at himself, reacted with dismay at his nakedness. He tried to cover himself with his hands. He said, haltingly but without slurring of syllables, "I'm sorry about this. I want to go home."

"Clothe him," Vorselus commanded, "and take him to his people.

All is well with Lanso." Makeshift coverings having been produced, those delegated led the fellow away. The rest of the townsmen clustered about Vorselus, joyfully commending him. They cried, "The Gods sent this wise one to us." They invited him—practically carried him—into a tavern, where they urged upon him their version of a royal repast, joints of beef and a bottomless jug of wine. Vorselus accepted all they sent him, the meal and the praise. They crammed his pack with their choicest comestibles, gave him a handful of their scanty coinage. They feted him and questioned him generally, eager to know more of their benefactor. Perhaps the wine loosened his tongue; perhaps he admitted too much of his personal difficulties; he did not subsequently remember the fine details of their intercourse, but whatever the case, he began to receive worried stares, oblique questions hitting home on sore points. He began to wish that he were gone from them. Then came a clatter of many galloping horses, hooves pounding gravel. A stentorian voice bawled to all who could hear:

"We seek the traitor Vorselus, who unlawfully fled from Dyrezan and the justice of his King. In the name of Skyrax, I order you to acknowledge if you know of this fugitive." Vorselus' new-made friends had dashed outside at the interruption of their gaiety. Vorselus, hearing those words, sneaked a look out a window—saw a squad of armed soldiers on horseback, men of the Guards— scooped up his pack and darted without a moment's hesitation through the empty kitchen and out the back way. He dashed between cottages, raced across a small field and dived into the shelter of the encroaching woods. As he ran he heard the rising commotion of hue and cry, ordered barked, shouts of hostile eagerness.

He connected the chain of logic behind the event. His flight from the city had been discovered; the troops at the terminals had talked, scouts had been sent out to search the valley. The good folk of Forian, he feared, would tell all that they knew. He did not think that he had told them—he prayed that he had not told—of his destination. Had his contact with Sragan been detected? If so, he would be taken when he attempted to escape the valley, presuming he made it so far as the pass.

He had no other hope. He must go on. Vorselus tramped through the woods, a narrow arm of trees between broad pasturage, reached a brook flowing from his intended direction, followed that into deeper forest. Once he saw two guardsmen spurring their horses across pasture near what he took to be the road out of town.

They did not approach his leafy cover.

Night found him miserable in the forest, wholly divorced from his own kind. There he slept, on a damp mossy bank, or tried to do so. He may have snatched a few winks from uneasy awareness. Regardless, the ensuing morn found him unrested and uncertain, feeling shabby, doubting his chances. He was not far from the foothills and the bottom of the pass—indeed, he had expected to reach it yesterday—but he dreaded what might come when he debouched, as he eventually must, from the forest that protected him.

When he did, emerging near what should be the right road, Vorselus had steeled himself to the wariness of the hunted. He did not tread the road. He slipped from wall to haystack, from haystack to tree, from tree to shrub, always watching for prying eyes. He had learned to welcome sightings of rustics who might aid him; now he shunned them, lest they know of the pursuit and wish to ingratiate themselves with their masters in the sky. One misstep, one betraying word, and he was done.

Vorselus reached, alive and free, the gradual slope leading up to the pass. The good road, with much rocky concealment to each side, lay unguarded, at least from within the valley. That comforted him; even now they could not conceive that he meant to vacate Dyrezan's precious precincts. Why should they? It amazed him. The mountains of the south-east rose like a wall before him, that single road promising egress. Up he went, ever scanning near and far for danger.

Vorselus had lived a life lacking in physical exertion. To him the word "strenuous" connoted intense thought. His efforts in recent days had ground him down. Now, by his own estimation, he suffered greatly. Climbing to the pass proved onerous work, a cruel ordeal so unnecessary in a justly ordered world. He was convinced that the air temperature escalated as he mounted the slope, though it should have cooled. His water supply dwindled at an alarming rate. He sweated; annoying grit worked its way into his sandals, the thongs chafed his flesh. Truly, those shoes weakened under the strain of sustained marching. He owned many fine pairs suited to the streets of Dyrezan. What good were they to him now?

Despite his misery he gained the pass. The mountain walls drew inward, steepened, enfolded him between vertical cliffs where two wagons could scarce pass one another. His view of the valley shrank from a panoramic vista to a narrow corridor, a thin window into the partly familiar. Strange as it was to him, the Valley of the Gods

59

linked him to home. What kind of world lay beyond?

Vorselus rounded a granite obstruction, strode into opening ground and almost walked right into a military post. He saw those soldiers in their primitive camp before they saw him, plunged in time into a dry thicket within a rocky cleft. There were not many of them—a squad, maybe, with horses tethered by a brick cistern, and a few purely functional structures of little account—but they blocked his way as surely as a host behind a battlement. Worse, at that moment came the tell-tale sounds of fleet steeds racing through the gap behind him. A horseman galloped into view, a slight man on a big horse laden with bags, accompanied by three mounted soldiers. They slowed, trotting into the camp, where they hailed the men of the post.

Vorselus overheard some of their exchange. "Communications from King Skyrax to the army," bawled the well laden rider. "I'm a courier, appointed by Minister Kardowan to convey political messages of import to Lord Nantrech. Here is my seal. Water and feed our beasts at once, and share with us your supplies, for I must be on my way." The growled response: "So be it. You'll reach bottom ere nightfall."

The name of Kardowan sounded as a curse in the ears of Vorselus. He wondered what that murderous rogue was up to now. The incident reminded him that he was still well within the orbit of his enemies. How far must he travel to escape their net?

For the moment, he was not going anywhere. Dyrezan did not allow just anyone to wander into its valuable valley; that guardianship also hindered easy exit. He would wait until nightfall. So deciding, he crept farther into the cleft, which became a rocky wash shielded by short, scrubby trees. There he spent the disagreeable remainder of the day, without the climb to warm him feeling the chill of elevation, hunched fretfully behind a boulder.

With the fall of darkness he made his move. He doubted there were more than twenty guards at the station. Most would sleep, a few remain attentive, hopefully not for his sake, but he would not bet safety on that. He inched down the cleft, sliding along the rocks, terrified by the reflections of a campfire flickering against rough hut walls. A shadow—no, two shadows—moved there. He heard muttered conversation. Tethered horses shifted, whinnied inquisitively. Vorselus hated that. So quiet was he, tip-toeing through the dark, that he imagined himself a ghost, intangible to men, detectable only by the keen senses of their animals. It had better be like that.

He did it. Without tarrying Vorselus congratulated himself, slipped back onto the road beyond the camp and picked up speed. He ran for a spell, down the outer slope of the pass, under the immense canopy of stars, into supreme darkness, a singular, clinging blackness of night that he had never hitherto known. Sometime later the moon rose, and by that pale light he guided his steps down the mountainside to the foothills beyond. It took him all night, but he reached the bottom and set foot in those mysterious lands outside the valley, lands foreign and frightening, regions he had never cared to know, but into which he must boldly venture were he to survive.

The dawn brought sights unfamiliar, but not especially horrid. The mountains towered at his back, while before a plain of waist-high grass stretched to the eastern horizon, its interminable expanse broken only by widely spaced clumps of trees and a thin ribbon of greenery that paralleled his road. He stood at a junction of sorts, the intersection of dusty lanes. His route ran due east, and he wasted not a moment in embarking upon it. He covered near a league before his nervous energy abruptly burnt out, and he detoured into the dense grass to drop insensible from sheer exhaustion.

So he crossed the grasslands, the journey of a week, a rather lonely march through lands largely unpeopled. The long green ribbon cloaked a stream which flowed down from springs among the lofty heights. Judging by the infrequent dwellings of good size and quality he glimpsed far off the road, and the teeming herds of various livestock—cattle, horses, even ostriches—that he skirted, Vorselus deduced this to be a region of great landed estates, another component in the mammoth food supply required to sustain Dyrezan. It pained him that the city in the sky could not be seen from this vantage, as the high rim of the mountains and the distortions generated by the uplifting magic blocked the view. Even that cherished glimpse was denied him.

Day by day the westward mountains receded and shrank. Few people passed him on the roads, and when they did he usually ducked into the nearest copse of elm and oak, which always shielded ponds for the herds. Occasionally a big caravan rattled by, parades of covered wagons rolling stolidly amidst driven herds moving west. Many of these folk were dark and strange to him, but in present circumstances he dreaded them less than his own kind, and he dared treat with them, swapping a silver coin embossed with the eagle of Dyrezan for a cooked meal. They told him the valley was their destination. He muttered something of a pilgrimage, which they believed as they chose. Otherwise he kept to himself, drinking from the creek, bathing in the cold waters (it kept off that maddening itching), doling out his rations with new-found parsimony. Mere days, he brooded, since he snapped his fingers to receive a surfeit of luscious viands! How could this be? Poor Lanso was home again, Vorselus supposed, perhaps happy; not he, not now, perhaps never.

He marveled that more caravans did not clog the roads, until he remembered that the civilized and semi-civilized subject kingdoms lay mostly to north and south of his home territory. West and east had ever been wild, often overlooked in the eternal sweep of history recorded in the scholarly halls of Dyrezan. The hundreds of generations he called his ancestors learned much in certain ages, forgot much in others. Vorselus bitterly admitted that he had ignored too many scrolls and traveler's tales that would have stood him in good stead now.

The great plain terminated at a forbidding wall of murky forest. The road ran into it, so he went into it, and for a dismal period he lost the sun on his face and tramped in shadow. Vorselus would feign believe that he had surpassed the limits of Dyrezan's sovereignty, though reason told him that could not be. Had he not heard of the great sea that marked the boundary in this direction? Through a sea of trees he swam, a desert of oppressive foliage. Dull-colored birds screeched at him, furtive beasts slunk through the undergrowth, rustling the branches and scaring him via the medium of dour imagination.

Yet within he discovered villages again. Inconveniently scattered, small and rude, but men dwelt here, men somewhat of his people, clearly related if not exactly like. Two habitations he slipped around, but by the time he reached the third, ten days into the murk woods, his food had given out, spells of reinvigoration no longer ameliorated his weariness, and in a state of desperation he showed himself. These folk were cold and wary, perhaps unused to strangers, especially those who offered enigmatic account of themselves.

This was, they told him, Claxis in the province of Fendar, and they acknowledged Dyrezan as master, a state of affairs older than memory, though it seemed to mean little to them except during the annual collection of taxes. Life went on regardless in ancient patterns, rough lives spent in their arboreal dwelling place where the effects of great events in the world scarce penetrated. Vorselus saw nothing to remind him of Dyrezan or even the people of the valley.

He asked of the soldiers. Did not troops garrison this far-flung province? They snorted, averred that the soldiers had all gone away, way off to the east, to the distant sea and beyond, out of the ken of men. It suited them, they confessed, to have the soldiers gone.

Vorselus, craving a bed, inquired at the dilapidated tavern after a room. The churlish landlord regarded him thoughtfully, pressed a few annoying questions, then turned to tear down a broadsheet nailed to the wall before agreeing to lodge him in that musty place. A room in the back, woefully unprepared, would serve him that night. Vorselus accepted with forced graciousness. Two coins—his last two—bought him a room with a cot and an ill-cooked dinner.

The mage ate what he could, surreptitiously stuffing extra morsels of bread into his pack. He repaired to his room in the middle of the afternoon, eager to rest those bones of his body that always felt out of sorts now, only a muted hubbub from the airless main hall disturbed him. He sensed that the tavern was filling up with customers, supposed that they had naught better to do of a lazy day. Snatches of conversation drifted to his ears. "I tell you it's he—." "—pay much for his—" "—unawares in sleep—" "—dead or alive."

Vorselus snapped to awareness. He had slept. Dim daylight still filtered through the sagging shutters of his window. He laced together what he had overheard, tied that to the furtive sounds of approach at his flimsy door. He fancied heavy breathing on the other side, surely heard exchanged whispers. He rose from the squalid, filthy cot, donned his pack, braced himself for what he knew was coming.

The door burst open under the impact of meaty shoulders. The first assailant tumbled headlong into the room. Vorselus shouted an ugly word of import terrible and mysterious, laid his open palm on the man's breast, decreed magical death. Weird green light flashed. The man shrieked and went down heavily, not dead, still writhing, but insensible. Dealing death demanded mighty magic, and Vorselus had not his precious materials, nor the innate power to seal fate. Great Kardowan could do it with a word, perhaps Albragon and a few others; Vorselus could not. His attackers were not so aware, however, so they fell back a space, until they nerved themselves to advance in a body with knives gripped in their fists. "Kill him!" they bellowed. "He's the one the sky lords seek! The wizard's head for a cask of gold!"

No doubt a promise guaranteed, Vorselus instantaneously reasoned, by the proclamation hidden from him by his esteemed landlord. He picked up the light, rickety cot, flung it at the posse. Lunging to the window, he smashed the fragile shutters with clenched hand. The thin wood disintegrated. He flung himself through the gaping hole, hit face first in mucky loam. Struggling to his feet, he saw one livid, sneering face thrust after. He screamed the hurtful word again, pressed his fingers into that hateful visage. The man squalled in pain, fell back into the room.

Vorselus laughed, made as if to go for his tormentors, recollected his situation and ran. There were too many of them, their greed fueling them with a power that he currently lacked. More came around the side of the tavern as he raced across the squalid yard toward an alley between wretched huts. Vorselus splashed through dumped filth, heard a woman's voice shrieking from a window. Footsteps pounded behind him, punctuated by fierce cries.

Then he was in the forest, again a fugitive lurking in the wilds on the pathetic fringes of civilization. To the immense relief of his tortured nerves he heard no more sounds of pursuit, but the nature of his situation horrified him more than ever. This time he fled with scanty supplies and the sure knowledge that every hand within reach was raised against him.

Half a league to the east he regained the road, tramped hopelessly for the rest of that day, dreading any meeting while suffering from aching loneliness. The next day he detoured into the spooky forest again, avoiding another village populated by men he dare not trust. His food gave out. His worn sandals fell apart. He drank from the stream until it turned away, cupped handfuls of silty liquid from woodland pools, felt queasy afterward. His sleep that night was abominable.

Another day, and he picked up the eastward flowing creek once more—despite its small size, its surprising length suggested river to him now—that and the long road being all that tethered him to his receding homeland in the west. His former life (any former life!) seemed a mirage. Hunger took big bites out of his stamina. He walked half in a fevered dream, knowing only the straight arrow of road and the passing trees and weird faces born of confused memories that thrust into his and spoke to him of senseless matters. Once, maybe, those matters had mattered, but they shrank to meaninglessness now.

He fell flat on his face, gritty sand in his teeth. He pushed himself up on an elbow, reached for his pack. It was gone, discarded during a bout of delirium. The intense sunlight stabbed his eyes.

64

Where were the shadowing trees? He heard distant voices. Did his pursuers come? He rose to his knees.

Was this crazed fancy? With bleary eyes he gazed across a wide expanse of low dunes which gave onto a sloping beach, and beyond that he beheld a lapping sea that stretched from north to south and away to the eastern horizon. A stiff wind from that sea blew sand in his face, and the smell of salt. By the shore a huge, formal encampment, almost a town in its complexity, teemed with men. Several approached him.

Vorselus raised his hands, cried out for help, announced himself with vestigial courtesy. These men were soldiers of Dyrezan! In his madness he instantly accepted them as saviors, declared to them in frenzy, "I am on a mission to the army of Lord Nantrech. I seek him, and Lord Morca, and the other great ones who faithfully serve our sovereign, that I may report to them of conditions in the city. Take me to them, I beg of you."

Rough hands seized him, held him callously upright as a red face redolent of coarse brutality glared into his own. This fellow, an officer of lowly rank, snarled the query, "Call yourself Vorselus?"

"That I am. Indeed, I am he, ready to report. Give me food, and lead me to your masters, that I may speak with them."

"Satisfactory identification," snapped the officer, drawing his dagger of office. "It's as the King commands. I'll take his head this instant."

Vorselus writhed futilely in the grasp of the soldiers. "You dare not!" he screamed. "I must see Nantrech, you fool!"

A chilling laugh shut his mouth. A higher ranking officer on horseback towered behind the group. He said, "So, this is the dangerous fugitive Vorselus, enemy of Dyrezan and foe of the good. Little did I expect to make your acquaintance. Know, sir, that I am Kenko, commander of my Lord Nantrech's base this side of the water, also arbiter of your fate."

Said his subordinate, "Let me cut his throat now. We'll send his head back as a gift to King Skyrax."

"'Kill him, if necessary,'" quoted Kenko, "'otherwise detain and hold him for fitting punishment.' Believe me, they have a rare entertainment planned for this fellow. What a treat that would be. The Gods grant that I find occasion to attend! Errant wizard, you choose to arrive at a bad time. I can't spare good men to escort vermin west. On the contrary, the supply barge leaves this noon on schedule to cross the water to the army, and I must see to its manning." He turned to scowl at the large, flat-bottomed ship, with furled sails and unattended banks of oars, wallowing in the surf. "Either I keep you here for an indefinite period—a scheme which suits me ill—or I send you on to my Lord Nantrech, as you profess to desire, if you can find him. That possibility amuses me. Men, I so order. Nantrech, ever wise, will decree when and how this animal is destroyed.

"Guard him. Feed him, that he live until the moment of deserved doom. Have him ready for the noon boat. He sails on it, to the wilds beyond the outlands." Kenko leaned close, grinned nastily. "Enjoy your voyage, Vorselus. Look out there, you scoundrel. There's hot work beyond the seas. Vicious war rages there, at the ends of the earth. What is happening out there? Who knows what may happen? If you're very lucky, you may die with an enemy sword through your breast."

VIII. A PRISONER OF NANTRECH

As the heavily laden barge rolled and heaved its way across the great sea, Vorselus found much to complain about his current lot. That his captors would deign watch closely a reputedly despicable criminal surprised him not; they made known readily enough how ill they thought of him. That they might decide to forgo granting liberty of the ship to such a viper he would have endured with stoic grace. Under the best of circumstances, to be sure, he must take as insult their feeding him on their leavings. The circumstances, though, were not the best, were of a caliber to be endured only under duress, which they supplied in plenty. They held him like a dangerous monster below deck, stripped of his grimy garb, cached in a cramped hold, dark and airless, a slimy cavity wedged in a sealed gap between compartments of rowers. There they kept him, his weak, skinny body festooned with chains fit for ravening beasts. Wrists, ankles, and neck were so encumbered, with relief afforded from necessity a mere ten minutes each day. Only the numeration of those precious intervals gave him awareness of chronology. Many such passed. He thought much, to little purpose, speculated lamely on fate and the future. He lived still, which considering what he had lately endured was a feat worthy of some slim satisfaction.

Came a day (was it seven days into the blind voyage?) that he felt a throbbing shudder not fostered of wind and wave, and the small, square plank door to his cell was thrown open out of schedule, and this time men entered with his stolid, voiceless keeper to unlock his weighty manacles and haul him roughly from that dank tomb. They dragged him onto deck; he cried out against the stabbing sun; they pulled over him a long, scratchy shirt and pushed him down the gangway to an unfamiliar shore. It took painful minutes for Vorselus to see clearly his surroundings.

If that be the morning sun, then this was the eastern shore of the sea. The wind kicked up the waves, which foamed and frothed on a steep beach of white sand that gave onto a flat strip of gravel littered with larger rocks. The beach arced in a kind of cove, giving some shelter to the dozen ships of war anchored there, abutting a wall of limestone cliffs that beetled in a series of natural terraces sprouting narrow clusters of lush greenery. Straggling along the edge of the lowest terrace he beheld a vast encampment, much larger than that of the western shore, fortified with a stockade, which he immediately realized marked the current abode of the military expedition of Dyrezan commanded by Lord Nantrech. Soldiers in familiar gear were everywhere, some at rest, others at attention, on watch, or busy with the minutiae of camp life. Above them, within caves or shelters in the cliffs, he discerned other people of a type unknown to him. They were squat, swarthy folk, horribly primitive in appearance, unclothed save for loincloths among the men, short skirts of drab linen for the women, the few children in evidence going stark naked. They regarded him, or the ship, impassively.

Several vessels of war hugged the shore. Sailors running from them flocked to the barge, commenced the unloading. Vorselus was not granted time to observe more. At a curt order from the captain soldiers ringed him, shoved him up the beach toward the walled camp.

They pushed him to the open gate. Gruff communications with the stockade guards established his identity and status. Handed over to this team, they again drove him along, threading a path among well-ordered tents to the center of the camp, where stood a large pavilion of silk, white with blue horizontal stripes at the corners and flaps. The golden eagle banners of Dyrezan flanked the doorway. Fierce warriors blocked the entrance, tall, brawny men whom Vorselus recognized as troopers of the Royal Guard. A soldier growled, "Here's one for the disposal of Nantrech." The pavilion guards searched him efficiently, brusquely hauled him indoors.

It was, after all, a kind of culmination to his quest. There, at long last, Vorselus found and met and treated with great Nantrech, lord of Dyrezan, adventurer and scholar whom the lesser mage had respected and adored for his incredible achievements, and mighty Lord Morca too, renowned warrior magician, and other lords of great repute; Harmon, scribe of strange folk and bosom friend of Nantrech, and Theodises, wizard of the Eclarion Circle, and more, all wise, learned, important. They were there, or they presently joined the gathering, at which they would determine the fate of Vorselus.

At first he feared a quick decision. Vorselus entered that house of silk—lavished with furnishings suggestive of good living in the far away Sky City—dressed and dealt with as a low born knave, human refuse deserving of summary attention. They brought him before Nantrech, seated at table with wine and wizards, in converse with Morca. Vorselus knew them both by sight and occasional greeting. Liege-men stood at their backs, servants flitting about at command. Nantrech was an elderly man with a full, straggly white beard and fussy mannerisms, draped in colorful robes indicative of sorcerial prowess and high rank, leaning back in a camp chair. Morca also stood out in that assembly, a large, muscular fellow, his youthful, clean-shaven features harsh and intense, crouching forward over a map with his massive arms resting on the table. A great wizard, in addition every inch the warrior, accoutered even in council with his weapons and his chain mail bearing the emblem of the Royal Guard. Both appeared focused on weighty matters.

Vorselus' identity was announced with precision and deference. Nantrech paused in his meditations, squinted at the prisoner, snorted unkindly. "Five days ago we heard by King's messenger of you," said he, "the first communication in a long while, but I did not think to see you here, of all places. Where, though, does a traitor hide from his just fate?" Vorselus blurted a protest, and Harmon slapped the table, crying, "Life is too short and chancy to waste precious minutes on renegades, especially one so malodorous and bedraggled as this. Run him through now, or ship him back to the King for loving disposal." Morca shook his head with a grunt, thrust out a pugnacious jaw and said, "With what is afoot now, I can spare nary a man to watch him. It is death or nothing."

Morca eyed the captive dubiously. "I know you," he said presently. "I remember you well. Are not you the Vorselus who won the prize for conjuration at the Festival of Prafinias, when I was just a boy? I recall begemmed birds in flight over a shimmering rainbow of transmuting colors. The crowd roared its approval of the spectacle. That was you."

"Indeed it was," replied Vorselus, "in happier times. I have cause to be thankful for much in my past. Lately, my lord, life takes an ill turn."

Interjected Theodises, "Assassination disagrees with me. Seek not sympathy here."

"I am no more an assassin," insisted Vorselus, "than yourself. You have been told lies by those who fatten on same."

"These lies are told by Skyrax," observed Nantrech crushingly, "in official communication to me."

"Written in the hand," retorted Vorselus hotly, "or at the instigation of Kardowan, who has made himself my enemy, and acts as the enemy of us all."

"A ludicrous alibi. Our esteemed monarch would not advance that brute over us. Perhaps you are the fomenter of those hateful rumors."

"I have experienced the reality of my assertions. I am a hunted man, because I dared oppose him in meager fashion. If he reigns, I lose all, which is much."

Morca grimaced, an alarming sight from a man whose merest frown caused hardened warriors to quail. "These tales disturb me. It is strange that we hear so little via regular channels, not even proper replies to our couriers; stranger still what reaches us borne on winds of rumor. Lately I keep hearing of Kardowan. That festers in my guts. If there be truth in the stories, then an honest man might needlessly suffer."

Nantrech responded with impressive gravity, "Our King is good and gracious. He would not submit to the dominance of evil."

"The best ruler," Vorselus almost shouted, "is no better than his advisors. Kardowan strives to conceal the truth in my case and yours. What of your couriers? Do they ever return? Kardowan pretends to receive no news of your expedition, put it about that you are all dead. Now he sends you a malicious message from the King. I beg of you, do not act in haste on commandments rooted in prevarications."

Nantrech muttered into his dense beard, "I grow bored. The next stage of our expedition begins. I would discuss that, and the learned submissions of Harmon, and other vital or interesting business. Lord Morca, I delegate this tiresome duty to you."

69

That one gravely said, "One more head missing from its shoulders will not shake my world. Vorselus, you are to die. Tell me, why strike at your King? Where is the gain to you?"

"There is none whatever," Vorselus replied with intense emphasis. "I am a quiet man, leading a quiet life. Big matters are beyond me. Surely you all know enough of me to believe that."

Morca rose, his eyes bright, a hint of a smile on his lips. "That has been my impression of you, to the extent that I deigned notice. My friends, recently I voiced concerns relating to the odd reports reaching us from home. This tedious business of Vorselus appears to connect, in some fashion, with that flighty scuttlebutt we have discussed. I would know what is fraud, what is genuine. With this man in our custody, truth may be rendered available. I suggest an experiment in magical interrogation."

Nantrech shrugged, grumpily replied, "I see where you go. You are a busy man, one on whom I rely. I take it ill that you would waste scarce hours on this craven scum."

"Humor me, my lord," Morca gruffly requested, "as a favor. I ask for a minor diversion to pick this mind. What say you, Phillipan? Can you quickly arrange it?"

"That I will do," said this personage. Vorselus paid real notice to the young officer at Morca's back, started as if stung. He knew the man—knew him—like yet unlike, but something akin to recognition smacked his psyche.

"It is you," Vorselus cried, "the missing one, the third member. Truly, it is! Look at me, boy. Strain for the knowledge. You have seen me before."

"What goes on here?" Nantrech caustically demanded. He reacted with heightened attention to his prisoner's outburst, and to Phillipan's white-faced, flustered response. "Morca, what are we learning? What should I deduce?"

The warrior mage turned to study his fellow soldier with a critical eye, shrugged. "It passes my understanding, my lord. Vorselus is no stranger to any of us, I grant, but I am unaware of close ties between him and my aide. Phillipan, explicate for us."

Phillipan was tall, stringy, clean-cut, every inch the dutiful, budding officer. He stumbled over his words before he answered coherently. "I can't properly explain," said he. "I know Vorselus to look at, as do you all, but there's something more: a memory, as one derived from a dream."

"And the girl?" Vorselus pressed. "The other one, boy; tell me of her."

Theodises sniffed. "Sounds like confession of conspiracy."

"That's a lie," Phillipan snapped with haughty disdain. Morca offered him a cup, which he downed at a gulp. "Thank you, my lord. I'm blameless. I believe this man is too. The why escapes me, but I feel it, deep in my soul. The girl; there's something about that, but I can't make heads or tails of it. A filament of recollection, maybe, but I haven't seen her."

"She resides in my house," said Vorselus, "in Dyrezan. Safely there, unless the agents of Kardowan have acted against her. She calls herself Teresia." Phillipan struggled with this information, shook his head hopelessly.

"This case bounds forward in delicious complications," Morca mused. Fiercely he said, "Prisoner, I will have the truth. I shall—with the acquiescence of just Nantrech—explore the corners of your brain via stern magic. Submit, and upon verification of your claims I may intercede for you. Be warned: any resistance, any noncompliance, and I shall pestle your mind to mush. What say you?"

Vorselus replied, after a deep breath, "I willingly accede to your just demand."

Nantrech waved a hand dismissively and nodded. Morca said, "Phillipan, accompany me. Guards, hold this one gently until I call."

Came the dusk, and Vorselus was led to a large but utilitarian tent near the pavilion of Nantrech. Outside its heavy folds the involuntary guest shrank back from the specter of a dreadful creature that paced aggressively before the door. It resembled—nay, was—an unusually large, sleek tiger, only clothed in glossy fur of night black with bright white stripes. A sudden yawn bared a red mouth harboring horrible fangs. His guards pushed Vorselus past this ominous apparition, leaving him grateful not to face savage feline judgment. Within the tent Lord Morca and Phillipan awaited him, seated at a bench behind a plank table loaded with exotic devices and vials of mysterious powders and liquors. This, the prisoner realized, was the mobile form of Morca's magical chamber, stocked with, at the very least, a fine selection of that wizard's arcane materials. Hearing an insistent growl outside, Morca declared to a soldier, "My Treenya grows restless. Feed her fresh meat," then barked at Vorselus, "Sit down," indicating the near bench. Vorselus settled himself, almost panting from tension. The lord said to Phillipan, "Mix the elixir." His aide sifted a grainy, striated earth from a sleeve

71

of silk into a crystal tube of amber fluid. On contact the substances momentarily seethed. "Give it to him." Vorselus accepted the proffered tube. Morca asked, "Do you understand, accused, what we do?"

"I am acquainted with the concept," Vorselus whispered, "have used in my own way a lesser form. I suppose this greatly exceeds the fruits of my education."

"Make sure wager on that. You drink. I will recite the words, which I discovered printed in olden hieroglyphics of gold on a parchment wrapped within a mummy's bandages, the mortal remains of an honored mage who dwelt in the latter days of the Early Kingdom. Nantrech knows this secret, a handful of others too are privy, those few I trust absolutely; you, unless I wildly mistake, know it not."

"You are correct, in essentials. I drink." Vorselus swallowed the fluid, rather tasteless, though it sat in his belly like hot lead. Morca commenced. He spoke the spell in the ancient speech, the tongue of the old script that Vorselus had wrestled with in tattered documents, but had never heard from human mouth, nor could he decipher much that he heard. He observed that Phillipan clapped hands over his ears, wondered at the danger of corollary influence. Then he saw, and wondered about, nothing.

The close view before him receded, the near image of Morca's face seen as through a long tunnel. Vorselus felt, vaguely, the bench beneath, the rough floor on his soles, a wooziness in his head. Presently a voice spoke to him, like a distant shout echoing from mountain crags. It was Morca's voice.

"Do not be afraid, if you are honest and true. I circumnavigate the psychic pathways of your brain. Do not speak, nor move, nor think; relax, and allow me untrammeled access to the most secret corridors of your entity."

What happened then? Vorselus could never afterward with certainty describe the experience. All conception of time lost, he nevertheless sensed the passage of hours or ages. He sensed his place within a dark volume, or rather he was that volume, and something moved or floated within it, something powerful, questing. That inside voyaged long, tacking across a formless ocean, putting into unreckoned ports, calling and departing, moving on, drifting up rivers through murky lands to unexpected destinations.

The world suddenly rushed back to expand around him. Vorselus blinked at grimy canvas, feeling tired, enfeebled. A face hove into view, that of grim Morca. "You are well," said he. "The interrogation is over. You will be returned to your quarters. The dawn nears. Later we will talk. It has been a stimulating night, my friend." Phillipan was there too, and he, with others, helped the enchanted mage, who sagged boneless in their grasp, to his feet and to the small tent assigned to him. There he slept, until he crawled forth, considerably revivified, to find the sun high over the sprawling camp.

They fed him and allowed him to wash—on orders of Morca, the guards explained—and gave him raiment befitting one of his station. Afterward, feeling better than he had for a long while, they escorted Vorselus back to Morca's temporary citadel of magic, where that lord shortly joined him, Phillipan in tow. Morca was almost kindly in demeanor, surely ebullient and eager. The terrible cat Treenya stirred at his feet, massaged his seated thigh with her big head, licked with a huge red tongue at his dangling hand.

"Treenya and I have journeyed long together," Morca explained. "I took her as a cub in the southlands, when I crushed a tribe that abused her rare kind for cruel sport. This orphan adopted me, you might say. I love her as she loves me. Others, she tolerates, unless I recommend otherwise.

"No debilitating effects I take it, Vorselus? Nothing lingering to grate on you? Good man. Here, take wine, from my own vintage. It possesses marvelous restorative powers, both from its superlative quality and a private charm. Well, that was indeed an unconventional odyssey, was not it, Phillipan? How about you, Vorselus? Recall you much of events?"

"Very little. I am well. Sleep restored me."

"Thus I expected, if you cooperated fully." Morca paused, as if to marshal his thoughts. "That you did, with a vengeance. Vorselus, I know that you are innocent of crime. I learn from you that, to the best of your understanding, your recital of Lord Kardowan's pernicious activities is objectively valid. Your inner mind confirms my worst fear. A terrible stew simmers at home, ready to boil. Were I there, I could take remedial action. Nantrech and these other worthies here constitute the firm pillars of Dyrezan. The King—bless his name!—there are things I could say, but not in company; never in company. I am afraid that counselors count.

"And here we are, at the butt end of nowhere, acting at the behest of Skyrax, with business unfinished. We are duty bound to proceed to the victorious end of this campaign. We must go onward! Only then may I gaze elsewhere.

"I have advised Nantrech concerning your case. Technically, Vorselus, you remain a prisoner, in charge of Nantrech. However, until we see Dyrezan again, you may throw in your lot with us, on parole. Stirring deeds lie ahead. You may make yourself useful."

Vorselus said, "My lord, I serve at your discretion."

"Excellent. Now, for the tricky part. Vorselus, you are, despite your lack of criminality, not what you seem. I delved into your mind, entered a peculiar maze, a labyrinthine network of psychic passageways. A time or two, I frankly admit, I lost my way in there. Who are you, really?"

"I scarcely know any more." A sigh punctuated the simple admission. "I could have told you much before of my worries pertaining to that matter, without resort to your elixir, but would I have been believed? My situation is precarious enough, without the spouting of crazy tales."

Morca chuckled. "What, such as your puzzling two-fold nature? Grant credit, man, to the long intensity of my arcane studies. I have uncovered marvels that, by comparison, render yours trivial. Mystery abounds! That is the way of Dyrezan here and now, and of other times and places as well. Strange things happen; one of them has happened to you. We must accept reality, however bizarre."

Morca shook his head in frustration. "I guess I know as much as you, perhaps more, for Phillipan here tells me a little. You are the man of this world—knee-deep in difficulty!—and another, subdued but unquiet, both living in the same brain. I understand your motivations; they are natural, accountable. What of his, this Vorchek? He is like us, I think. Lesser, yet keen, and actuated by desires we can appreciate. What does he want?"

Vorselus replied, "To go home, I expect."

"Aye, a sentiment we all share. If he succeeds, what becomes of you?"

"I dread the discovery. Bear this in mind, my lord. If I face arcane danger, so does your man Phillipan, who I assure you is also more; and one other, my slave Teresia, who—incredibly—matters to me more than any human being in this world, or any other."

Phillipan grinned. "Pretty, is she?"

"Valuable," said Vorselus. "I must protect her, and make all well for her, if it be not too late."

"That transpires or not," declared Morca, "as the Gods decree. Vorselus, you do intrigue me. Come an age of peace and quiet, I would like to delve with you into this tantalizing business. Now, my friend, let us indulge the present. I am to work. Phillipan, he must know what we face. Give him the grand tour, bring him up to date, forewarn him. That is your appointed task for this day."

The young officer showed him the camp, where well over half a thousand soldiers of Dyrezan, mainly valorous warriors of the Royal Guard, prepared themselves for mighty deeds. Beyond the camp on the beach rose the cliffs and terraces of the Peoki, with their gay orchards, ribbons of fruitful fields, rustic thatch houses set into the rock walls. This was Rongia, one of their many villages clinging to the rugged coast. The Peoki were plain, unassuming folk, fishermen and farmers, short, swarthy people who boasted legends of greatness from a bygone age when they commanded the land to the east and dwelt in plenty with fine cities and feared naught. Those days were past as if they had never been, as if they never could have been.

Vorselus met them, mingled with them as he and his guide climbed the weathered limestone ramps linking the terraces. Through scholarship supplemented by magical art their language had been revealed, a knowledge quickly imbibed by Vorselus. The Peoki proved overtly friendly, ever gracious to the strangers from the west. Vorselus learned why. Atop the highest point, overlooking the mighty salt sea and level with the inland plains, Phillipan told him the story.

There had come from the interior of the eastern land—be it island, continent, or an extension of the territory known to Dyrezan—centuries ago a fierce and warlike race of conquerors, utterly unlike the races documented by the scribes and adventurers of the Sky City. Inhumanly pale they were, and misshapen, deemed men by default only, for they were horribly more than animal. The Peoki claimed from old report of those elder days that they crept from caves and hidden burrows in the ground, infesting the fair land before the rightful denizens could act. They were noted for their fiendish savagery to which was added some repellent art, for they knew magic, of a kind, and wielded it in disgraceful fashion. They overran the Peoki kingdom, slaying and burning, exterminating most of the inhabitants, reducing the survivors to primitive thralldom along the coast. Bad as this was, there was more to the discredit of the conquerors; Phillipan obliquely referred to certain assertions, picked up from the natives, alluding to nauseating dietary practices. Such was the lot of the Peokis within memory of life and many generations of the dead. Their masters demanded hideous tribute:

75

the living bodies of captives, oft herded away to a nameless fate in the hinterland, never more seen by those who loved them.

Into this abysmal situation intruded the expedition of Nantrech and Morca. This invasion became known to the dark rulers. They sent messengers who, breathing hatred and scorn, demanded subjection. Morca sent back their heads in bags, accompanied by haughty missives. A force came down from the hills beyond the plain to crush the western intruders. The heroes of Dyrezan routed their fell opponents, refusing to accept prisoners from those unclean ranks. Now a gigantic army of those foul ones gathered over the eastern horizon, preparing for a fateful encounter.

Said Phillipan, "The Peoki have flocked to our ranks, at the behest of their village chiefs, adding near two thousand spears to serve in the coming war. Within days, Vorselus, we march to meet the foe. Sword against shield, magic against magic, we will fight, and if we overcome their horde we shall march into the heart of their empire, lay it waste, claim it for benevolent Skyrax. We need every strong arm, every wizardly mind. That is where you come in."

Replied Vorselus, "With such colleagues as the prestigious savants gathered here, we cannot fail."

"We must not," insisted Phillipan. He lowered his voice, with an ominous glance toward the eastward marches said, "Something more than crude barbarism reigns here. There are olden tales from legendary expeditions that set foot hereabouts in half-forgotten millennia, long before the age of the ancient Peoki. May we doubt the legends now? Listen to this, Vorselus: these hideous men—these creatures—style themselves the Rhexellites."

Vorselus cried, "Have you taken leave of your senses? How, Phillipan, know they that name?"

"As they would have it, according to their late embassies— speaking in the name of their great King Gorgras, who rules from a palace on a mountain away to the east—they are the lineal descendants of those long lost old ones, an ancient power re-establishing itself in the world. What think you of that, Vorselus?"

"It sounds a grim fairy tale come to life. One that should terrify children, I grant; but what of men?"

"Word has gotten about. There's confusion in the ranks. Lord Nantrech has his sages investigating. He wishes to pay a call on their king in his fortress of Tsathgon—by force of arms, if need be—in order to uncover the truth. For that reason alone we will fight."

Vorselus nodded soberly. Rhexellites! It was a word spawned in

76

blackest myth, derived from tales half-told in bygone days which were themselves partly mythical. Every scholar of history, Vorselus among them, knew something of the Rhexellites, that fabulous race of wizards who ruled the world before the greatness of Dyrezan, before Dyrezan was dreamed. Grim they were, and cruel, and cold, and merciless, yet they had among them great minds, and they scaled in dead, dusty eras epic heights of civilization, rising high to despise the Gods, whom they would trample underfoot for their own glory. Magic they mastered, and the secrets of the earth and heavens, reigning in evil glory until hubris blinded them and a nameless fate overtook them, destroying their empire and annihilating their race, wiping their scourge from the planet. So went the story. The Rhexellites were gone, a shadow of the past, a corpse of dim history. Or were they?

Vorselus wondered aloud, "Does that skeleton still dance?"

IX. WAR ON THE FRONTIER

After a fortnight less a day of hectic activity the combined army of the Dyrezanian expedition and its Peoki allies marched. During that span Vorselus lived, with the doubtful forbearance of Lord Nantrech, as a paroled prisoner, free to come and go so long as he proved himself a worthy patriot and useful mage. Agreeing to these terms, Vorselus was accepted into the team of learned sorcerers whose abilities were channeled into the stream of onrushing war.

From the region of the coast ran inland a road of sorts, a wide, leveled path of loose dirt and gravel, and along this the troops tramped, with their commanders and officers riding by and to the fore on horseback, inquisitive mounted scouts racing ahead across the barrens to spy out threats. In the van marched the Royal Guards, armored and armed with bright steel, their muscular thighs swinging in drilled unison. Behind them straggled in eager semblance of order the mob of Peokis, dressed in rags and armed as they were able with spears and knives and hastily fabricated bills, with their chiefs in gaudy feather bonnets urging them on, lusting for vengeance. At night the designated wizards, in the charge of Nantrech or Lord Morca, stewed their brews, fingered their charms, muttered the words and peered into crystals, that they might see with the mind what the eye could not. They verified what had been previously suspected, that a veil of magical darkness hung over the land, that away to the east a countervailing force strove to blunt the efficacy of their mystic vision. Much that should have been seen was not; they knew only that power, a furtive, black danger, loomed before.

On the second day of the advance an embassy met them on the road, and Vorselus garnered his first sight of these who called themselves Rhexellites. This glimpse did not foster easy mind or untroubled rest. Truly they were a loathsome race, these brutal conquerors, with their pale, fishy skin which spurned the golden sun, their lithe bodies and sparse, wispy hair on their scabrous heads. Their faces were the worst: large dark, round eyes, pointed chins, slits of mouths, no noses to speak of save flaring nostrils, and no ears but holes. They spoke among themselves in a sibilant, reptilian hiss. Were these indeed men? Possibly once, but the sight of them made Vorselus think of the Peoki tales, that the olden Rhexellites had destroyed themselves through dabbling in rites of extreme vileness, and their survivors had fled to escape their just doom in nighted sanctuaries within the bowels of the earth, festering there through black ages, emerging after countless millennia changed: lesser, corrupted beings, devotees of still coarser and most base tastes, yet greedy for their remembered glories. He wondered what they retained, if anything, from their mighty past, and what they had acquired during their long, subterranean exile.

The ambassador, as he might be called, rode up with his gaggle of mounted spearmen, bedecked in barbarous finery, and in a rasping approximation of the Peoki tongue gave vent to dire threats and warnings. "Turn back, you cattle," he hissed, "back to your pens by the sea, to await our coming. Great King Gorgras, he who reigns unchallenged in the invulnerable hold of Tsathgon, demands his due. He bids you gather in his honor levies of corn, and fish, and fruits of your trees. Collect these dainties to whet his palate, and also the tribute he truly craves, the required number of youths and maidens in full, healthy and fat of flesh, to be sent him for his pleasure. Go back; lay down your arms, lest retribution visit you. Prepare the banquet. So he commands."

To this Lord Nantrech responded with a fine speech, praising the majesty of King Skyrax and the virtues of Dyrezan, outlining at length the lofty goals of the expedition and urging on the enemy the freedom of the Peokis. The ambassador's mirth at this presentation he expressed in the most outrageous of terms. Never in his life had Vorselus heard such filth poured upon the sanctified name of Skyrax. Quick-tempered Morca cried out in anger, yet Nantrech would have resisted hot impulse, save that the monstrously ugly ambassador would not stop, but went on to indicate with unbounded relish a possible fate for Skyrax in the indeterminate future; a fate bearing culinary implications. From this suggestion the nobles and wise men of Dyrezan physically recoiled in dismay, as if stricken a devious blow. The ranks of the Guards seethed with barely controlled fury.

Even Nantrech, of the cool head and sober mind, cracked under this verbal barrage, and out of unleashed ire visited upon the ambassador a cruel spell. The lord bellowed in anger, motioned with his hands—nay, with his whole arms, a flurry of frenzied motion—and thundered an incantation which streamed at its subject like a misty cloud driven by fierce wind. The ambassador shrieked; he reeled in his saddle; he covered his face with abnormally thin, spidery fingers, and when he removed them, sobbing and gasping, the whole host in the van of the army saw what Nantrech had done. He had inverted the offender's face, turned it inside out.

Nantrech sagged, spent, so it was Morca who galloped forth on his armored steed and imperiously declared, "Return to your master, tell him that we come. Woe to he who opposes us! We march to Tsathgon, smashing all in our path. Explain to Gorgras that we cancel his banquet. Instead, the buzzards shall feast on the corpses of his warriors. Skyrax is great, Dyrezan invincible. Tell him this. Go now!" Treenya roared her approval. The ambassador, moaning horribly, was borne away by his retainers.

Presently the march continued. Camp they made that night. Before dawn the Rhexellites struck. An indeterminate force of the enemy—Morca later estimated their numbers at two thousand—surged out of the darkness against the southern and eastern ramparts of the hastily built stockade. Despite an alert defense and probing spells, the attack burst out of the night a full surprise. Cunning magic, undoubtedly, had masked the advance. A hornet's swarm of arrows, the thrusting of a myriad of iron spear points, a press of deathly pale bodies at the wall; then the stout warriors of Dyrezan manned the line, swords flashing in the glow of the torches, and by break of day the Rhexellites drew off, leaving hundreds of their own heaped under the stockade or strewn across it. Morca summed the cost: "We took our licks, but we swapped them one for ten. I count that a fair ratio. These Peokis are quick to die, poor knaves, but they do not quit. Hate drives them on. I wish we had more of them."

The expedition pressed on all that day and into the next, entering a region of volcanic hills where the first villages of the Rhexellites were encountered. They were squalid affairs ensconced in dark ravines, dirty dens where the sullen, hateful-visaged inhabitants glared silently at the passing invaders. During the night gangs from the villages crept close, infiltrated, tried to raid or spoil the stores of supplies that moved with the army in wagons. They were caught; all were killed save ten, and these Morca ordered spared. He ordered also that their hands be lopped off, and the maimed brutes sent back to their folk as a warning to all who would raise a hand against the heroes of Dyrezan.

Early afternoon of the fifth day confronted them with an especially large, round-topped hill, and upon this loomed the enemy host. Lord Morca scanned the scene. "Five thousand if a man," he observed to Nantrech, "or maggot, as the case may be. They do not test us this time. This they mean as the big show."

"Let us await their charge," suggested Lord Nantrech, "on ground of our choosing, and butcher them as they come within reach."

"Nay," replied Morca. "Let us convince them of our sternness. Do they believe themselves safe atop that slope? I would take the hill. The blood of our men burns, and my Treenya hungers for a frolic."

"As you will," agreed Nantrech.

In passing to Vorselus, who stood near, Morca said, "This day you pay for your keep." Indeed, the previous night attack passed so quickly that conjurations had played no part. Morca went on, "I assemble the sages, that we may put the fear of the Gods into these insects. Praise Xenophor, Who ever watches over us, that our victory may delight Him."

Vorselus joined the team of wise magicians, who accepted him by now as an equal, taking station directly behind the lines. Harmon explained the plan of battle, so as it pertained to the employment of arcane art. Meanwhile the army drew up in formation: Dyrezanians in the center, Peokis in the wings, a small reserve of the Guards in the back. Nantrech and Morca rode to the fore, both in fighting armor. Treenya cavorted playfully until heeled by her master. Morca addressed the ranks.

"They dare defy us!" he roared. "Soldiers, today you determine the penalty for their insolence. Teach them manners. King Skyrax commands that we grant him victory. Will we disappoint him?" The troops howled in throaty negative. "Will we conquer?" ("We will!" shouted the troops.) "Will we slaughter the foe like so many rabbits?" ("We shall!" boomed the troops.) "Let us have at them!"

The Guards advanced in lock-step, the Peokis keeping up in looser order, a scattering of Dyrezanian officers ensuring that the allies kept ranks. The army climbed the slope. The mass of the Rhexellites grew distinct: pale creatures, swathed in untanned leather wrappings, a forest of spears jutting above, standing silently. Then nasty voices hissed from up there, many voices in ugly cadence. Bright light flashed across their front; a wall of flame! It rolled down the hillside at the advancing soldiers!

"Lie down!" Morca screamed, hugging rambunctious Treenya to the earth, his officers echoing the order along the line. The troops threw themselves down, hugged the ground, biting dirt. The barrage of fire swept over them and passed, fading away behind. Here and there, especially among the Peokis, a man groveled in pain or beat out a smoldering flame, but none were killed nor even incapacitated. At command they rose, steadied, resumed the advance. The Rhexellites, having commenced a guttural cheer, quieted.

Over the heads of his men Morca called to Harmon, "Show them what we can do." The wizard acknowledged the order, delivered his own, began reciting the words. Vorselus chanted with the rest. Theodises, with his fellow mage Candor, fired a hellish brew of stinking solution in a brass pot they carried between them with the help of Peoki servants. It belched sulfurous vapors. The chanting concluded.

From the empty sky suddenly descended an inky black cloud that fell like a toppling wall upon the crest of the hill, blocking all sight from within and without. Hissing shrieks could be heard up there, as the noxious fog tormented exposed flesh. Vorselus smiled grimly. Not showy, like the magic of the enemy, but vastly more effective. Great was Dyrezan!

"To the left!" Morca snapped, and the entire army swung round, picked up speed despite the incline, moved quickly toward the obscured enemy right flank. The awful black mist roiled before them. At a shout the unified mages made cutting passes with their hands, willed the cloud away. It vanished on the instant, revealing the disorganized ranks of the Rhexellites. "Charge!" cried Morca, and the assault went in.

It was a grand, hard-fought fight while it lasted, arrow for arrow, sword against spear, spear to spear, fury clashing with fury; but the

Dyrezanians and their liege-men Peokis took the initiative, held it, pressed into that ghastly mob, hacked and stabbed, thrust and slew, killed and kept killing, piling up a tally of slaughter that swept over the hill and down the other side over the mangled bodies of their foe. The Rhexellites fought valiantly, with fiendish cruelty when they got a man down, yet their numbers and assurance of victory could not balance their shaken confidence when faced by superior skill. They broke—they ran—they died in droves. Not one of Morca's gallant host gave thought to prisoners.

Dusk found the men of the west in victorious possession of the hill, amidst a litter of shredded sinews and chopped bone and weltering blood, the scattered remnants of the Rhexellite army fleeing madly to the east. Treenya went about with damp jaws, angrily spitting at foulness, having relished the sport more than the prey. Near a hundred warriors of Dyrezan, and four times that of the Peokis, were no more. Many others suffered serious wounds. "This is a great day," announced Morca.

Without delay the expedition began again its forward operation, forging onward with the dawn under lowering clouds, entering a land of well-watered plains cut by streams and studded with villages. These were deserted on the whole, cubic stone shells of houses, the sites offering evidence of hasty departure by the majority of the inhabitants. The old remained, and some women and children, to spit at the invaders, who scorned to tarry, ignored insult and marched on.

That night Vorselus talked with Phillipan. Round the campfire where they fed themselves the young officer unburdened himself. He said, "O wizard, you have unsettled me with your tale, giving rise to strange thoughts that peep at me from dreams. I think I know you, as much from another life as this. You were my teacher, in that other."

"Indeed I was," replied Vorselus, "and a good one, I would say, if the fragments of he floating in the soup of my mind mean anything. A man of another time, with ideas foreign to our own, ideas unusual and at whiles nettlesome. That other face of mine is an ignorant one, but questing, ever questing. That is how, by some stray formulation of art, he came to dwell within me, and his machinations drew you— the secondary you—likewise through the years and the spheres."

"Now a voice mutters to me, questioning my actions, my existence. It isn't helpful. I have much to think of these days. My concentration is strained. He—that one, Philip—frets for himself. I don't know what to do."

"What works for me," Vorselus said, "will work for you. When I have the time I will sort this out. Vorchek belongs elsewhere. He realizes that. There must be a way to send them all back."

"Yes. There's the girl, too. I see her now, in sleep. That's a sweet image. And she's really here, with us?"

"A long ways away, in terrible peril, I will be bound. I like not that. It hurts me to have left her to her devices. I console myself that the one I knew in another life—Theresa—was artful, in her own way, expert in taking care of herself. I trust that this Teresia has picked up a thing or two from her unwanted passenger."

On the eastern horizon at dawn a lone, angular mountain showed itself blackly against the red fog that smothered the peak. The advance of the army resumed. The mountain rose higher, the heavy mist lifting, revealing itself a volcanic eminence with craggy top. Certain crags appeared too regular, cubic, unnatural. The road ran straight to the base, then switch-backed up the sides of the vast cone. At the summit sprawled a massy pile of carved basalt, a black fortress with crenellated walls and embattled towers. Beyond rose greater towers, dark stacks of giant blocks with few windows. On the walls, on the slopes below, waited an awe-inspiring host, ten thousand or more Rhexellite warriors. The ominous force stood at attention as the Dyrezanian expedition reached the base of the mountain.

The pale ranks above opened at the road, allowing space for a heavy, ornate chariot to issue forth, surrounded by a company of armed riders. The driver, flanked by armed companions, reined in. Cased in silver was that chariot, the gleaming metal thickly studded with uncut gems, and driven by six black horses that reared and strained against that load. Atop the chariot in an ebony seat squatted a pale man, very tall for his race, whose accouterments and sneer of assured command identified him for who he was before ever he spoke. He wore a black robe inlaid with silver fibers in the design of a spider's web, and on his bald white head perched the heavy ring of a big iron crown bearing in front, like a baleful third eye, a single large ruby. He said:

"I am Gorgras, king of the Rhexellites, monarch of all lands to the great sea, lord of life and death over my domain, descendant of the great ones of past times and present keeper of the ancient secrets. I welcome you as guests, and bid you freely enter my citadel of Tsathgon. Come, noble friends from beyond the sea, with all your legions, into my matchless abode, where cheer and merriment await."

83

Said Vorselus, "This be merely a trap." Nantrech nodded, saying, "That is surely his intent. We have no friends here." Morca patted Treenya, said, "I am like to accept the offer. Already I pondered how best to storm that high wall, and I cared little for my thoughts. Let us get in, even if it be by false invitation, then consider our options."

Lord Nantrech stated, "Great deeds demand great risk. So be it." To the king, "With gratitude, and open hands, we come." So it transpired. The hosts of Gorgras drew away from the road, and he rode back the way he came, and the army of Nantrech warily followed, up the steep slope, through the immense, frowning gate which appeared chiseled from the thick obsidian walls, and into the black heart of the Rhexellite empire.

Within, the expedition from Dyrezan was granted reasonable accommodations along the huge courtyard that faced the gate. The troops went into barracks, the lords and sages into apartments hard by. Through every step of their settling in messengers moved freely back and forth between the contestants, avowing happy tidings and desires for lasting peace. Despite these poses of kindness the warriors of Gorgras in great numbers manned the near wall, lurked at a moderate remove outside the square of the Dyrezanian camp. Morca laid out a perimeter, quickly but intelligently fortified from the materials transported in the wagons, told off a hefty percentage of his total force as guards, ever vigilant, their weapons drawn in showy, intimidating fashion.

This was the citadel of the Rhexellites, fortress and city, capitol of their dark kingdom. Said Vorselus, "I style it a mathematician's dream, and an architect's nightmare." Phillipan was not wont to argue. He said, "It's a piece of the lowest hell, where even Azamodeus dare not tread." What sort of place drew forth these responses? Picture the scene: the great courtyard gave onto the castle of Gorgras, girded by its own bleak walls sliced from volcanic glass, against which the apartments of Nantrech and his companions abutted. An inconsiderable distance beyond that wall rose the royal keep, the tallest tower in the city, like the rest a sheer, cubic monstrosity of single huge blocks stacked one atop another, black and purely functional, lacking ornamentation, featureless save for infrequent vertical slits of windows. Other structures were of similar construction, black, hard stone, cubes on cubes, cubes laid by cubes, aggregates of cubes. Harsh angles, darkness paramount, shadows seemingly fostered by a mad brain, made for an oppressive and heart-sinking vista. Beyond the radius of the camp all was the same.

84

Officers, then scholars, who went into the city by invitation strode linear basalt streets, beheld block after block of cold, dreary black edifices. The folk dwelt in dispiriting chambers, the Rhexellite nobles in large, ugly piles, the lesser orders in small stone hovels inside squalid districts where they plied their common trades. Big or small, it was the sameness that intruded on the mind and soul.

All went well that first day. The quarters giving onto the castle wall possessed inner doors communicating with the royal interior, passages zealously guarded by watchers on both sides. Through one of these came a courier bearing welcome to a lavish feast to be held that night, where (the king's mouthpiece espoused) eternal amity would be sealed. All the great ones of Dyrezan were invited, along with sufficient liege-men to make them feel safe. Said Nantrech, "So long as our backs are secured, and retreat covered; so long as they make no questionable move; with certain exceptions from our assembly, who shall stay behind to maintain order in camp; I will accept and attend."

"I second the gambit," growled Morca. "It is our chance to study them."

Vorselus was one of those honored to attend this meeting of the most high between the two empires. Gorgras truly set out to provide a fine and daunting show for his guests within the stark confines of his castle. His lackeys raised up a grand rectangular pavilion of polished red wood and many soft, ornate hangings in the yard into which he, his courtiers, and his guards entered from one end, while Lords Nantrech and Morca, their esteemed companions, and the picked company of Guardsmen and best born Peokis, entered from the other. There the fools of Gorgras gibed and capered, and desirable women (all captives of other races or tribes, including the Peoki, which caused bitter muttering) lasciviously danced, and the king himself regaled with a show of magic. He first performed a series of minor tricks that would have bored any tyro of Dyrezan. The chiefs of the Peoki seemed impressed, but Nantrech made a point of ostentatiously yawning. At this not so subtle rejoinder his people laughed out loud. Seeing this, Gorgras, with some show of anger called for materials, and shortly made for his guests a stronger brew. This time he, after mixing ingredients in a cauldron and hissing unintelligible formulae, opened a hole in the air above the paving of the court, from which plopped a revolting greenish monstrosity as big as a bear, a mass of bulbous eyes and writhing tentacles, which squatted heaving but otherwise motionless until Rhexellite spearmen thrust out from their midst a cringing, weeping captive; a young girl, as pretty in her way as the dancers, only her features naturally distorted with terror. The horrid thing immediately lunged at her, moving quickly and glutinously across the intervening space, then leapt somehow, taking the girl into its substance. She disappeared with a scream within—there was a commotion of slippery, animate surface—and she was gone! The king clapped his hands, and the guardsmen began menacing another captive with their spears.

Vorselus, aghast at this horrific display, could not contain himself, but whispered to his leader, "O Nantrech, wizard beyond compare, conjure us a champion who will slay this escapee from the lower hells." Nantrech would not, attesting that he chose to keep his enemies in the dark as to the full powers of Dyrezanian magic, also commanding the infuriated Morca—himself a grand sorcerer beyond compare—to refrain from displays of esoteric prowess. "So be it," cried Morca, and forthwith he sprang from the gallery into the yard, sword in hand, vowing at the top of his voice to best the hateful beast. His people, Dyrezanians and Peokis all, roared their delight. The Rhexellites gave vent to their own anticipatory glee. And Morca fought the monster. Though called from unhallowed spheres beyond sane conception, it was composed of matter, flesh and blood, if seemingly more foe than one man could handle; save, conceivably, that man be Lord Morca. The thing rushed at him, waving its awful feelers. Morca dodged, spun, circled, and slashed . . . and slashed, and cut and ripped, until a final thrust into the vitals laid low the monster, leaving it a quivering, subsiding heap of suppurating gelatin. The Dyrezanian company cheered deliriously. Gorgras sneeringly spat a word, which caused the mound of green ooze to vanish.

Then the king, feigning graciousness once more, commanded that gourmet viands be served. Morca rejoined his folk, grinning proudly. Thralls brought among them the food. Quickly arose another cause of contention. Cared not they for the foodstuffs served on those silver trays, for though much was concealed by sauces and complex preparations, the aspect of certain whole joints plainly revealed the nature of the repast. The men grew unruly, murmuring their hostility. Unable to control his disgust Nantrech stood and raged, "Do not dishonor us with the comestibles of fallen savages. As men, we repudiate this filth, and those who offer it, and in no wise will have it." Thought Vorselus that the Rhexellites would fall on them then, but their lord restrained his soldiers, though his nasty face was a frigid mask of evil intent, and he offered instead dishes of vegetables.

This the majority of his guests would have accepted, only Morca opined that he feared the broth, thus rejected the substitute, in which Nantrech concurred, giving order that his party return to their encampment, to partake from their own supplies. In this wise ended, sourly, the entertainment.

X. THE CITADEL OF THE RHEXELLITES

Vorselus thought the truce—for such was all that unnerving peace could ever be—was like to end then and there, but fear or cunning prevailed on the opposing side, and no hostile moves were yet instigated by the Rhexellites. On the contrary, next morning they brought fresh produce, of a healthy and decent sort, to Nantrech's men with the king's ostensible blessing, and for the remainder of their sojourn in Tsathgon the Dyrezanians ate as men. Now began a period of watchful waiting and tension while the invading party strove to learn the ways of their reprehensible hosts. Lord Harmon, scholar of strange folk, led the sages among the inhabitants of Tsathgon and the members of the court to investigate current practices and glean something of their history. This Gorgras allowed, though little pretense of friendship endured past that first unpleasantness. His spearmen ever surrounded his guests, manning the keep and the walls of the fortress, dogging those granted leave to wander, and with the passing of days their numbers grew. Minor incidents flared—taunts and private combats—which kept all on edge. Craving action, Morca counseled a surprise move, while Nantrech demanded caution until he had gained what useful knowledge he could.

Vorselus marveled to find himself among such fell folk, exotic and evil, he who had in former days taken so little interest in foreign matters. The Rhexellites were a fearsome race, a curious compound of fallen nobility and wretched barbarism, a people whose ancient fathers may once have surpassed Dyrezan in the great arts of civilization, if old tales and new boasts be valid, yet who had sunk low throughout the eons of their exile from the sun. This irruption of their might onto the surface must, he felt, represent the last gasp of their better elements, as from what they claimed he deduced that only the more unwholesome types, scarcely human still, remained in the dreaded caverns beneath that land, living like animals in a weird twilight world lit solely by the glowing emanations of subterranean fungi. Once theirs had been a glorious empire of magic and majesty, one which dreamed itself eternal, until their delvings into cosmic secrets carried them beyond grasping after sane knowledge and into a pursuit of forbidden mysteries. The ancient ones went too far—their brutal children of this day had forgotten how—and it was to escape some pitiless horror dredged up from the limits of the universe that they fled into the underworld. Now they had returned, to a small degree, changed in body by long isolation from the sun-kissed human stream, refashioning a pathetic mockery of former greatness, bringing with them the abysmal practices fostered by the extreme conditions in the bowels of the earth. From such grand heights of pride, fallen to such pitiful depths; Vorselus could not refrain from falling to his knees, praying to the good Gods that in the fullness of time his people's fate be not theirs!

It was their cannibalism—so repulsively confirmed—rather than their too common cruelty, that made them loathsome in the eyes of the loyal subjects of Skyrax. Proper food they would eat, but only to supplement their desired diet. Vorselus, in the course of his studies and observations, had occasion to behold the sumptuous feasts of the nobility, the simple meals of the poor, ever the same main course. The king and his cronies preferred fresh meat, red with blood, lightly cooked after being slaughtered for amusement before their eyes. Oft times they would boil their victims whole and aware, as civilized men did lobsters, casting them shrieking into vast, bubbling pots; or they would roast them living over coals inside bags of hide. They did not inflict this degradation on their own folk, at least not before their guests, although he supposed that in the lengthy centuries underground they must first have learned to prey on their kind. On the surface, perhaps, as a result of their extensive conquests, they had too great choice of foreign morsels to plague their own.

The explosion of violence that shattered the uneasy truce came following the sojourn there by the Dyrezanians of well-nigh a month. The winds of destiny blew but one way during the interim, with the lesser officers of the surrounding, ever growing Rhexellite army shouting, at those they came to openly deem their "prisoners," vile insinuations pertaining to their ultimate fate, while many of the armed visitors, despite the remonstrations of Lord Nantrech, taunted back what they proposed to do with the Rhexellites once they had been subjugated. Nantrech held off so long because he remained a scholar first, soldier second, keen to continue his intellectual delvings until he concluded his findings of fact. Key matters of relevance had been learned concerning the Rhexellites in those quietly ominous days: much of their language, impressive portions of their history, something of the sinister cast of their minds. There was more to know, so much more, but when pressed Nantrech conceded that the campaign season was slipping away, and had at last reached tentative agreement with his lords and officers and the Peoki chiefs on the necessity of a quick and bloodless coup, when suddenly all subtle plans were thrown over by the renewed outbreak of crimson war.

It was valiant but reckless Morca who did the deed, on the evening of an exotic Rhexellite religious ceremony. Vorselus saw it all, took part despite misgivings, an experience no man present could ever forget. The pale folk swarmed into a high, massy cube of a black temple, far across the open yard of the court, maybe a fifth of a league from Nantrech's camp. Priests dressed in gaudy scarlet robes (one of the few splashes of color in that dismal realm) led the way bearing torches and silver staffs of office, along with what appeared the majority of the noblemen of Tsathgon. Amidst the wildly shouting and chanting throng numerous guards herded hundreds of miserable chained captives, evidently being taken into that place for sacrifice, feasting, or both. As the cavalcade passed by and beyond the Dyrezanian onlookers, illuminated by a thousand flaring torches, hostile soldiers on the fortress walls above called down evil jests, snickering loudly among themselves as to the identity of the next victims chosen for the ceremony. The mob of Rhexellites disappeared into the temple, cramming themselves within the building, from which ominously regular chanting presently arose, punctuated by recurrent and lingering screams of unendurable agony.

Morca reached the breaking point, a situation in which he had much company. He feared, as he explained later, that the rites of the black temple were a disguise for an onslaught against his position; that there were too many people, too many natural leaders, too many spearmen pressing close. "Do we wait until they slit our throats?" he cried to Vorselus and Phillipan, who observed with him.

"Consult Lord Nantrech," Phillipan advised. Vorselus seconded the idea.

"I have sought his rede," said Morca, "twice sent messengers, but Nantrech cannot be quickly found. I am told that he walks the perimeter, discoursing science with fellow savants. Too long I have waited. We must not lose more time." In what he considered a moment of extremis, Morca decided to initiate swift action in order to forestall what he deduced or imagined as a cleverly laid scheme of attack.

He threw open the makeshift gates of the camp ramparts and charged across the gloom of the flagged yard at the temple with almost half the military complement. Vorselus felt it his duty to join the fray. Two hundred men of Dyrezan advanced in phalanx with shields interlocked, first at stride, then at trot, finally at a run, backed by many hundreds, perhaps a thousand of vengeful Peokis, as they rushed the three large doors facing them in the temple wall. The Rhexellite guards went down with barely time for a warning cry, and then the men of Dyrezan burst inside, to behold a ghastly sight within the single large, multi-tiered room or amphitheater that comprised the temple interior. In a flash of disbelieving insight Vorselus took in the incredible scene. The thousands of celebrants sat or stood on a sloping floor ringed with circular benches, gesticulating and chanting crazily as scores of victims suffered butchery at a stroke in the arena or central dais. Those unfortunates were killed with spears, or burned by magic spells of the priests, or fed to creatures not unlike the one witnessed at the feast of Gorgras, spawned of sorcery. The Rhexellite troops within turned and dashed at the intruders, who mad with righteous blood-lust began a massacre of all Rhexellites within, both those who made opposition and those who, stricken with fear, endeavored to flee. The crude martial virulence of the enemy combatants was no match for the exquisite tactical training of Skyrax's Guards, backed by the many furious Peoki. With Morca leading the way, swinging his sword and reciting cunning charms of confusion against the foe, the warriors of Dyrezan swept all before them, hewing down the enemy and trampling their bodies in red ruin underfoot. Vorselus fought as the others, with borrowed sword in hand, as best he could, between bouts of minor magic which he composed on the fly. A few Rhexellites only escaped through doors in the other three walls. Their priests were slain with enormous satisfaction on the part of the slayers. When the ground level had been cleared of life—except for a pitiful handful of rescued captives—Morca led his ferocious host up the broad stone stairs to the higher levels. No Rhexellite escaped alive from there.

Morca returned triumphantly with his men and, when confronted by Lord Nantrech, boasted of his exploits and his slight loss.

90

Nantrech upbraided him for his hot-headed audacity. "You have ruined everything!" he screamed.

Retorted Lord Morca, "You are in no position to argue the merits of the case. You did not see what has fouled our eyes and souls forever. Tell him, Phillipan, tell him, Vorselus."

Phillipan said warmly, "They are fiends, deserving only of death." Vorselus replied diplomatically, with a shake of his head, "It was madness."

As they spoke a tocsin resounded, clanged, reverberated over the fortress. Hundreds of torches flared from the battlements above the camp, and from a high perch in the royal keep a familiar commanding voice sibilantly bawled, "Death to the interlopers! Kill them all!"

The Rhexellites, demented with rage and the fervor of unleashed hate, charged in their thousands. Vorselus later, when time allowed, gave thanks to the eternal benevolence of watchful Xenophor, Lord of All Creation, that his people were awake and aware, under arms to meet the onslaught that came, whether it was a long plotted design or the fruits of irate fury. Nantrech, helpless but to accept the situation, buckled on his armor and, with weapon in hand, joined the fight. The stampede of bloodthirsty retribution stormed across the dark court, the bowmen among the Peoki raining arrows into the packed ranks. The Rhexellite wave crashed in a foam of blood against the rocks of Dyrezanian fortitude. They clambered up the ramparts and met death at the hands of cool, military competence. Steel swords bit into their mercifully thin armor, those that wore any, and slashed at their flesh; bronze shields pounded purple their skins. They retreated, leaving scores of the slain behind... and came on again! Over and over throughout the interminable hours their immense numbers broke against that thin but hard line. Then lights, weird colors and ethereal radiances, flickered from the slit windows of the keep. Vorselus knew those signs; Gorgras conjured battle magic to smash down his enemies. Leaving Morca in full command of the combat, Nantrech repaired to his chambers where, with the aid of Vorselus and his scholarly colleagues, he commenced a counter enchantment. Meanwhile blazing fireballs rained down on the camp, with hideously unnerving specters wheeling among the stars through the night sky, calling on the men to cower or flee lest they face doom.

Nantrech, that wizard of wizards, with his fellows of the arcane arts, brewed from the unseen spheres the corrosive rain that eats flesh and pocks stone and metal. Rapidly the spell consumed the bulk of the magical substances at hand, but faced by such oppressive numbers they could but hazard the utmost on a single roll of the die. He cried out, "Xenophor the Mighty, and the Gods who serve You, protect Your devoted children and smite these wicked ones." And a mysterious gust of hot wind burst forth from nowhere, and about the ramparts black sheets of acidic droplets pelted down from the clear sky, and the Rhexellite soldiers howled and squalled in their pain and choler. They fell back, and with the break of dawn it seemed they would come at the defenders no more.

Nantrech, rejoining Morca at the battle line, took rapid stock of the situation. They had suffered casualties, more from the fires of Gorgras than the spears of his army, but the ranks were largely intact, the greatest losses being absorbed by the Peokis, who fought unarmored like the majority of the foe. In Vorselus' mind loomed the immediate question: what to do now? They were, at first reckoning, trapped within the citadel of Rhexellite power, cut off by a wall of hatred propped by the formidable arts of the king. What to do? This was, too, the issue before that hasty council. Morca said, "Carry the war to the enemy. Each man of Dyrezan is worth ten of them, and we have the Peoki warriors at our side. Let us extend the reach of our strength, as the cornered tiger leaps from his lair." Treenya throatily growled approval, as if she understood. Nantrech the wise, ever ready to face reality, however grim, agreed without reservation. He said, "I came to suppress the Rhexellites, and any chance for subtle diplomacies is past." So the ranks were reformed, a small company being tasked with holding the camp, while flying columns surged forth to take the castle and pierce the heart of the enemy empire.

Two columns stormed to the left and right, bashed their way up the steps on the inner wall and in a brutal fight cleared that portion overlooking the encampment. Vorselus, his unaccustomed wildness utterly spent, held back from the cut and thrust, devoted his activities henceforth solely to arts magical, in which he gave a better account of himself. The main column advanced squarely against the keep, where Gorgras lurked with huge forces and unguessable secret powers. The gate was thrown down with charmed rams, the potent force being supplied by Lords Morca and Nantrech, Harmon and Vorselus, in unison. The barrier gave, but with significant resistance, indicating a counter spell applied from the other side. The king, and whatever mages he supported, were still active in the contest. Then the warriors of Dyrezan and the legions of the Peoki entered that human beehive. The soldiers hacked and thrust their way through a dense wall of Rhexellite bodies. They attained the door of the keep, crushing their enemies beneath them, then forced passage into that perfectly square portal, where a conjured monstrosity splashed to the floor and scrabbled toward them. Vorselus thought that grisly king of the Rhexellites relied too much on fear. Frightful was the thing, but swinging blades chopped it into convulsing lumps of slime. The subsequent clash cleared the barbaric throne room on the ground floor, where a gilded seat stood empty among the reeking refuse of those who had fought to defend it.

Up the harshly diagonal stairs they climbed, destroying opposition on one floor, then the next. Many a worthy subject of Skyrax or Peoki ally fell, for the enemy were bold and, quite rightly, expectant of no mercy, so they fought and slew like devils. The Peokis, when they advanced to the fore, suffered horrendous casualties, yet they battled on cheerily, ever eager for a go at the foe. The thirst for revenge of infinite miseries inflicted drove them on. Came they all at last to the topmost level of the royal tower, where they grimly hurled themselves against the final barrier of men and fortifications. A frenzied spasm of killing led them into a great gloomy chamber of shelves bearing arrays of scrolls and instruments of magic, the walls of the chamber adorned atrociously with the hanging bones of royal victims. There stood the king, Gorgras, amidst the last of his guard, hissing vicious commands, intoning desperate spells. From a steaming cloud of yellow mist rose up a black spirit champion, armed with knobbed mace and loathsomely curved hook to protect the royal person.

Lord Morca thrust through his fellows and, laughing heartily, strode forth to do battle with the entity. "Watch," he cried, "as light defeats darkness!" He would not use his arts, insisting as he passed that no man, soldier or mage, interfere. Nantrech gave him his head, and he made the most of the opportunity. Vorselus pressed at the packed ranks from behind, striving to behold this epochal event.

What a duel that was! Morca's lust for combat flamed as he fought. Steel rang on steel, and once Vorselus thought the hook would tear out his companion's vitals. The spirit champion could not be killed as readily as men perish, but it could be rendered into fragments, and this Morca laboriously performed. When that strange one was entirely dismembered Morca, scarred by the bout and leaking blood from numerous wounds, stumbled away and fell gasping against the wall, utterly spent. Then Lord Nantrech gave the order, quietly, in a toneless voice, that all within be extirpated. In this

93

wise ended the life of Gorgras, king of the Rhexellites.

Tsathgon had fallen to Dyrezan, the terror of the dark kingdom forever broken. The fortress was secured in short order, for the common folk—all who remained alive in that place—had more hate than fight in them. Much of that day was spent in a wild rampage of looting, of merriment and drinking. The Rhexellites boasted a potent sauce that, of all their wonders, most impressed the troops, and under those joyous circumstances restraint could not be thought of. Indeed, such was their renunciation of discipline that unseemly atrocities were forestalled solely by the instinctive distaste felt by the men for the local women.

Nantrech commanded, to the few remaining under arms, that the keep be ransacked for secrets and marvels, and this they did. He hoped to carry back to Dyrezan a train of priceless booty to placate King Skyrax, to startle the multitudes, and to increase the lore of the wise. Surely there was much to justify his wishes. Even Vorselus, brain-sick from strife and bloodshed, could not help exclaiming aloud at the wonders uncovered in the despoiled castle, the treasures pecuniary and, most importantly, the intellectual. To the expedition commander he admitted, "Our full lifetimes can be spent analyzing these riches."

Much that had occurred in this dark land caused him regret and filled him with dismay, but Vorselus felt profound relief that the struggle was over. He could allow himself to believe what seemed impossible a short time before: that his way was clear, that with immediate perils quashed, and his good name restored among these great men by faithful service, he could march home with them sharing their triumph and freshly earned respect, restore his reputation in Dyrezan, and aid them in re-establishing safe and proper government back home.

Came that baleful night, after that fleeting day of hard-earned repose, when all his fond dreams of glory and wisdom were shockingly dashed. Exactly how the events transpired he was not to know. In latter days of desperation he had spare moments to reflect that a few Rhexellite survivors of the battle, priests or noblemen maybe, knew of one weapon remaining to them, a power to be unleashed solely when human might had failed and all hope had fled; a weapon of suicide. Possibly they hid themselves within underground chambers of the keep—there were such, which he and the other savants intended to explore at leisure—or utilized tunnels within Tsathgon that the conquerors never had time to locate.

94

However it happened, Vorselus first became aware that something was horribly wrong when a single Dyrezanian warrior, one of the garrison squad guarding the keep, dashed breathlessly into the encampment, unarmed and bleeding from odd wounds, babbling a morbid tale.

With blood leaking down his face he gasped, "Monsters, monsters from the nether pits among us!" Quickly he related, in broken sentences, how from corridors in the lowest level of the keep had come an irresistible tide of barely glimpsed beings, a mass of squirming shapes surging out of the darkness, taking the men unawares as most of them drunkenly slept. He could not describe them, though he had seen, for a moment, and gazed upon them by feeble fire light. These things clawed and bit a path through the soldiers, slaying silently, chewing on the bodies of the hale and the dead. The man shrieked that they were already eating of him when he broke away and ran for his life.

Scarcely had he choked out this wild story when the bitter truth presented itself. There burst from the broken gate of the keep a living tempest, a rampant river of forms that only in the murk of night, at far remove, could be mistaken for human. Akin to the defeated Rhexellites they were, but it was a distant kinship, one that even the beaten foe, perhaps, would fain have disowned. And more came, a teeming horde gushing from the black temple, and then from all points. Nantrech in his shirt came running up shouting orders, and Morca in partial battle dress appeared to marshal the men for renewed battle as they could.

This was not a period that Vorselus ever desired to recollect. The unimaginable terror of that hideous night, when creatures of the ultimate darkness stalked abroad! He must forevermore flinch from the ghastliness of the memory. These were the true children of the primordial Rhexellites, the most debased and despised specimens that still crept through burrows and caverns beneath the lands smiled upon by the Gods. Down there they festered, as he could testify in astounding numbers. He doubted not that they had been released or liberated in some fashion, for their murderous appearance at that juncture could not, he later reasoned, be the work of happenstance. Fast it occurred, terribly fast: the irruption from the keep, then the temple, and from the common folk's quarter, from which some of the less polluted subjects of dead Gorgras ran for their lives, accompanied by those Peoki—stationed only that afternoon among the little cubic houses—who were sober enough to seek safety. Came

95

a torrent of mindless bestiality! Naked they clawed toward the men, with hairless, corpse-white bodies, lean and hungry looking, with repulsive spidery limbs sporting curved claws on the wiry fingers of their misshapen paws. Below their low-domed pates gleamed monstrous eyes, big as saucers, glared faces of pitiless hate with noseless nostrils, mere holes in those evil masks, and the filthy red mouths filled with long needle-like fangs.

As the outliers among the troops were swept up and torn apart in that verminous maelstrom, Morca barked furious commands. "Form up, all ye who hear me!" he roared. "On the double, secure the city wall." Vorselus, who had again taken up a sword, this one dropping from the fingers of a dead hero, realized soon enough what Morca already understood in those critical seconds: that this was not an enemy to be opposed, but a menace to elude at all costs. The men fell in; how many Vorselus wondered—perhaps a couple or three hundred sons of Dyrezan, maybe five hundred of the Peoki—the rest already cut off, dead or doomed. They carved a path through blood and gristle to the main gate which opened upon the road of salvation. Most of them reached it. They could hack the things down, but unless firmly dead they would not stay down, still biting at their human opponents as the severed heads of ants are wont to do. Many a man who could have stood against five civilized opponents went down screaming, stricken in terror when enmeshed by those skinny, clawed limbs that wrapped around their prey like binding web. Nevertheless the soldiers opened the gate, struggling frenziedly to hold that position while the rest of their people passed through. Behind them a living carpet of insanity, stretching to the limits of vision, pressed closely at their heels.

Said Morca to Nantrech, "Give me fifty of our best, that I may hold the gate until you and the others escape the mountain via the road." Nantrech, that noble man, hesitated to accept the offer, but after an agonizing moment agreed to the plan. As Vorselus with the larger party ran down the royal avenue toward the far away plain, unseen in benighted mist, Morca held his ground, Treenya snarling at his side. With his last glimpse Vorselus saw the great lord conjuring thunderbolts in the darkness.

Morca's sacrifice was valiant but fruitless, for the main body fleeing in the dark were scarcely halfway down the steep slope when the pale troglodytes appeared from all sides. Vorselus blamed the mountain, which could not have been solid, but rather honeycombed by the dwellers down under. At this moment all organization, any semblance of order vanished, replaced by a pell-mell scramble for life. Battle-tested heroes ran like scared children. Vorselus saw Cressus the wise, and Nemedas the philosopher, and many another worthy sage perish on that cursed mountain, prey to things unspeakable and unclean. Vorselus fell in with a band of Peoki, scant protection against the peril, but companions at a time when he dreaded being alone. The cavern horrors closed in, slinking over the stones to get at them. Out of his nightmare delirium Vorselus remembered Morca's thunderbolts. He guessed then, as that lord mage must have guessed, that the denizens of darkness emerged only in darkness, for true light was anathema to them. Within the folds of his robe he carried a handful of fire globes, useful for producing light and fire by night, kindly lent him from the presumably dead Harmon's magical stock. He cast one to the heavens and spoke it alight . . . and the vile creatures gave back, cringing from the glare!

"It works!" he inanely shrieked in the tongue of Dyrezan, which no one within earshot could understand, but the Peokis cheered, because they grasped the import. While the globe hovered above, Vorselus used the miraculous chance to gather the handful of allied warriors and descend the slope. A few furlongs more and the horrors came on again. Another globe repelled them. The dwindling party advanced, slicing their attackers into steaks as they barreled through. Fight, kill, flee; what Vorselus would have given for his hoard of magical supplies, or the abandoned potions of Gorgras, that he might have conjured a wall of flame to stand off the creatures. He used the last globe near the base of the mountain. A relative few of the filthy ones still leapt from the deepening shadows to bar the way. Against them the retreating men steeled themselves and charged, Vorselus calling on the great Gods of the universe, the Peoki crying out to their imaginary deities.

He met the dawn alone, having lost his last companions, dead or fleeing, during the final dash of the night. He cowered against a boulder poised on the lip of a great ravine, with the featureless plain stretching before, the evil mountain looming above, the insidious mist shrouding its top, concealing the unbearable scene of unexpected tragedy. Tumultuous clouds raced across the heavens. Vorselus was exhausted, cut and bruised, shivering with more than cold, the normal functions of his mind stunned and disabled. And he was alone—horribly alone—not knowing quite where he was, nor whether aught else of the grand expedition had survived.

97

XI. THE WANDERINGS OF VORSELUS

An unseasonably torturing sun beat down on Vorselus as he tramped alone and lonely across a wide open volcanic plain. Hard, brittle rocks slid beneath his feet, sparse, spiny shrubs caught at his legs. He moved south, by necessity rather than choice. He had tried to make for the Rhexellite road, where he estimated it to be, considering that his best chance to regain contact with what was left of the expedition, but unfriendly villagers chased him away in the wrong direction, and he was never able to make good the detour. The loathsome troglodytes were gone—thank the Gods!—dead or floundering back into their burrows, hopefully never more to disturb the surface of the world and its dwellers, but Vorselus faced natural perils in plenty. In the midst of enemies he had no food, no water.

It was the latter requirement that drove him still further south, far off the path followed by the army on its initial eastward march. Early that first morning a light rain left dirty puddles among the rocks from which he sipped; then, nothing. The weather turned, the sun blazed, and away from the fields by the villages he thought near the road he fell into parched, unfriendly terrain. Toward the end of the second day he suffered on the brink of death.

He came to a broad gully, into which he dived for shade, lying panting behind rocks, then pulled himself up as the sun descended to cover distance in the relative cool. The gully steepened to the south, became a ravine which plunged among rock walls into a narrow chasm. Here he chanced upon a spring seeping low from the wall, the water trickling down the gorge in a little clear stream. The sparkling water invigorated him enormously. He guessed he would not die that day, so long as no enemies chanced upon him.

That was good, he supposed, yet he could see naught else to cheer him. Such a chore life now seemed! He spent all of his time jumping from one hot danger to another; nothing ever resolved, no event of any consequence save that it momentarily menaced him or briefly aided his survival. This was no way for a civilized man to live. What of his aspirations? Did they count for nothing in the wide universe?

Next day he followed the stream south, although only Xenophor knew where it led him. It meant life-giving refreshment, which was plenty for now, if hardly sufficient. By this time Vorselus felt in dire straits for nourishment, but in this sun-scathed land, its sere nature marred solely by the minute rill hugged by thin greenery, that was a problem. He occasionally spied wholesome creatures furtively drinking, but they were too quick and wary for him. Having lost his sword in that final scramble down the mountain, Vorselus plodded on totally unarmed. Makeshift magic, of course, was customarily useless against the beasts of nature, and so it proved now.

Dusk gathered, heavy and quickly chilling. At the limit of vision he spied two men squatting by the stream ahead. At the same moment they saw him, rose, approached cautiously. Vorselus did not run—he had not the strength, and the walls of the small canyon were difficult to scale—choosing instead to steel himself for trouble. The first man came at a lope. He was not a Rhexellite, thank goodness, but a healthy man though clothed only in the rags of a loincloth, and a Peoki, and—fancy this!—one whom he recognized. Before the amazed wizard advanced Fenji, a Rongian fisherman who had attached himself to Nantrech's headquarters as a go-between to the Peoki chiefs. Vorselus had known opportunities to admire his prowess in combat, had given him up for lost with Morca's detachment. The fellow hoisted a long spear with ill intent, shouting his battle cry, then stopped and stood down when he realized he faced a normal human being. He called to the man coming up behind him, called him by name.

"Phillipan!" cried Vorselus, coming on to close the gap at a staggering run. He marveled that he should encounter this man of all men. He felt the hand of fate grasping him.

"Well met, wizard," replied the young officer in kindly tones. The three came together, shaking hands and slapping backs, Fenji also, as a comrade in arms.

The dark native said, "We be two, thought we all. Now we three. Anymore?" His Dyrezanian, obviously picked up in camp councils, was not the best, but he made himself readily understood. Phillipan seconded the question.

Vorselus ignored them, warmly shot back, "By the Gods, I must eat. I am famished. Have you food?"

They did, having borne away from the final cataclysm a march-sack of rations, supplemented by infrequent kills on the trail. They took him to their camp, a stone-ringed fire on soft loam by the creek, and there they fed him, giving him in their generosity more than his share, which he greedily devoured. Replenished, Vorselus could properly respond to questions, and field his own.

Said he, "I have seen no one since that unforgettable night, except for those despicable villagers in the vicinity of the mountain."

Phillipan said, "Likewise, my friend. I came through with two guardsmen and three Peokis as companions to watch my back. Fenji is left to me."

"But you live. That is more than I dreamed. I gave little for Nantrech's chances; for yours, none. You live. Does Morca?"

Fenji looked crestfallen, cast down his eyes. Phillipan sighed, stirred uneasily, said, "Surely he does not. When the rear guard collapsed, and those beasts poured over our shattered ranks, Lord Morca released us, told us to run for our lives. He would not run. I last saw him mobbed by those things."

It took a minute for Vorselus to absorb this awful news. "So what comes now?"

"We follow the water," the officer advised, "until we can safely turn west. We must get back to the coast. We should be all right there. We can head up to Rongia, catch a ship."

"We leave this place," Fenji blurted lugubriously. "No good here."

Phillipan chuckled without mirth. "He's right, of course, but he means more. Fenji's heard stories about this area. He tells me it's haunted."

"I could say that much about the entire Rhexellite kingdom," Vorselus replied.

"He means this place in particular. The notion derives from the Rhexellites. There aren't any villages out here, you see. They shun the area."

"That is great," grunted Vorselus. "If even the Rhexellites are afraid of it, I want no part of it."

"I'm sticking with the water," was Phillipan's decisive answer. "Without that we'll be dead in days."

All three stuck. Next day, following the stream, they reached a point where the little canyon opened into a wide valley. Springs fed the creek, expanded it, its course wandering through marshy bottom land. Fat trees dangled willowy branches, tall reeds grew densely, all serving to block the view ahead. Black clouds gathered, rain fell in bursts. They pushed on miserably through the morass.

At night strange lights reflected into the sulking sky from somewhere down the valley. To that weird glow was added infrequent flares of greenish radiance arcing into the heavens, then dissipating. Fenji shuddered, in a burst of his native language augured doom.

Phillipan whispered, "I don't like it. There's something odd around us."

"Much magic here," explained Vorselus. "These are signs, indications of the stirrings of force nearby. The question is what kind, and who controls it?"

"If it's the Rhexellites, we're done."

"Very likely." There was no warmth in Vorselus' response. He had given up on himself long ago.

At daybreak the clouds lowered, forming the semblance of a solid black ceiling over the land. Vorselus imagined that he could reach up to touch it. Thunder rumbled, loud rolling growls accompanied by sporadic flashes in many colors. Vorselus thought these unlikely to be of natural constitution. His companions said nothing but, taking the gauge of their behavior, he reckoned they felt likewise.

The stream broadened into a large pond surrounded by dense stands of trees, enclosing a small island overgrown with trees and shrubs. Skirting the edge of the pool, they spied a clearing at the edge of the island, a sandy beach narrowing into the interior. At the back of that they glimpsed a hint of artifice.

"It's a hut," muttered Phillipan.

"More than that," said Vorselus. "It is a marble structure. That is fine stone. The raw material is not native to these parts, judging from what we have seen."

Whispered Fenji, "Nothing here for us. We go."

Phillipan retorted, "If someone's home, we may get food and information. Let's risk it."

At that moment a bright red flare rocketed from the island to burst overhead. Vorselus grinned hardly. "The pond does not appear deep. We can wade it. We had better go on in. I suspect that someone is waiting for us."

Fenji required argument, but he would not be left alone, so they went, sloshing through the water which never rose to their knees. From the beach they beheld the building more closely, observed that it was of plain construction, angular, but of striated marble, with a domed roof, quite unlike the harsh Rhexellite style. They approached. Nothing moved thereabouts except winging insects, no sound save their low buzzing. Then quietly spoken words of song drifted to their hearing from the interior, a curious chanting refrain:

"Thus spins the cycles of Time round and round
For those still living, for those in the ground
They do not wait for the bold or the lost
Nor for these three whom Fate has cruelly tossed."

Said Phillipan, "Do I hear oddly pointed music yonder? Who sings to us?"

The arched door, closed by a mere hanging drapery, provided ready access. Vorselus noted that the material was good silk. For a period the three tarried on the threshold, then Vorselus thrust aside the curtain and led the way inside.

Within they found a single large, oblong chamber, its walls faced in pearly stone, with tapestries hanging at intervals bearing cosmic signs: crescent moons, star-bursts, radiating suns, comets. The stone floor was bare except for a structure at the far end. Slits in the dome allowed enough light to reveal the thing, as they came up, to be a stone-rimmed well, a rather curious sort of well. The water was crystal clear, and they could see the sandy bottom, but through some cause—possibly a trick of diffraction—that bottom appeared far away, at a dizzying remove. Fenji croaked an untranslatable Peoki word and stepped away, Phillipan muttered an oath and turned aside, Vorselus pondered darkly but continued to stare. It was too easy to see into that well; the waters generated their own light; the lambent glow intensified. Now Vorselus moved away, greatly concerned. Bright power flowed from the well, swirling in the air like a whirlpool.

Said a solemn voice, "Welcome my friends, to the temple of Xenophor, seat on this Earth of the Most High." The words emanated from behind the nearest tapestry, not six feet away. The curtain parted. A man sat within a little alcove, squatting on layered rugs of various thick furs. He was a strange man. Not Rhexellite, certainly, neither of any race Vorselus could definitely identify, yet a true man, with general features that haunted with their subtle familiarity. He wore a long black robe that concealed all but his fine, slender white hands and his exquisitely young, clean-shaven white face. That face was a marvel: youthful yet not fresh, a mask of vitality through which oozed a suggestion of extreme age. The eyes were dark holes, black and deep, reflecting twinkling lights not in evidence.

He said, "Welcome, Fenji. Do not fear; I will not bite. Welcome, Phillipan, as you presently style yourself." When he spoke, his words penetrated directly into the mind, readily understandable, as if he

102

spoke through a vocal apparatus hidden in the hearer's brain. "Welcome, sorcerer Vorselus, mage of Dyrezan, or do you prefer Professor Anton Vorchek?"

Vorselus felt an electric shock course through him. Meaning to sound authoritarian, he demanded with a nervous stammer, "Who are you? What are you? How do you know me?"

The man laughed with genuine humor, a tinkling sound like the shattering of ice. "How could I not know you? I know all, though I rarely attend. You drew my attention to you. You employed my book."

"Your book—"

"*The Black Book*, it has been called. Greetings, Vorchek. I am Jacob Bleek." Vorselus wavered, was like to pass out. Phillipan and Fenji took him in hand. For a time he must have lapsed into unconsciousness. It seemed mere moments passed before the three were seated on furs before the well, with the remains of a meal in ceramic platters, and Bleek sitting above them on the lip of the well, the ghostly whirlpool of throbbing lights playing about his head. He said, "It appears you have heard of me, Vorchek. I appreciate your intense reaction."

The one to whom he spoke asked weakly, "Is it truly you? You are not of this time; indeed, from much closer to mine. This era is as foreign to you as to me."

"Come, come, wayward scientist, you should know better than that, having read my book, or as much of it as the vicissitudes of time granted you. My research has opened to me all the doors of time and space. In every sense, I am ageless. You need only ask how I come to be here, at this unlikely juncture.

"You called me to you, Vorchek. That is the price, apparently, of a too intense application of my works. I became aware, was drawn through the spheres to await you. It was ordained that you would reach me."

Here was a strange and interesting fact: throughout the duration of this bizarre meeting, Professor Vorchek was equally in command of his persona with the wizard Vorselus; he knew himself, knew his history, as did the other, without any conflict at all. Both functioned mentally, feeling no restraint or selfish opposition. Only in thrall to frightful magic of limitless power could such a thing be. The professor could not fathom it; this truth superseded his science. It mystified the mage; in his heart Vorselus realized that he confronted arcane art which triumphed over all the magical lore of Dyrezan.

103

That was most disquieting, even insulting.

Said Bleek, "I treated with the Gods, as had no man before me, nor any since; yea, even stood at the throne of Great Xenophor, in His realm beyond matter and sanity, and there I demanded the totality of knowledge and wisdom. I received it. My book, as it has come down to you, embodies the surviving fragments of that power which can destroy a universe, or fashion one from nothing. You tapped into that, Vorchek, in a very small way, seeking knowledge. Of your stance, I approve. I must say, however, that you made a serious muddle of the matter."

"I did not understand," Vorchek exclaimed. "I meant to observe the great deeds of the past, follow a line of research. I did not realize I was thrusting myself directly into hazard, becoming one with this world."

"The complete chapter would so have informed you." Bleek smiled. "Through my eon-spanning studies I delved into the pristine magic of the primordial Rhexellites, learned their greatest secrets dating from their final age of glory. They taught me the method."

"The Rhexellites!" sneered Phillipan. "I don't hold those creatures in high account."

Muttered Vorchek, "The old Rhexellites, he means, Phillipan, from a past that even you have forgotten. Of course that name set off alarm bells in my mind, but the connection meant nothing outright to my alter ego. Thus it came about, eh? Regardless, Bleek, despite careful preparation, and dedicated attention to your writings, my plans did go astray. I thought I had it all figured out."

"Really, Vorchek, you must get your facts in order before you commence theorizing. You hurled yourself into pointless danger, in the process dragging your two foolish companions with you. What of Theresa, that helpmate of a girl you stranded and abandoned? What of Philip, who has practically disappeared into Phillipan? What say you, soldier? Have you benefited by this rash experiment?"

"I haven't," replied a sullen Phillipan. "I've been weakened, when I most needed all my wits and strength. Part of me is troubled, the other . . . lost."

"Just so. Your other half never emotionally or intellectually involved himself in that enterprise to any serious degree. It is quite different with Theresa and Teresia, more so still with the professor and his unwilling host. If amends are not made, there psychic battles will flare in time."

"I would like nothing more," shot Vorchek, "than to correct my

104

error, get my people home, and leave these folk of my dead past to work out their own destinies. Of course I would help them if I could—Vorselus is almost a brother to me, in spirit, and I hate to think of Teresia's travails—but I cannot. I am not master of the magic that rules their world. My insights pale before their own. I am not accustomed to being in that position, will gladly put it behind me. How do I undo your spell?"

"There is only one man of this age," intoned Bleek, "who can aid you in that task."

"Naturally. I am speaking to him."

Bleek chuckled. "I am not of this age, I tell you, nor any longer of any age. Time for me is a well-built carriage—or a fine-tuned sports car, as you would say—conveying me smoothly and in extreme comfort to any destination I choose. Look not to me to fish you from the shipwreck of your errors. There is another, I assure you, to whom you must turn."

"But you can do it!"

"Of course I can. I do not particularly care to do so. Pointless meddling never suited me. Deal with your own problems. Then again, an exercise of my power, to amaze and confound, might amuse me."

"Then amuse yourself," retorted Vorchek. "Do this thing. It costs you nothing, but will make a big difference to me."

"What will you have?" queried Bleek.

"Take me and mine home."

"Just a minute," cried Phillipan. "It's too bad about this Vorchek's troubles, but I have my own. I'm Phillipan, not this Philip who counts for nothing with me, and my concerns lie in this, my intolerable present. Many good men of Dyrezan have perished; others may face peril. I hear terrible stories of civil disaster at home. If you, man of mystery, choose to act for us, then I beg you to wield your mighty arts in the favor of our glorious empire."

"Dyrezan," said Bleek, "is a single tawdry heartbeat in the life of the cosmos."

"You lie. Dyrezan is eternal, and grand, the center of all conception."

At this point Vorselus could stand no more. Sagely holding back until now, that he might listen and learn, he broke in at last. "Unbounded wizard," he said to Bleek, "I stand with Phillipan against this Vorchek, who means well, I suppose, but has not in his heart all our interests. Our situation becomes increasingly desperate.

105

I know, from tragic experience, that our great home totters. I crave information. Tell us everything you can of how matters stand, and I will be content."

The sorcerer Jacob Bleek nodded. "You ask only for knowledge. That pleases me. Knowledge has ever been my goal. I gained, to my endless regret, far too much of it. I can spare you a little.

"Vorselus, since you left Dyrezan dire doings have proceeded apace. The situation there has since deteriorated, become worse than you imagine. Would you care to see with your eyes, hear with your ears, what has transpired there?"

"That I would," said Vorselus. Vorchek raged, "That is not what I ask!" Vorselus scoffed, "We know your selfish position. Phillipan, speak!"

The officer looked doubtful, confused by the shifting personalities of his companion, which made for a weird dialogue, but he spoke up with confidence. "I will have it Vorselus' way. Fenji, how say you?"

The poor Peoki shook his head, was long in speaking. Finally, after much thought, he said, "I stand with live men, not ghosts. My friend says true."

"That's it, then," cried Phillipan. "O great Bleek, show us these things."

"Let there be no more delay," said Vorselus. "We will study and learn."

Jacob Bleek said airily, "So be it. I have conjured." He rose from his seat on the well, strode to his alcove, pulled aside the curtain. "Peer into the well. Stare long and hard. A window shall open for you." He withdrew from the chamber.

His three guests crowded around the well. Lights moved down there, darting sparks that flared and vanished below the water. The surface eddied. A pale yellow glow shimmered, arose from those infinite depths, expanded and intensified to obscure natural vision. Light was all, dazzling light, and then it began to resolve itself into form. Fuzzy shapes emerged from the radiance, focused gradually into clear-cut objects. Now they gazed as through a window into another physical aspect of the world. The scene unfolded before them.

XII. THE CASTLE OF KARDOWAN

Vorselus recognized the locale, once he adjusted himself to the unusual angle of view, like that seen from a bird on the wing: the Avenue of Azamodeus, in all its glory, in wondrous Dyrezan; the scene lit by street lamps and the lights from the many windows of fine houses, for it was night there. It was the far northern end of that great street, away from the heart of the city, a district occupied by the noblest and proudest of mages. No sooner had he established this than the image wavered—as if viewed through crystal water into which a pebble has been dropped—and he beheld the street-ward front of a distinctive edifice, the gloomy, gray castle of Lord Kardowan, a princely abode fit for such a powerful and dangerous man. There were the extensive grounds lush with concealing shrubs, the territory patrolled by private guards; the high, bare walls, with the towers of the castle protruding into the sky beyond. It was mostly dark there, save for the torches of watchmen pacing along the crenellated tops of the enclosing walls.

All images looked remarkably realistic and clear to Vorselus, as if he had been returned to his homeland and gazed upon these things in the flesh. This reminded him uncomfortably of Jacob Bleek's unique magical prowess, that this singular man could, with so little effort, conjure marvels that surpassed those achieved by the grandees of Dyrezan.

Another change of scene, one which seemed to bore in a flash through walls to arrive at a cramped, square brick chamber, illuminated by dull globes of magic in the corners, with one small door of oak fastened with a heavy iron bolt. Most of the available space within the room was given over to a square table of stone, on which rested silver flagons of wine and golden goblets. Seated about the table, with the backs of their plain chairs almost touching the walls, were five men, two of them dressed in stately fashion, the others attired in common stuff and wearing short swords from their belts. Vorselus knew three of them by sight or acquaintance: the small, hawkish Lord Kardowan, the large, decadent Lord Albragon, and the brutal Garok, his face hideously scarred.

The latter was speaking, harsh of voice, yet in the manner of one deferentially reporting to his superior. Vorselus grimaced with morbid amusement at the coincidence—no, surely design—which made him the immediate topic of discussion. Garok said, "Vorselus

107

is dead; at least, that is the tale we've spread about the city, and if it isn't true yet, it will shortly be. I tell you, my Lord Kardowan, by this time he's lying in a ditch, somewhere along the eastern road, with his throat cut. There's no way that fool could escape our net, nor any place for him to go. Forget him."

"Have I already," replied Kardowan. "Never meant he anything to me, being merely a tool by which I could make the point that opposition to me proves instantly fatal. He served his purpose. Some who were inclined to balk at my ascendancy have shown themselves remarkably friendly since his feckless flight. What of the girl?"

Albragon irritably interposed, his great bulk shifting uneasily. "Wise sorcerer, we gather here not to discuss the fate of slaves. You ask of a broken instrument. Let us forget her as well."

"An instrument with a tongue," Kardowan declared. "She, too, were better dead. I had this stupid Teresia under my thumb, yet somehow she turned, was pulled astray. I tried casting my mind after hers, only to receive peculiar results. There is strangeness in her case. Garok, what of her?"

The thug deferred to one of his cruder colleagues or subordinates, addressed as Lukas. That one said, "She remains within the refuge of the house of Vorselus. Not so much as a step has she taken out the door."

"Seize her the moment she does. Regardless, soon I expect to be able to send in soldiers after her." Kardowan took up a document from the table, studied it, cast it down. "All right, Albragon, to our real business. May it please you. What do you hear of me from the King?"

Albragon said, "Naught but words of love, friend in wisdom. Your advice stands as law unto him, like pronouncements from the Gods. He will not act without you. He decrees as you bid."

"Excellent. My position, so far as it goes, becomes secure. Yet still," Kardowan's voice rose to a shout, a surprisingly thunderous sound from that small mouth and those delicate lips, "still the Grand Council defies me, works to undercut me, sends to me these outrageous missives! Wait, they say, wait for the return of the army with Nantrech and Morca, wait before we commence major shifts in policy. Their obstructionism begins to annoy me. Albragon, that seals their death warrant."

That lord shook his head nervously. "We must proceed with due caution at all times, and perspicacity. You have gained much at no cost. Beware of the heavy fees attendant on risky action."

"Indeed? Shall you smile and nod your way to the kingship? Your blood courses not sufficiently royal for that, noble one. You will have what you seek, and I my prize, which I value the more, but first we spend treasure to gain the more. The Council remains the single organized force standing in my way at this time. Therefore, they must be removed."

"How is that to be managed?"

"Ostensibly, by your methods, Albragon: the sweetness of honey, the glad hand extended in bountiful cooperation. I will treat with those men as boon comrades. I shall open my arms to them, welcome them as honored guests to my domicile, and here—mark you—they shall attempt to betray me and the King. O, Albragon, such a cruel rejoinder to my fawning hospitality!"

"I see not that," sniffed Albragon. "It is not their way. Of course you could crush them then, but they will not act in that fashion, nor, I think, take any earnest measures until the Lords Nantrech and Morca return."

"You mire your brain," jeered Kardowan, "in gross realities. Think, for the nonce, only of appearances. The desired result will unfold."

The murky scene closed; another image developed: the plaza before the court of Skyrax, in broad daylight, typical doings of the people in those familiar surroundings. Now a crier strides forth from the royal castle, flanked by mages who release into the air exotically colored pigeons from the King's aviary bearing messenger globes. The crier shouts his news, and as he does the airborne globes echo his words:

"Citizens of Dyrezan, subjects of Skyrax, favored of Xenophor and His Host, harken to this revelation. Last night evil deeds advanced against our fair city, assailed its goodness, only to be repelled by the fortitude of loyalty. The King commands that it be made known how his faithful servant Kardowan smashed a ring of criminals operating against the welfare of the empire.

"Long has treason festered within the closed chambers of the Grand Council, a vile conspiracy headed by the false patriot Malfador. Long had he conceived it; cunningly he engineered it; in the dark, while we slept, he attempted his stab at King and country. Demanded he and his scheming Council audience with Lord Kardowan, noble consultant to the King, that they might trap him in his very home and slay him there, thus removing the sole obstacle to their nefarious plans.

"Wise Kardowan struck back against their attack, relying on his arcane prowess and clean heart to surmount the vicious powers arrayed against him, defeat them, consign them to oblivion. It is done! Let the bells ring out our joy! Treason meets its indelible fate. The Council is no more! The villains are dead! A new Council, composed of decent men who love the King, will be established to aid in our governance. Happy day! Let all men shout their approval; let the women and children sing their delight!"

The pictures in the waters of the strange well of Jacob Bleek faded away like a dream that refuses to wait on memory. Phillipan cried, "That isn't correct. This amazing instrument makes pretty pictures, but spews nothing but lies. It's worthless." Vorselus agreed, "Something is not right. We miss too much. Sorcerer Bleek," he called to the vague form huddled behind the drapes of the alcove, "you toy with us. Granting that you show us true, nevertheless you vouchsafe mere surface knowledge, unworthy of your magical might. It is the core reality I would see."

Bleek chuckled distantly. "So you may," came his amused whisper, "yet it is important that you know how others may not. You heard what the people were told, two weeks thence. That image is fact. You ask, however, for the fact before the fact, that which intervened between midnight plotting and sunny proclamation. I forget that your common minds still function in terms of absolute chronology. Before time, after time; what are they to me? So be it. Attend, Vorselus, to the sickish reality behind sweet words."

The waters re-activated, swirled in pearly eddies, coalesced into another scene, identifiable from visual hints and casual comments as the great dining hall in the castle of Kardowan. The master of the house sat there at the head of his table, in his gold and black robe, with retainers and scribes about him; and down the long table, which bore evidences of a finished meal, sat the twelve esteemed and elderly men of the Grand Council, dutiful old Malfador among them. Kardowan was offering a toast to the greatness of Dyrezan and its continued prosperity.

"Enough of this," grumbled Malfador. "Kardowan, you invited us here—summoned us, more like—in order to discuss the health of the state. You promised crucial disclosures. So far I hear naught but that akin to buffoonery." His colleague Kakion agreed. "We are not dazzled by the splendor of your entertainment, nor fogged in mind by your plentiful wine. Come to the point." Said another, no less than Menzias, "Hear, hear, get on with it. If there is aught we should know, make haste to inform us, that we may confer and promptly act. I grow weary of these shenanigans."

"As do I, noble friends," Kardowan replied coldly. "I asked you here to tell you a tale of monstrosity, the story of treason uncovered, of double faces separated and stripped bare, of justice surely wielded like an ax. A conclave of Dyrezan's worst enemies have been brought to book at a place prepared, lured there by sugared tidings, and corralled to their destruction. This I tell you, and this you may shortly confirm."

"Who are these enemies?" demanded Malfador.

"Why, my dear magician, adept of the strange arts, I speak of you and your unworldly crew."

Kardowan snarled, "I stand at the King's side, by his direct command, yet you oppose and impede me at every turn. Under the new regime, that constitutes the ultimate infamy. You exhaust my forbearance, strain my mercy to the utmost. I unmask the hate behind your pasted smiles!"

"We stand against tyranny," snapped Malfador. "You cannot browbeat us. We are sorcerers all, potent and studied. You are but one man, however skilled." He rose. "We take our leave of you. The King shall hear of this drivel and your antics. Do not try to molest us."

Kardowan's sudden, shocking, maddened laugh screeched throughout the spacious chamber as he struck with the full force of his well-studied magic blow. One man, yes, but one of superlative power, in his own arena, his plans coolly laid, his program long formulated, tested, assured. Kardowan had calculated every factor.

The initial blast of blazing energy caused the men of the Council to reel in their seats, Malfador falling against the table. They seemed stunned, defenseless. How could that be? These were clever fellows, trained in the arts of magical warfare. They would not have walked into the den of danger helpless or unready. One could imagine—yes, this must be the answer—that Kardowan had impregnated the very fabric of the room with disarming charms, spells that sapped the strength from arcane shields. Indeed a cunning trap! That would explain the apparent weakness, so odd, among the victims. Did not they prepare for that? Had they been too thoroughly lulled by oily flattery to expect such a deep, devilish scheme? They were old, and sure of their security, there in the heart of the great city that of long standing belonged to them. They might—and the Gods must

111

weep!—have made that terrible mistake.

Also, it would have galled them to admit that Kardowan was the greatest of them all. If they chose to underestimate him, then they decided unwisely. It was a fatal mistake. Immediately he commenced the clash of wills. Blue sparks crackled in the air as Kardowan lashed out murderously with his focused mind. Menzias went down, clutching his temples in agony, and another, the renowned Debicet, breathed his last. Now Malfador, and the remaining nine who sprang to their feet, recovered from the first surprise stroke and struck back. The Grand Council of Dyrezan hastily fomented, from their vast innate resources, their own psychic missiles, and the chief of the Council (perhaps more ready than the rest) conjured on the instant a small but frantic thing that flew at Kardowan's face. It was a bird, but no such bird as adorned the aviaries of Dyrezan. Its head bore a ridiculously large beak pointed like a honed dagger, and its drab gray feathers were oily, its body elongated and twisting like an aerial snake, and it lunged at its prey with a terrible screaming cry. Kardowan shook as with ague when the ferocious forces smote, and he wildly slapped at the fluttering monstrosity that pecked fiercely at his throat, yet he quailed not before the counter-attack, but maintained the fight. His magical defenses were up and charged, blocking those killing strokes. Whatever charm he used to unman his enemies did not affect him. He steadied; he crushed the snapping thing between clenched hands in a spray of watery gray ichor.

Kardowan renewed his assault. Kakion crumpled, then good Quenfal, then more. The fight had gone out of those standing. Now Kardowan produced from his robes a whistle which he raised to his lips, blew with a shrill, piercing shriek. Every door to the room flew open. In charged Garok, commander of Kardowan's armed liege-men, with the ruffian Lukas at his side and fifty picked men, rushing toward the tottering guests in full armor and with swords flashing above their heads. The great minds of the Council had not sensed the near presence of these brutes? More fiendish magic, another layer to the trap, level atop level of weird charms that encompassed the destruction of men who deemed themselves invulnerable. Wonderful old Malfador possessed still strength for one last rally, brought his wide eyes to bear on Lukas who, bellowing in the fury of blood-lust, bore down on the aged mage. Lukas died in mid-swing, the helmet flying from his head as his skull ruptured and his brains spurted out. He fell, and fifty more wavered, but Kardowan screamed out his anger and urged them on with foaming lips. "Kill

112

them, kill them all, you fools. Kill them while you can!" They lunged forward, Garok leading the pack, mobbed those old men, butchered them like cattle. Swords rose and fell until nothing resembling the human form remained in that reeking pile of bloody meat about the fine table in the dining hall.

Kardowan, alone against all, had triumphed. He had slaughtered the Grand Council. Surely even he must have been amazed by the feat, unique in the surviving annals of the city. The Council, venerated, inviolate; not only abolished, but wiped out; it was a great, if infamous, deed. Truly Kardowan staggered, though not from dismay at the astounding effrontery of his ambitions; no, swayed and sagged from sheer exhaustion induced by magical combat to an extreme degree. He had bested them all, but for the moment there was little left of him. He stumbled, groped for his chair, collapsed like an empty sack. He shouted for Garok, only his commanding cry came out a pathetic squeak.

"Bring me wine," he gasped between stentorian pants. "Fill the glass full. No; I will have the jug." His spare frame vibrated with weakness; a vein pulsed on his shiny, sweat bedewed pate. "Clean up this offal," he said presently. "We must arrange the scene, bring it into unison with the tale I shall fabricate for the court. Some will demand proofs of the dead ones' crimes. I shall see that they have it."

The image of Kardowan's cruelly grinning face faded into darkness. The waters of the magic well grew still. From his remove Jacob Bleek said, "There, my friends, as you would have it, is the actuality concealed beneath the varnish of proud and noble words trumpeted to the populace of glorious and eternal Dyrezan. Not pretty, I say, although I am aware that tastes differ. I prefer the public version. It suits better my sense of aesthetics."

"It can't end there!" shouted Phillipan, who angrily thrust aside the curtain to face the man whose revelations tormented him. "There must be more. My people are not so supine as to cravenly applaud this brazen deed of murder. One braying speech will not quell their doubts."

"A speech authorized in the King's name, seconded by his devoted Grand Councilor Kardowan. That is a blunt stick against doubt, my friend."

Fenji the Peoki warrior, who had observed in silence the mysterious unveiling of images from past times and far places, muttered as to himself, "Wonderful this, and Dyrezan like a dream

113

from the Gods, but I think the Rhexellites better enemies. They hated my people sure. Never did they trick us with smiles."

"I do not think the tale concluded," said Vorselus. "This is old information, which saddens me, for much time has passed, and we are far from home, helpless for a long while to intervene. However, come we home if we can, to do what we can, what we must. I will know more."

Bleek said, "There is much more. There is more to everything that exists: deeds, ideas, desires; endless ramifications, complications, minutiae heaped atop imponderables. What of it? The details of infinitude bore me. I have known them all, infinitely. You need not."

"Let us see," insisted Vorselus.

The well stirred again. Once more they gazed on the castle of Kardowan by night, entered with their eyes its forbidden precincts. In another room, a small chamber decorated with curious painted designs and heaped with books, Lord Kardowan sat at table, looking smug as a sated vulture. Near him paced Lord Albragon, his corpulence cloaked in a drab robe, a broad hat clamped down low on his head. Albragon seemed worried. He muttered something, his words accompanied by nervous gestures. The image closed with him. He burst out loudly, "I did not expect it this way. I thought to rope them, chain them up, put them out of the way. By Xenophor's righteous rage, a massacre, Kardowan! Have you lost your senses? This sinks all boats."

"Undoubtedly, if we falter for an instant. Instead we go forward with vigor, hesitating not, lest we perish. Only one road remains open to us. I shall pave it with mortar fashioned from the ground bones of my enemies."

"Unless the city rises against you."

"Against us, Lord Albragon." Kardowan laughed. "We are renegades together, you and I. We sink or swim, together. Throw your notable weight fully behind me. Only thus will you attain what you crave."

"If I will have the crown," observed Albragon, "I require a head on which to perch it."

Kardowan gave another laugh, one which lingered. He seemed wonderfully jovial. "Stick by me, and your head squats safe. Therein lies your sole guarantee."

"I do not see it. The Royal Guard is strong. Its officers and ranks bow to Morca. They are not fools. They will see through your masquerade."

"I forgot to tell you, indomitable friend," said Kardowan quietly, "of my audience with Skyrax this afternoon. I pressed upon him the necessity for weeding out disloyalty among the ranks of his warrior protectors. The document is drawn up, it is signed by me, awaiting only the morn for the King's seal. Key officers shall be replaced, and Garok takes command. My henchmen will be officially incorporated. Guess you whose orders they shall obey without question?"

Albragon weakly smiled. "You think of everything. We should not fear arrest from them."

"There will be many arrests, however. With the Guard tamed, I predict the incarceration— and, perhaps, the entertaining punishment—of any contrary citizen who disturbs our straight path to power."

"That's it," growled Phillipan, turning to his companions with wild eyes and features contorted by fury. "Kardowan's got it all. With our best leaders dead or missing, he'll make a clean sweep of Dyrezan."

"Words," said Vorselus, "schemes and dreams. We know what he means to do, or meant to do, at this point. We have not seen him do it. Dyrezan has not survived this long, throughout the misty ages, because it gives up its soul easily to a madman like Kardowan. There are good men at home, even if they be not the finest nor the most heroic. They will stand against him. And we are coming; somehow, whatever it takes, we shall return, even if armed only with this strange knowledge."

XIII. THE CONSPIRATORS STRIKE

Finally Professor Vorchek could stand it no more. "Enough of this!" he cried. "Devilish doings, to be sure, and my heart bleeds for all concerned, but a personal matter torments me, and I will not be denied my sip of the well. Stand aside, Phillipan. The little bit of Philip within you drowns in your personality, but my awareness is strong. I demand satisfaction. Jacob Bleek, my loyal assistant is stuck in that hornet's nest; Theresa, sharing a body with the dancing girl Teresia. What of her? Did Kardowan ever pause from his imperial machinations to seek her? Does she still live? I want to know!"

Vorselus tried to silence him, but after a fashion he shared the concern, neither could he surmount the heights of Vorchek's powerful need. The wizard drew back, letting the scientist storm. "Show me, Bleek," he pleaded. "Offer me hope, if you can."

Jacob Bleek nodded. "That is naught of difficulty. All knowledge is equal. You may see her, Vorchek, and in pursuing her activities learn much else. The girl became more than a bystander in this affair." Vorchek cared not to hear that, yet it relieved him to know that she lived, that there was a story of her left to tell. The mystic well glowed with peculiar throbbing light, and he saw.

The house of Vorselus, its upper windows darkened, the lower shuttered, the modest shrubbery of the narrow yard facing the street, unkempt. Inside the house, within a nook off of the dining hall, where the mage had been wont to lounge and study his scrolls, sat the girl Teresia, dressed in a simple shift pulled loosely over her tempting curves. She nibbled at dainties, a sweetbread and sugared fruit. She looked woefully bored.

She started at the sound of a door thrown open beyond the corridor connecting to the foyer. That was the front door. Rapid steps of sandaled feet slapped the floor tiles. Ling-das dashed in, hair unruly, features flushed. He looked shabbier than in the days when he had a master at home to please. Nor was there in this scene a trace of his customary deference. He addressed the girl as an equal, saying, "Teresia, I bring bad news of terrible doings in the city."

She shrugged. "What, have you misplaced another batch of councilors?"

Ling-das snapped, "It's no time for levity. This could be serious for us both. The streets fill with soldiers! The army, backed by the Royal Guard, marches as on campaign, yet they wage war not against the foreign enemies of Dyrezan, but against their own people. Kardowan and his hired swine lead them! Magic fire flames in the skies, black mist shrouds the towers, and below resounds the clank of armor and the swish of swords! They're arresting everybody who's anybody, and I pray that's all they do." He paused ominously, then went on in an awed tone, "It's being said—there are criers everywhere, sent straight from the palace—that the eastern expedition has met a tragic fate, been destroyed by horrible enemies out in the wilds beyond the sea. They say the army was wiped out in a single night, and the Lords Nantrech and Morca slain along with the rest. I didn't pick up any details, but Kardowan must be sure of his information. Otherwise, he wouldn't dare this onslaught upon the city."

116

Teresia sprang to her feet. "What's it mean to us? What do we do?"

"I don't know the first; as to the last, we'd better do it fast. They're in the next block, coming this way." Ling-das paused, obviously thinking hard. "Already I've hidden my master's secret things, and such money as he possessed, in a place underground, beneath the floor of the cellars, where only determined magic or digging would reveal them. I count them safe until he returns; if he does, that is, for surely he died long ago, in some awful land on the road to nowhere."

"He lives," Teresia insisted, "and will come to us when he's ready. Our master Vorselus isn't a normal man. There is more to him than your people realize."

"Not my people," Ling-das replied bitterly, but then he sighed, said, "only they are, now, after all. Dyrezan is my destiny. Yours, too, girl. My master gave me one charge: that I protect you from harm. Thus far we've been lucky. The house has been watched, not violated. I think, today, our luck's run out." He called in a shout for the lesser servants. They came at his beck with near the alacrity they would for Vorselus himself. He said to them, "Check that the doors are bolted. If anyone demands entrance, don't resist them, but volunteer nothing. Don't give out any information. Direct them to me. On your lives, forget the existence of Teresia. As you know it, she was never here."

"It will be done," they responded. Ling-das told off their tasks, and they went.

To Teresia he said, "Now to hide you. If they come here, you'll probably be targeted. I doubt that high and mighty Kardowan has forgotten your escapades. He's a vindictive goat, I reckon. Of course you're familiar with the dungeon?"

"Quite enough, thanks," Teresia spat. "You're not going to lock me up."

"I'm going to lock you in, maybe lock others out."

Darkness, eddying of the strange waters; then the well displayed a fresh scene, apparently immediately following the last. Pounding on the door, harsh shouts; the bolts drawn back by quaking hands; the soldiers bursting in, not the Guard or regular soldiers, but a team of Lord Kardowan's liege-men, headed by the wolfish, scarred Garok. His men manhandled the slaves, bellowed threats at them, roared questions. Ling-das showed himself, fawning, the eidolon of ingratiating politeness. Garok screamed at him, "What news of the traitor Vorselus? Where find we him or his corpse?"

Ling-das looked abject. "As all the world knows, master, he ran away long ago, surely to meet his fate alone in unknown lands. We've heard no more than you."

"That's about right," Garok growled. "So, to the real business. Where's the faithless girl of my Lord Kardowan, this slut Teresia? It's her day to feel the lash, and that's just for starters. Hand her over, slave, or I'll prick out your eyes with my blade."

Ling-das radiated frightened helplessness. "Gone, master, back to her people in Vincalnac, I expect. She deserted us weeks ago."

"You lie. When I prove it you'll lose your false tongue. No one's gotten out of here without our seeing them. She's here. Men, find her. Tear the place apart!"

Kardowan's hirelings ransacked the house, kicking in doors, tearing down tapestries, chopping with axes through wooden panels. While they perpetrated these enormities Garok pressed other points upon the apparently eager to cooperate Ling-das. Ramming fist into palm, the hulking henchman said, "If you want to keep breathing, you'll fork over Vorselus' stash of magical junk. For some reason my master wants it. Also, slave, deliver up the traitor's gold." Garok laughed. "That's my fee for your continued health."

"There's nothing," Ling-das whined. "Vorselus fled with his tricks. He must have taken his treasure, too. Never was there much."

Garok grunted, swung a mailed fist at the servant's jaw, smashed him against the wall. "Give it, or you're dead. Make up your mind. I want the stuff."

Ling-das groaned from the floor where he had fallen. He rose to his knees, hands upraised for mercy, gasped, "My master's magic items are gone. I can't obey you. The little gold, the few jewels—"

"Yes?"

"I will take you to them."

Garok drove the poor fellow at sword's point through the house, up the stairs, into a storage room already despoiled by looters. Ling-das ignored the gutted wooden walls, proceeded to the back wall of stone, dragged out a heavy block. It dropped with a crash. Two coarse fabric bags lay within the revealed recess. Garok shoved him aside, greedily seized the bags, unbound their mouths. He snorted happily at sight of the precious contents. He poked around in the hole. "This all?" he gruffly queried.

"All."

"Not enough. My beggars are already collecting the valuable

118

ornaments. I've got to have a bigger cut than this. Take me to more."

"That's all there is," said Ling-das. "Liar," sneered Garok. "These wizards keep piles of good stuff." Said Ling-das, "Not all. My master was too studious to horde wealth. He squandered it on knowledge, always buying materials and scrolls." Insisted Garok, scraping his sword against the stone wall with a flaring of sparks, "I want more. My master wants the funny goods and the girl. I take the rest. You aren't cooperating."

"I can't."

"You can die." Garok thrust his sword through the slave's belly. Ling-das sagged, slid into a balled crouch. He chuckled weakly.

"You lose," he whispered. "These trinkets are nothing. Everything of value is safe from you. Vorselus will return. He'll make you pay, all of you."

With one ferocious stroke Garok chopped off his head. Wiping the blade on his thigh, he returned to the ground floor, where his men assured him that the house had been completely ransacked. They had seized nothing pertaining to magic, nor any hidden slave girl, but an oddly miserable quantity of gold and silver pieces.

"Knock holes in the walls," Garok ordered, which they did, but nothing more turned up. Eventually they departed in angry disgust, committing more random destruction as they abandoned the despoiled house.

All was quiet now. It seemed that time had passed, an indeterminate period. The old dungeon, remnant of a former age; the floor of the lowest cell, a musty cubicle of rough granite; heavy paving blocks, big squares of massive stone; but one not so heavy. It creaked upward slightly, revealing two wary, emerald-blue eyes. Teresia peeked out from her hiding place. She lowered the stone. Inside she crouched in the tiny, forgotten oubliette, surrounded, crowded by the real treasures of Vorselus. She had food, water, a supply of candles. She stayed down there—how long?—there were indications of many days. Eventually her candles ran out. That plagued her more than the steady diminishing of her life-sustaining stores. She squirmed in utter darkness. When she could stand that increasingly noisome chamber no longer she threw open the thin, cleverly balanced stone and emerged into the dungeon proper. Long she tarried there before she tremblingly ascended to the living quarters.

The place was a shambles. No one else remained, all the servants

119

dead, kidnapped, fled. She found the body of Ling-das, did what she could to honor his memory. Food stocks were largely untouched, some still edible. She made herself a den in a closet, where she might quickly abscond from the eyes of stray visitors. She waited.

She had time for thought, and not much else. She spoke aloud her mind, in that dreadful living tomb. She thought of her life as dancing girl, the baleful sequence of events that took her from her family, her land and race, to dump her into the current muddle that was Dyrezan. She thought of lost Vorselus, and when she did other, stranger ideas encroached upon her mind. She knew him as another—Professor Anton Vorchek, infuriating man and consummate scientist—the man who, without adequate explanation, had contrived to drag her—the other her, that pesky young lady Theresa—to this improbable, impossible mess.

Images of the city: splendid Dyrezan, grown gray and sad; no more the festivals, the strollers in the parks, the boisterous throngs; the bloody sword governed in Dyrezan. Kindly proclamations issued from the palace of Skyrax. The citizens heard them, hoped for a while, cheered those winning statements... then felt the brutal reality that mocked the golden words. The army, erstwhile heroes of the city, held it like an armed camp, detachments stationed along all the main streets and public centers. The homes of the great ones—save for a certain obsequious few—were occupied now by the swordsmen of Kardowan, the former owners dead, jailed, in hiding.

Kardowan strutted like a king in the royal palace. Only he received audience of Skyrax. All others came to him. He announced the whims of the King. They suspiciously resembled his own.

A dreadful image of the King: dicing with the court lackeys, carousing with slave girls. Off-hand he would ask, "How goes it this day with my people?" When he so deigned to ask, there would soon be noble Kardowan to assure him, "All is well."

A series of fleeting images, glimpses of a veiled young girl in her travels about the city, always near dawn or dusk. She pauses here to observe, tarries there to question a citizen. Who is she? Once a wandering patrol of Guardsmen stop her. She throws back her veil. They recoil, bow low, march on. Who is she?

The scene zooms spectacularly, a sensation of rushing flight. There is her face writ large in the waters of the sacred well. It is the Princess Lora who moves about in disguise, darting from one place to another in the city. She journeys throughout Dyrezan, invading even those districts where no proper princess ought to go. She talks

120

to many people. Most tell her nothing of consequence. A few reply in furtive whispers, speak with gestures, point covertly to indicate directions. Repeatedly she mentions the names of lordly men and noble sorcerers. She asks not of those killed or known to be rotting in prison; she asks after those missing, their fates unknown, those who may still be at large.

Always she says, "What you tell me, Kardowan shall never know." And, very occasionally, this promise bears fruit, yields useful answers. The scarce informants direct her to certain places. Doors open to her. She disappears within, to re-emerge later, her face beaming.

Dyrezan is an immense city. A series of pictures provides little knowledge as to the duration of her adventures. Dawn and dusk, dawn and dusk, slipping in and out of the palace, her maid-servants wringing their hands; avoiding the soldiers as best she can, facing them down when she cannot; at last she comes to the unguarded door of the forsaken house of Vorselus.

Teresia watched her from an upper window, where she observed the street in the gathering gloom. She seemed puzzled by the approach of that little girl. When the visitor entered the house Teresia scampered below, to lurk behind a big chest in the main hall. She watched as the intruder entered the room. On an impulse she sprang out from behind, grabbed her roughly.

The girl did not cry out. She said, solemnly, "I am the Princess Lora. Unhand me at once, knave." Released, she whirled around, dropped her veil, stared dubiously at her attacker. "Who are you?"

"Teresia, the sole remaining servant of the wizard Vorselus."

Lora nodded. "I seek him. I always wondered what really happened to him."

"He's gone away this long age, to avoid murder."

Lora sighed happily. "That is good. I wish others had been so lucky. Tell me how to reach him."

"Only the Gods know that."

"Do not trifle with me."

"Don't play me for a fool," Teresia retorted. "I know there's a price on his head. Who are you, child, that I should tell you anything?"

"I," Princess Lora said proudly, "am the enemy of the traitor Kardowan."

In the best comfortable den, they talked long. This was how the Princess told it. "These bloody apes do not yet dare molest me. So long as I am circumspect, I come and go as I please. Since the outrages began I have established contact with many of the true patriots who survive at liberty, nobles and mages. I have explained the situation to such of them as had not deduced it for themselves. Kardowan reigns in Dyrezan, not my illustrious father. Somehow that evil man tricked him. That was not so difficult as it should have been. Dear father was always inattentive, always, I fear, at the mercy of his advisors. To his credit, he formerly chose men of glory and wisdom."

"He's slipped up now," Teresia acidly observed.

"It was a sad day," sniffed Lora, "when our great ones left us to go gallivanting in wild places beyond the map. Lords Nantrech and Morca knew how to manage my father. His good heart served him well enough with them as guides sincere; I pray that the recent news is yet another falsehood of those who scheme to enslave us, for Father fares ill, I grant, without them. Now Kardowan panders to his worst instincts. I suspect Albragon as well, though I cannot be sure of him; he is a slippery character, that one. I just do not trust him. Regardless, Father plays while the evil ones work, revels while they plot fresh indecencies. Kardowan tells him soothing lies. I try to reason with him, but he will not hear me."

"So what, then?"

"Others do hear. Listen to this." Princess Lora described her recent activities, eagerly telling of her exploits. "There are plenty of good men and true still here to oppose these scoundrels. Each man has been isolated by fear, scarcely daring to speak in private lest he fall afoul of Kardowan's spies. I speak to them all. I bring them together. They begin to organize. There is the Lord Varador, and Ganlin, and Feesham, and several others, big enough men, preparing to act."

"To do what?"

"Resist, any way they can. They have their liege-men; too few, I admit, but collectively they make up the core of a modest army. They have their magic. When they rise—soon, I think—others will join them. Not all of our citizens are supine cowards. They believe what they are told or, if they doubt, they fear frightful retribution. Given a chance, though, with arms in hand, the people will fight."

Now Princess Lora plied Teresia with questions as to her circumstances. In time her whole story tumbled out, which filled Lora with sweet compassion. She said, "It is a miracle that you have survived this long. Shortly you must go forth to eat, and then they would catch you. You believe this despicable Kardowan would punish you?"

Teresia said flatly, "He would kill me for kicks, laughing while he did it."

"I will not stand for his laughter," Lora said stoutly. She giggled as at a private joke. "Would you like to have some fun? Would you be willing to try something silly, but that just might get you out of this mess? O, how Kardowan would howl if he guessed! But he will not, I promise you. Teresia, come back with me to the palace of the King. I can smuggle you there, and hide you there while the great deeds of the patriots unfold. You will be safe among my servants. No one would dream to seek you there, right under the nose of Kardowan. He would not think to look for you there in a million years. Is not that marvelous? We shall laugh, you and I, from inside the lair of the wolf, while that mangy dog blindly flails his claws!"

XIV. WAR IN DYREZAN

Jacob Bleek showed his guests the beginning of what came next clearly enough; as for the rest, it came to them as a jumble of chaotic, turbulent images. There was artistry of sorts in this presentation from the depths of the well, as of a grandly produced entertainment, but the magician Vorselus was in no mood for aesthetic considerations. "Amuse yourself not at our expense," he complained to his mysterious host. "This is tragedy you show us, not farce."

Bleek shrugged. "I have come to think them one and the same."

And Professor Vorchek exclaimed, "No more plague us with these horrors. One of mine faces death in this madness. I would see her more, but you tease with cinematic tricks."

Bleek laughed his sneer. "I have little enough jollity these days, nor any others. You contain in that body two self-important minds. Vorselus the mage, apply your studied acumen and piece together the logic of what you see. Vorselus, time-spanning scientist, bring to bear that arrogant logic of yours and deduce. I present you with the facts of immediate history."

The uprising against the enormities of Kardowan commenced with a well-laid ambush prepared and led by Lord Varador, staunch champion of Dyrezan's glory and personal friend to the missing Lord

Morca. In former years they had campaigned together against the barbarians. Varador was old now, long withdrawn from public affairs, but his patriotism burned brightly, never more so than on this evening, when the henchmen of Kardowan were called by lying report to quash an imaginary street disturbance. On the way to the presumed scene they marched through a narrow black alley. Suddenly archers let fly from overlooking windows. Swordsmen, stout fellows of Varador's household, accompanied by faithful men of the houses of Ganlin and Feesham, charged from doorways and streamed into the exits of the enclosed passage. They hit hard and fast, shrieking their fury, and they slew every man who opposed them. It was over before the defenders could begin to react.

With the blood of the oppressors successfully shed, the proclamation went out into the night, by word of mouth and magical transmission, an appeal to the people of the city to rise en masse and do battle with the lackeys of the tyrant. The rebellious lords revealed their names, dedicated their lives and fortunes to the cause, swore to fight to the death or until they had erased the arch-traitor Kardowan from this world.

Every man in Dyrezan heard those brave words, learned of the victorious counter-attack, and many, dreaming of hope again, reached for rude weapons and, shouting with combative joy, poured into the streets. Dyrezan came alive again that night.

"The tale is true," said Lord Kardowan to Lord Albragon. "My men have not returned, not even a lone messenger. The fools dare defy me! A handful of upstarts and has-beens go to war against me, with all the power of Dyrezan at my back? Such lunatic tomfoolery demands a cure, prompt and thorough. I shall administer the physick."

"The fat burns in the fire," muttered Albragon. "I receive reports of ominous stirrings in all quarters. How do we explain this to Skyrax?"

"Go to him, my friend, kinsmen of the King. Concoct a story. Make it good; give it a dollop of honey, but ensure a free hand for me. Now comes the time when the merest pretense of formality may be shed."

Daylight: armed citizens, forming into small bodies in the public squares. A handful of deserting soldiers join them. Much speech-making, bragging to wives and children that the reign of "King Kardowan" is over, that the jackal has lost his fangs. Another grouping, smaller over all by far but more concentrated, crowds into

124

the great plaza before the Royal Palace. A hard lot these, boisterous and vulgar, those men who by inclination or fear side with the ruling power, believing in its strength if not its cause. They are issued arms from the stocks of the army.

Such is the imbalance of popular desire that within twenty-four hours Kardowan appears to have lost his grip on Dyrezan. Everywhere—save for the armed camp about the palace, where the majority of the army and the Royal Guard stand firm, obedient to their new officers, and a few more isolated posts—the rebels have seemingly triumphed, largely without a fight. They mock the pronouncements of doom emanating from Kardowan's chambers. There is gaiety in their boasts. They speak of marching forthwith on the palace, striking down the usurper and his gang, liberating the King from his unknowing bondage. Surely, this war is over scarcely before it begins.

Kardowan struck back. Did it take him a day, two days, three to swing his sledgehammer? He waited for the moment of maximum effectiveness, then hit hard. Weird magical visions in the dawn sky stunned the senses and inspired terror in hearts. These horrid wonders were the works of Kardowan and Albragon conjuring in unison to achieve the most magnificent and nasty effects. Monsters swooped and howled, corpses lurched and gibbered, demons glared fiercely, breathing flames and threats. Flying squads of mailed cavalry surged down the avenues from the palace, spearheading grim columns of professional infantry trained to kill, and companies of hard-hearted henchmen eager to do so. They overran the flimsy, poorly guarded barricades before the rebels were aware. They chased and slew the amateurish detachments stationed about the center of the city, dashed through the park along the winding River Tethe, rampaged into the quarter of the nobles from three sides. They lifted the siege of Kardowan's castle (held for him by vile Garok and his swordsmen), then assaulted the grand houses of the contrary lords. Their retainers fought, and they died, to hold those majestic homes, but in each case after a bitter battle those edifices fell, to be given over to the flames. No mercy was shown by the victors. Resistance, coupled with defeat, meant death, sure if not always quick.

On the rebel side, confidence surrendered to despair. Ganlin perished in his burning house when his amateur soldiers deserted him; Feesham they took captive, to face public execution of the grisliest sort on the Plaza of Kings, his life stripped from him by a ravenous swarm of conjured insects; Lord Varador, grievously wounded, was dragged away by his people, barely eluding a like fate. The now leaderless citizen warriors ran for cover. Without a head, the body of that hastily fabricated army seemed quickly doomed.

So prognosticated Kardowan. "A show of force," he explained to the King (while minimizing the extent of the conflict), "is all that we required. I have crushed this fresh league of traitors against you. In your name I order judicious arrests and fitting punishments. Fear not; your person and kingdom are safe in my hands." Indeed, of a sudden Lord Kardowan has regained most of the city. A few inconsequential districts have been ignored for the moment, the oldest and densest quarters of Dyrezan where the common folk dwell, yet otherwise it has been a clean sweep. To all intents and purposes Kardowan has restored his rule.

Night: do appearances deceive? The troops calling themselves the royal forces have withdrawn into fortified camps about the city. They rest, secure and confident. From the tops of the towers of the inner city magic beams illuminate the nearby streets, affording early knowledge of potentially unfriendly movements, which do not arise. In the outlying quarters the situation differs. Couriers gallop to and fro, bearing news and commands. Not one of them reaches his destination. Slung nooses bring down riders, knives flash in the torch light. Opposition still lurks out there in the darkened city. More instructive force is necessary.

At the palace Kardowan dressed down his hand-picked officers. "Why did not you act to complete your mission?" he demanded. "I sent your orders. You disobeyed."

"We did not receive them," they protested.

"A few lingering criminals," snarled Kardowan, "halt my mighty machine. This I do not tolerate. I will send magicians to accompany you, with whom I may esoterically communicate. This day you finish the task. Kill them all. Burn down the city if you must. Finish it!"

The next, or another day, and the army moved out from its scattered strongholds, marching everywhere, unto the walls that overlooked the void at the edge of the city. Single squads tramped down the empty streets. Pillars of black smoke rose from various locations. The squads became increasingly separated.

Amidst a tangle of archaic lanes in the most ancient and squalid district one squad, filing through a maze of antique houses, turned a corner to confront a barrier of stones and wood barring the way. A mere half a dozen heads showed over the top. The squad advanced at a rush, climbed onto the low wall . . . and died in a shower of arrows and the thrusting of crude spears from the concealed masses behind. Elsewhere battle flared, small-scale engagements each, the combination the equivalent of a major battle. Fighting raged throughout the area. The advance slowed to a crawl. Come the night Kardowan's army sullenly returned to its safe camps.

That great lord is furious. "Smash them!" he screams. "Do not hesitate. Slay and burn! Outrage their women. Such delicious activities will break their morale." He ponders. "There is, in that region, only one structure worthy of our attention: a stone temple dedicated to Xenophor, a large building, one dating back to the earliest eras. That must be their headquarters. On the morrow make for that with your concentrated force. Fight your way to it, seize it, level it to its foundations. Smash its stones to fragments. That will make them gasp. That will choke them!"

The bulk of the army marched as a unit. They penetrated the district without a fight, seeing no one. The area was completely deserted. Zigzagging through the crazy streets they gained the temple, a squat, solidly built structure hoary and stained by time. It stood empty of worshipers, vacated by its priests. So massive were its blocks that the occupiers faced a serious quandary in their allotted task of despoiling it. They did what damage they could, firing the few furnishings—pitifully few, as most had been removed—knocking down columns, yanking out the rare weak stone. It looked somewhat worse for wear after their diligent endeavors. A deal of time was spent in accomplishing that much. Then they turned to march away.

Barriers confronted them on every street. According to the best military principles they planned, calculated, then assailed each one, burst through with little loss, caught and killed a handful of defenders. A couple of court magicians had consented to join the army. Their conjured flames cleared a path. The counter-march proceeded. The army ran into more roadblocks.

These they likewise overran. Victory, constant victory, one small triumph after another. News of success they sent winging from the court mages to the sorceric mind of Kardowan, who relished the soundness of his scheme. The army moved on. Dusk gathered.

Victory, they cried, only their triumphant march ran well behind schedule, and with the fall of darkness their situation turned gloomy for more than one reason. First, a strange opaque mist collected about them, one that curiously swallowed the light of their torches. They guessed it was not a normal mist; someone directed magic at them. Murmurs and grumblings arose from the ranks. Surely the big magic was all on their side? Second, the resistance of the rebels barring their way mounted spectacularly. Their numbers grew, and their determination. Those pesky barricades multiplied; the taking of each required a pitched battle. March to camp, return to camp . . . escape to camp! Before they knew it the soldiers of Kardowan were fighting, not for victory, but for their lives.

They cut their way through. They battled grimly through a maelstrom of unrelenting combat, assaults and counter-assaults on all sides, fury matching fury. It took them all night to get clear, and they were good for nothing that day. Their commanders boasted of their skill in leading the army back from its difficult position, noted that casualties did not exceed ten per cent. Claimed one, "The glory of this night shall be forever remembered!"

With a curse Lord Kardowan retorted, "A few more such victories and I will have no army. It is the enemy who must die. This is what comes of disobeying my orders." The officer who boasted shot back hotly that the entire expedition had been Kardowan's idea, and he imprudently suggested that proposals of that kind henceforth be vetted by military council. "Perhaps the lord will make allowances for the wisdom of others in the future." Kardowan, unable to control his anger, spoke three words of arcane power that melted the man into steaming paste.

Lord Albragon, who beheld this atrocity, could stand no more. Pleading indisposition, he retired to his great castle, promising to return when he had recovered adequate strength to wield his magic in the service of his eternal friend and colleague. Kardowan sourly let him go. He said to himself, "That one has not the stomach for ruler-ship. Why should I make him king, even as my puppet? When all is settled I shall change my name to Skyrax."

The war—for such it surely was now, full blown—assumed a new cast. Kardowan's army controlled chunks of the city, the rebels others, with skirmishes sparking daily along the battle lines drawn across roads, through neighborhoods, even through major edifices. Royal forces seized a manor house up at the far end of the Avenue of Azamodeus; the rebels countered by destroying the post at the Upper Terminal, quickly reinforcing that position so as to shut off their enemies from the outside world. An attempt to recover that place failed in ambush. The rebels held on to it. Lord Varador, who lived and recovered sufficiently to resume command (it was he who planned, from his sick bed, the trap of that wonderful night and orchestrated the magic mist), led from an unknown hide-out.

The attempted destruction of the old temple consecrated to Xenophor reverberated throughout Dyrezan. Varador's propaganda screamed of sacrilege: the despoliation of an undefended holy site! Numerous soldiers deserted from Kardowan's ranks; officers likewise, a few, mindful of what had happened to one of their number who crossed words with their enraged lord. Many men he still had, and they dealt death regularly, matching blow for blow. The war settled into a stalemate. Neither side could muster the numbers or the magic or the schemes to decisively tip the scales.

Kardowan, the great mage, had the edge in magic, supported by the craven sorcerers of the court. He employed his powers to spy out the city, to track the movements of the enemy that the friendly forces might block them. Lord Varador and his few magicians lacked the superlative skill of their foe, and yet they seemed able to deduce the actions of their opponents and react accordingly. This troubled Kardowan, to the verge of red-eyed madness, until he forced himself into calm that he might dissect the evidence. The gigantic ambush of that fell night: the enemy had known, in detail, the scope of the operation. So much was apparent. They did not derive the information via magic, which he could block with his spells of protection. Therefore, he astutely reasoned, a spy lurked close to home, a traitor in his camp. Once reckoned, his superior intelligence experienced no difficulty in tracing the source of his problem.

In her chambers in the highest tower of the Royal Palace, with her genuine serving maidens dismissed, Princess Lora said to her secret companion, the ostensible servant Teresia, "It is all up with my game. The ogre Kardowan is on to me. No more will I be allowed out of the palace. For my own protection, he tells Father, but make no mistake, I am his prisoner. My spying days are over."

"What of me?" asked Teresia. "I may be sent on short errands. From those I may, with luck, wander too far. It's a chance. What needs doing?"

Lora chortled with delight. "Precisely what I wished to hear! You are my true friend, and so much fun. The beast intends another stroke at the terminal, a bigger one this time. His hirelings must have their rations and their entertainments, and with all transport from without the city closed down they begin to whine. Imagine that! Such nerve; think how it is for our friends. Anyway, the patriots must be warned. I tried to slip out this last hour, but that was when he slammed the gate on me. Perhaps, if you were very careful, you could attempt it this night?"

129

Thus Princess Lora instigated Teresia's grand adventure. With the report she must deliver memorized, the girl departed from the tower at the lowering of night, conveying a bag of dirty linens that justified her movement through the palace. She darted through an ancient door that communicated with a forgotten tunnel running under the plaza to a small temple on its margin. There she emerged from darkness into peril. Henchmen of Lord Kardowan were all about her. She risked capture at their hands, or death, or worse still if it be Kardowan's retainers who caught her. She proceeded slowly, never showing herself to passersby, however harmless they might seem. She spent most of her time hiding motionless in the shadows.

Her direct route lay straight along the Avenue of Azamodeus, past the district of the nobles, beyond the warehouses of the tradesmen, to the vital post overlooked by the city ramparts. That was a long way, most of it patrolled, much of it a potential battleground. A stroll that far would have taken hours in the best of times. Dawn found her barely halfway, nervous and exhausted, with the faithless sun exposing her to her enemies.

The realization of her current location thrilled her with abject fear. She crouched opposite the hated house of Lord Albragon, her one-time master, that man of filthy mind and questionable inclinations. She did not want to be near his place, nor approach the dreadful castle of Kardowan which loomed close by. Imagination drew for her images of the snares that lay in wait. She slipped into a side street, made her way past several minor intersections, all mercifully vacant, to a point opposite the house of her latest master, the lost Vorselus. The sight angered her. The vandals of Kardowan had burned the upper stories of the house. The stone shell remained, and something of the ground floor, pitifully dilapidated and stained with soot.

There she took refuge for the day, revisiting scenes she scarce recognized. She dozed at intervals. Twice enemy soldiers marched past in the lane, never heeding the abysmal wreck, one like so many others in the city. Toward evening she prepared herself for another go at her destination.

In the dark Teresia got quite close to the friendly fort at the Upper Terminal before trouble snatched at her. The soldiers of Kardowan crowded the vicinity. They were everywhere, in packed ranks, resting easily now, but obviously gathering for action. She feared her efforts were too late, for these troops seemed poised to strike by daybreak. She circled around the camp through a block of musty, empty warehouses, seeking an opening.

Rough hands fastened upon her, yanked her into shadows. A broad hand stifled her squeak of alarm. A husky voice growled the query, "What's this? Does Kardowan employ pretty girls now as spies? I didn't dream they'd choose to serve that ugly fiend."

Bundled into a side room, a cluster of black figures surrounded her. Freeing her lips, Teresia warmly whispered, "I don't work for Kardowan, you dope. I came to warn our men out there of impending attack. I have it on good authority."

"Who's your source?" demanded another voice.

"A loyal servant of Dyrezan in the Royal Palace," she replied, adding significantly, "one very close to the King."

With her eyes adjusting to the gloom Teresia observed the knowing glances and nods. "She means the Princess," said her captor. He released her, turned her to face him, said, "Quickly now, tell all you know." The girl, confident that she was among friends, related the particulars of her message. The man, apparently the leader of the little group, said, "Plenty of men and magic too, this time. This'll be the real thing. I figured something was up, with all that commotion earlier today. Xanto, get word to Lord Varador. Advise him we need a potent brew at the ready this time, otherwise our boys can't hold. Now girl," he continued, "I'm Jaracy, scouting for the army of Dyrezan. Those men in there require warning as well. That was your intention, wasn't it?"

"Sort of," Teresia replied dubiously, "but it looks hopeless."

"It probably is," Jaracy admitted. "However, it must be attempted, and a little girl like you stands a better chance of sneaking in than big fellows like us. You've cloaked yourself darkly; that's good. Are you hungry? Eat something, feed your strength. Then, I want you to try for it."

It was not quite as impossible as it sounded. Camp followers accompanied Kardowan's force, including many drab, lowly specimens associated with the irregular units of armed retainers. Teresia brazenly sauntered into the hornet's nest, doing her best to avoid eye contact lest she invite any sort of unwelcome attention. She eluded the sight of the outer guards, who watched mainly for bodies of hostile troops; she wended her way past clumps of soldiery lolling beneath walls; she approached the improvised ramparts erected by the besiegers to shut in the defenders. That area was crammed with troops.

A harsh, unkind voice called to her, "Hey, girl, get back from there. You want a spear through your head?" Cruel laughter bubbled up from loungers behind her. One oafish shape rose from the darkness of a sheltering wall, hissed gleefully, "Come over here, I say, little one. You'll be good for what ails me. Don't worry, mates, we can take turns with her."

Teresia sprang onto the barricade, dodging under a hefty arm that swung out to take hold of her, leaped down the far side and ran for the friendly lines. Those were not far away, but the enemy were closer. Hostile forms jumped down after her. A spear whistled through the night, its iron point clanging against the pavement at her heels. Torched flared, casting wavering shadows before her; her own, and others close by and closing. She screamed piteously, "Help me, please help me!" The friendly barrier seemed a million leagues distant.

It was not. Arrows zipped past her from the front. Fingers clutched her flying hair, then came a grunt of pain, and the fingers relaxed their grip. Another spear rattled to earth from behind, sliding ahead, then more arrows from the opposite direction, another groan commingled with curses, and she hurled herself over the rough stone wall into the precincts of the Upper Terminal.

Hustled into a lighted room, she gasped out her story between rasping breaths to her rescuers. Several of them were professional, armored warriors, the best men on the rebel team. "You're safe now," someone said gently, "as safe as any of us, I guess." A tough, steel-helmeted soldier, to whom the rest deferred, mused bitterly, "That won't last long, if they're bringing up the magicians against us." Said another, "Whatever comes, Kozmak, we won't give anything away."

Teresia explained further about her encounter with Jaracy's squad, saying hopefully, "He'll get word to Lord Varador. He knows the stakes. They'll look out for us. They have to!"

So they did. With the morning came the big attack, heralded by a cloud of stinging green vapor that blew over the defenders against the wind. While the rebel warriors blinked and gagged the enemy hosts advanced at a run, bellowing hateful cries portending mayhem and slaughter. They came face to face at the wall in a shower of arrows and spears, followed by a crescendo of clashing swords, with the dead dropping in heaps . . . and then weirdly selective sheets of flame dove from the sky into the melee, driving back the attackers from the fray, leaving them exposed in the open space between the lines. Hurled spears and arrows from twanging bows decimated

132

them. They recoiled, the survivors stumbling back over the contorted heaps of their slain, their initial and best chance for immediate victory dashed.

"Xenophor fights on our side!" cried the rebel commander, Kozmak. "Stand firm, boys. We snubbed old Kardowan's nose, but these brutes aren't finished yet, not by a long shot!"

XV. THE COMPANIONS OF VORSELUS

The last image faded from the strange well of the wizard Jacob Bleek, leaving his rapt audience staring into shimmering water. The body of Vorselus stirred irritably; the persona of Professor Vorchek cried out, "What is this? Bleek, you cannot leave it there! I must see what becomes of Theresa."

And Phillipan rose, approached threateningly Bleek's alcove, said, "The city of my birth burns, yet you stop your hateful show at this juncture? Give me more."

Bleek cackled a spiteful laugh. "That I will not, that I must not, for you are not like me, a seer of eternity. For you all, past, present, and future possess tangible meanings, even the good professor, who dreams that he has defeated time. Know, you, that I have carried my charming tale to the events of this very day. You are, as Vorchek would say, updated. Henceforth the story of civil war in Dyrezan unfolds for you according to your iron-bound chronology. If you would know the future, my friends, then you must choose to live it."

"In that case we're done here," snapped Phillipan. "I'm for getting home, and it's a harrowing long walk. The sooner we get started, the better."

"Agreed," said Vorselus. "We should not tarry while patriots die for us. Jacob Bleek, can you advise us as to the course we should take?"

"Of course I can. An infantile question, that. However, I will not. This tedious intervention bores me. Go, all of you, and strive vainly against fate, dreaming your free will, and meet your destinies that were written on the fabric of the universe when it was conceived by the jesting Gods."

"What of you?"

133

"What of me? I will linger here," replied Bleek, "to ponder for another weary infinity the marvels of creation I once imagined fascinating. I shall stay for a day, or a thousand years, or a million, then move on. Our meeting did produce a fleeting instant of interest. That is something."

"As you say," muttered Vorselus. To Phillipan he said, "What can the two of us do, if we make it?"

"Every man counts," came the firm answer. "I've my sword, you your magic. We'll win through, we'll pitch in. And it should be three of us. Fenji, comrade, won't you join us in our quest? Our route isn't likely to lead directly to your village."

Fenji shrugged, said, "All life these days is adventure. Why not more? I would see the city in the sky."

"So be it. Wizard Bleek, thanks for the information."

They set out that very afternoon, to make leagues while the sun still shone. Before they left Vorselus accosted Bleek once more, but it was Vorchek who spoke for him. "Perhaps I was a fool to use your book. I had no idea, obviously, what I was doing. Let me ask you this, and I implore an answer: is there any way out of this fix for me and my people? Can we get home again, to the future where we belong?"

Jacob Bleek stood at the shore of the island in the river, staring at him with gimlet eyes gleaming in his pale, emotionless face. He leaned forward on his staff, said, "I have told you so. Those of you who survive this age, certainly, may return to your own. The proper arts will assure that much. My *Black Book* holds the key, but that is not available to you. Even I do not carry extra copies with me. If you had it, years of study might see you clear. There are alternative mechanisms, however, which, though they may not initiate the process, can reverse it. That alone requires unique magical prowess. Good-hearted Vorselus, sadly, is not so able. The capabilities of Dyrezan, for all her arcane glory, scarce rise to that level. Just one man among the reigning masters of this age possesses the requisite gift. Vorselus, you would free yourself of this unwanted intrusion into your soul. Cooperate, then, with your alter-ego."

"I will, truly," replied Vorselus. "Who is this man we seek?"

Jacob Bleek chuckled. "Look you for the dead man, Vorselus. When you meet with him, against all expectation, then you will know. Good-bye." He turned away, hesitated, hoarsely called over his shoulder, "Enjoy the mysteries of your future. The revelations, the surprises; these are all that make life worth living."

So their grueling march recommenced. For the next two days the trio splashed through marshes, trudged through sand or hopped over boulders, ever to the south down the drear valley, in a direction unfavored by them, yet mandated by the need for ready water. Then, providentially, the shallow stream turned to the west, toward the distant sea. They had reckoned that it must, sooner or later, and this gave them hope of early arrival on the known shore, from which they might journey to friendly territory.

The sere, brutal terrain receded behind, giving way to lands of field and pasture, but here new perils arose, for this land was not shunned by the natives, and though sparsely inhabited, its occupants were the Rhexellites, foes to all who differed from themselves. Those dreadful folk, while far removed from the heart of their ruined kingdom, were nonetheless cognizant of the destruction visited upon their kinsmen by strangers, and they reacted with bitter hostility when approached. Requests for sustenance met with threats, the brandishing of spears, alarming advances. The three were determined, hardened by suffering, ready to swap blow for blow, but they could not stand against whole villages. To be sure they tried, and managed to spill some blood, without worthy gain. Therefore they skulked, sneaking through the day and hiding by night, creeping from lonely camps to steal what was not freely given. Despite danger they hugged the river, which they knew must eventually pour into the sea that separated them from the great western civilization.

On the third day of their westward trek they espied from afar, on the summit of a curiously unnatural rocky mound overlooking the river, the figure of a man squatting on a boulder, peering down at them. The stones were impressively angular, many of them proper cubes, and they thought the mound resembled a fallen edifice rather than any work of nature. Faint traces of a road ran through the debris to the top, close by that motionless, silent human form. Said Phillipan, "I dislike his attention, and am minded to teach him manners. Also, I would study the lay of the land from that rise. Let us, with due caution, introduce ourselves."

"The sun sears your brain," huffed Vorselus. "Seek not trouble. I carry already on my back a full bushel." Phillipan would have it so, however, so they trooped up the mound, prepared to question or fight as circumstances dictated. The stranger rose to meet them, a sword in his hand, metal glinting on his body. When they came together all four uttered cries of astonishment and joy.

"Hail, my good fellows!" roared Lord Morca with unrestrained cheer, as they shook hands and embraced. A furry mass leaped from among the rocks: Treenya, scarred, lean but still ennobled with feline vigor, come to sniff curiously at the three. Morca restrained her with an affectionate word. "Ever she watches out for me, better than do myself, I think. Long have we journeyed through this forsaken land, oft doubting that we would see a friendly face again. Phillipan, Vorselus, and loyal Fenji; there is a motley crew, by the Gods' unfathomable wisdom! You survived the night of terror. That almost surpasses belief. I have wondered whether any of the expedition lived to tell the tale."

Said Phillipan, "Noble one, your glad reappearance reaches my mind as an abrogation of nature's laws. If any man was doomed to die during that tragedy in the darkness, I thought it you. Be you a shorn soul? Surely, you're a dead man walking."

Morca laughed. "My last day lurks in the unreckoned future, concealing its face from me, I trust, for many a long year. Not to argue the point, however. I gave myself over for dead twice that night; no, three times it was that I imagined great Xenophor condescended to receive my soul for such as it could gratify Him. Perhaps it has a bitter taste."

And Vorselus thought to himself, "When I meet the dead man, then I will know. Morca, the finest mage of our times, I counted surely dead, yet he walks. Whether he know it or not, he holds the solution to my dilemma. This is an opportunity of blessed fortune not to be gainsaid. I shall stick with him like a loving brother—nay, like a leech—until our business be done." Once they had settled themselves in the lord's shelter among the tumbled stones, Vorselus asked of him, "How is it that you come to be so providentially alive?"

"Grant me reams of parchment," replied Morca, "that I may set out the tale in many scrolls. I exhausted my supply of magical materials getting down that mountain of misery, saw my companions fall one by one, until I stood near solitary, only Treenya remaining, spitting filth from sodden mouth, those hellish monstrosities groping for my throat. So long had lasted our running combat, however, that dawn intervened then, to chase the creatures of darkness back into their hellish underground burrows. May they ever haunt by night the condemned towers of Tsathgon.

"Yet only then did my adventures begin. What remained, if anything, of the army had fled away ahead of me, and the foul country folk were up in arms, hunting lone survivors. My retreat blocked, I turned south, probably for the same reasons you did, found the water course, held to that from necessity. This you understand. I attempted sooner to strike west, got myself mixed up with hauntings in a region of latent magic, where warriors of forgotten ages danced at midnight and wished to entertain me with heroic personal combats to the point of death. Mayhap they nominated me as a suitable recruit. O, we had a grand time, they and I, indulging ourselves in the joyful arts of swordsmanship. Not much had they forgotten, despite their lengthy sojourn in the grave. Duty called, though, so at last I avoided their murderous beckonings, escaped to a lonely village peopled by what I believed fair folk, lost on an otherwise deserted plain, where I sought succor.

"Yet they too sought to satisfy my craving for adventure, for the populace of that fairy town proved again no more nor less than ghosts, who coveted me as a permanent resident. I won my way clear, with Treenya's aid I confess, as fortuitously those greedy spirits clothed themselves in fleshy envelopes which claws and fangs may rip. Have you ever heard the like, my friends? Mark well, 'tis a tale the minstrels shall one day sing!

"From there we made our way back to the valley, from which we pursued a course, I deduce, similar to your own. You must have been two full days behind me. I have holed up here that long, prizing secrets from this ancient pile where, according to obscure scrawls of eon-shadowed script, certain of our ancestors once communed with powers called out of spheres presently unknown to us. I would learn much here, given time."

"That we have not," exclaimed Vorselus. "Fascinating is your account, my lord, like none other I expect to hear in this life, and an honor it would be to study with you, but harken to our tale, so that you may understand why we demand haste." Vorselus told Morca their, if possible, even more curious account of unusual happenings, his relation supported by eager interpolations from Phillipan and Fenji.

At the last Lord Morca said, "These are dazzling wonders which you vouchsafe. Vorselus, you have proven yourself many times over a true son of Dyrezan. When we are free to consider our own fates I will help you, as I am able, to rid yourself of this mysterious linkage to this other personality, this Vorchek. Phillipan, also—my friend— requires such aid. All incoming tidings fill me with amazement. Indeed, the world grows stranger with each breath I take. Ten years off my life I would give to converse for an hour with this Jacob Bleek. A wizard greater than the best of Dyrezan, so he vaunts, and the indirect cause of your troubles to boot! My renowned library contains no tale like it."

Fenji said, "I learn these moons to believe everything. When I doubt, I'm wrong."

Morca grew pensive. "Let us put aside mighty amusements, however they draw us to them. I accept as fact your arcane sources of knowledge, which bluntly state that fair Dyrezan writhes in the grasp of a blood-hungry man. Never cared I for Kardowan, nor regarded Albragon as ought but doubtful. These news, strange though be the source, confirm my worst fears. Gentlemen, we must save Dyrezan, and therefore we must return there alive, and with all speed."

Vorselus and Phillipan seconded the motion, but the former could not help but vigorously express his concerns. While the group sat among the stones, sharing their scant supplies, he observed, "We are lost in the middle of nowhere, in dreadful country, with enormous barriers of terrain and distance separating us from our goal. Also, we are friendless, perhaps the only left living of the expedition. What, realistically, can we do?"

Morca replied, "We can shun weakness, laugh at peril, seize every opportunity. The river flows west, and westward we journey to the sea. That is a big target, to be sure; the arrow of our march shall not miss it. Let us strive to make the most of our resources, those we bear—pitiful enough—and those we chance upon. Trust in the Gods, Vorselus." He rose abruptly, slapping his sheathed sword. "Come, we go swiftly."

So they adventured together, the four of them and fierce Treenya, trekking by the river which gave them life, along the way encountering fell beasts and hostile villages of Rhexellites, troublesome obstacles certainly, only they had Lord Morca with them, a man born and bred to face dangers. They eluded or defeated these simple hazards, reached on the third day of their united trek the shores of the great sea. "We make great strides," averred Morca. "At this rate we will be home ere long."

"At this rate," Vorselus panted, "I will be worn down to dusty bones in no time." The hard marches, it chagrined him to admit, plainly told on him more than his companions.

Where they touched the sea was a flat land barren save by the river, in the vicinity of a squalid village. "Peokis," Morca decided; Vorselus not so readily convinced, yet Fenji, after careful observation, shortly agreed with the lord, who added, "See, this is not that ugly, deathful architecture of the Rhexellites. Primitive these be, but they are healthy human folk, and like to be friendly." Through Fenji's good offices acquaintance was soon made, and the Peokis of Tarabu proved not just friendly, but quite their comrades. These fishers knew all about the mighty expedition from across the waters, in which their own people had taken part to destroy the oppressors. Some men from this village had joined that campaign. A few had come back.

"Some survivors," told Fenji, "not many. The big chief—wise Nantrech—reached Rongia, way to our north, filled twenty boats of your men. Those our fishing boats, so two hundred."

"That's more than I dared dream," exclaimed Phillipan. "Our stand for them on the dark mountain of death served its purpose, however doleful the result. We'll join them in a rush and march home as an army."

"Not so easy," Fenji cautioned. "The great master from the west waited days for stragglers, then sailed in his big ships. He is gone."

"Counted me down," muttered Morca. He shrugged. "I should not blame him. Truly we have wandered a sad long time. It follows that we must cross the sea by our own contrivance."

"Which we cannot do," Vorselus stated bluntly, throwing up his hands. "The sea is wide, and the Peoki boats are not fit to sail the open waters. That is scant chance."

"And the only one we have got," said Lord Morca, "so that is the way we will do it. Fenji, we must purchase, borrow, or steal a boat. Buying is out of season with us, so that limits our options to the two. Do what you can."

As it transpired, the Peokis were eager to prove their generosity by offering a boat for loan, although not a man of them would consider undertaking the cruise, as they were all superstitious of the watery deeps out of land's sight. Also, as Morca observed with haughty disdain, they exhibited a deep-seated reluctance for the company of his alarming pet cat, who he would keep by him come what may. Fenji, as good a sailor as any of them, agreed to helm the voyage, though his heart sorely troubled him. Fatalistically he said, "I live, or die with brave companions. It's a happy way, either way."

No time they wasted. That evening they fed and labored to make ready the boat, a small, double-hulled affair with a single sail. They loaded it with food and skins of sweet water from the river, plus useful gear selected by their accompanying fisherman and warrior. They were off with the tide before dawn, four men and a tiger, venturing in that little craft into the uncharted regions of great water.

At Morca's bidding Fenji steered them west by north, the intent being to touch land as near to the old far side camp as possible. Often Vorselus thought they should not get so far. The boat rocked at the slightest swell, quite unlike the behavior of a big ship (which he recalled with distaste as sufficiently unpleasant), and its crew were ever exposed to the harshness of the elements. Treenya wholly disapproved of her circumstances, bruiting her ire for all to hear when dampness dared touch her paws, otherwise lounging fretfully in the bottom of the boat or indifferently nibbling on fish heads.

Twice the winds blew strong, and once the storm clouds gathered and burst overhead, deluging them with rain which must be madly bailed. Yet the winds, be they gentle or cruel, blew steadily in their favor, so day by day they made quick passage. Early on the morning of the fourth day—much earlier than Vorselus had hoped—they spied a dark line of land ahead.

They touched upon a forested shore, an anonymous landscape which suggested nothing of their location, save that they had conquered the salt sea and attained the vaguely defined edge of Dyrezan's sovereignty. This feat they cheered, offering rousing thanks to those Gods who especially favor the reckless. Treenya scampered like a kitten, celebrating with a lizard which she captured immediately after setting paws to earth. Morca felt that they had made fall somewhat to the south of their planned course, therefore commanded Fenji to take them north along the coast. The Peoki, amazed, despite all he had been taught by tribal tradition, that the great sea actually possessed limits, complied, and within hours steered them into a little shore-side village inhabited by folk Vorselus was enraptured to call his own.

These humble people of Laraco informed them that they had sailed pretty well, for the army camp lay merely a day's travel on foot to the north, according to them still manned by troops. A forest road, one on which a wagon could pass, connected to that point. This information gratified, for the hazards of sailing wearied the little band. Lord Morca, back in his own domain, wielded his vast authority to commandeer everything his party desired, swapping their boat as payment, and with scarcely a pause they loaded a rickety conveyance drawn by a single horse—the only one of quality to be had in Laraco—and all piling in set out on the trail, with Morca at the reins. They stopped for nothing, taking their meals on the road, jolting along the ruts between the pressing dark trees through the afternoon, into the evening. Full night had fallen when the forest fell away, revealing the broad, sweeping beach where stood the tents and makeshift huts of the old expeditionary camp. Campfires gleamed among the sprawl of low structures. As they trundled into the perimeter a lone sentinel hailed them with a challenge replete with crude oaths.

"Salute when you speak to me," snapped the driver of the wagon. "This is Lord Morca—aye, returned from the dead I am—and you can stop gaping at me, knave, as if I were a wraith who has skipped his tomb, and announce me to Lord Nantrech, if he be still here." With the demanding it was done, for in another minute the long sojourning party were ushered into the spacious hut that served as headquarters for what remained of the army.

Nantrech embraced his colleague with stark wonder and unbounded delight. "This be the age of miracles!" he exclaimed. "Yours is a face I never expected to see again, except in morbid and reproachful dreams. Phillipan, too, and Vorselus, and this one, Fenji of the fishers, our noble allies. Even your wild mistress Treenya returns, to once more terrorize my men. How can such things be? Tell all, my friends, but first refreshment. You," he cried to none and all, "bring food and wine, on the double, and tell Lord Harmon I send for him." Three soldiers scurried to obey. Nantrech added, "Aye, Harmon came through with me, as did so few of our men of mind. Brawn ruled that deadly night on the slopes of Tsathgon. He and I, mates of old however disputory, clung together like crabs, saving ourselves by dazzling monsters with magic tricks."

Nantrech had his stories to relate—of the bitter return from the bloody mountain to Rongia, the collection of stragglers, the final decision to re-cross the sea—but it was Morca's tale, supported by the accounts of his fellow adventurers, which took center stage. Nantrech marveled that any of them had survived their perilous trek through hostile territory, was flabbergasted by their mystic insights into the terrible doings back home, still so far to the west.

Said he, "These days I have tarried, unsure how or whether to move. I sent forth couriers, of course, bearing tidings of our travails, half expecting reinforcements that we might make another stab at laying under us the wreckage of the Rhexellite kingdom. None came, nor any direct word in response to my missives, save for confused accounts emanating from the court, advising me of public disturbances, counseling me to lie low with my men until detailed orders followed. Never did they. Your report is the sole intelligible account I have received as to conditions in the city, yet even now I scarce can accept that catalogue of horrors, and the means of gaining such wisdom continues to confound me.

Said Lord Harmon, who had joined them in amazement at the identity of these late visitors, "This unspeakable Kardowan wages war on our citizens! That must stop. Our expedition fought for glory, which we won at fearful cost; now it may do battle for justice. Let us march with the morn. We are few, though, good Morca, two hundred fighting men at most, plentifully armed, yet otherwise ill-equipped. It will make a slow moving army, and I fear that time presses."

"Have we horses?" asked Morca.

"Nary a one," replied Nantrech. "They panicked at sight of those ghoulish things on that hellish mountain, most bolting or dying amidst the pale tide of night monsters. During the retreat we had cause to slay the rest, that we might eat."

"We must round up more," insisted Morca. "Time is precious—already we come tragically late—and men on foot will never serve. Let us scour the villages within reach, mount every man we can, hurl them forward to Dyrezan."

"It will be done," said Nantrech. He slammed fist to table, decreed, "The men advance at sunrise. As we march, we shall collect horseflesh, equip them, push forward the mounted troops at the gallop. Morca, you take the lead. A foaming steed may reach the Mountains of the Gods half dead in a week; nay, in five days."

That was how they did it. Orders flew fast and furious all that night. The warriors of the shattered expedition forwent sleep that they might make ready. They grumbled and cursed their officers as soldiers will, but they labored diligently and with alacrity to break camp and prepare for the road. The first elements moved out before the sun gleamed.

Asked Vorselus, whose lack of sleep and rest made him querulous, "What can two hundred men accomplish, even should they arrive before the conflict be over? If we clear the way on the road we must break through the mountain pass, and if we succeed there, we have yet to win our way into the city, drifting among the clouds. There hateful enemies in number await us."

Phillipan replied, "Questioning isn't doing. If we don't try, we surely fail. Brave all, make our chances and take our chances; that's the only way. We have many friends in the city, if they haven't all been killed."

"May the Gods forbid that," murmured Vorselus. As he wearily trudged he whispered a fervent prayer to mighty Xenophor. Phillipan heard this, joined in the prayer. They begged that the God, whose limitless knowledge made the secrets of Jacob Bleek seem sheer ignorance, guide them safely and quickly to their destination, that they could there risk death against any odds which might please Him.

So few villages on the road, fewer hidden off the paths that disappeared into the great forest, but all within reach received stern visitations, and at request, by blandishments or threats, they gave up their horses, fleet steeds or knobby-kneed farm haulers, and Morca placed his colleagues upon them, then his officers, eventually a few troops. Nantrech and his surviving magicians rode with him, and Vorselus, Phillipan, and Fenji, the best company commanders and hand-picked warriors, those most keen for the laying about with steel blades. Treenya loped with them, complaining bitterly at whiles, yet despite her natural willfulness managing to keep up. Two full days and more it took to mount fifty men, and once they achieved that the cavalry spurred on, Nantrech detailing his remaining subordinates to carry forward the foot army, recruiting as they went. The fifty galloped away, thundering down the highway to the west.

Though life continued hard, Vorselus' spirits were lifted by the companionship of so many goodly men, not a foe among them now, nor hand in the grip raised against him. They rode in common cause, for the defense of their fair city and its people, and in the doing they made possible—maybe—the restoration of his own fortunes and well-being. Never could he have contemplated undertaking that effort alone.

The incident in Claxis amused and gratified Vorselus, who remembered well being hunted by those villagers during his solitary outward trek. Morca's advance guard there confronted a military patrol sent out from the distant valley of the city. Mounted men they were, who demanded the business of those shabby, care-worn riders from the east. The local folk gathered about the central lane where occurred the confrontation.

Said the gruff, blatantly unfriendly patrol leader, "I'm Pranfar, tasked in the King's name to hold this post, preventing egress from the east against all comers. Turn back or surrender as suits you, but you don't pass this place."

A village elder pointed and croaked, "That's Vorselus, a dangerous renegade with a price on his head. He slunk in here during his flight from the King's justice, ravaged our beautiful town. Arrest him and turn him over to us."

Lord Morca impatiently snorted at this, identified himself and advised, "Cleave that foolish talk to your tongue. Soldiers of Dyrezan, you recognize me. I come with my companions from the army of the east to rid our land of its oppressor. Join us or stand aside, but I order you not to oppose us."

Pranfar laughed and snarled, "We be men of Lord Kardowan, and we kill his enemies for our pleasure. Unhand your swords and submit to our will."

Phillipan cried, "Do we treat with the monster's hirelings?" And Lord Morca returned, "Assuredly not. Nor do I waste on them my conjuring. Men, at them!" And Vorselus laughed in wild abandon, declaring with glee, "Let it begin here!" With that he and his companions spurred to the fray, dashing in amongst their opponents.

The folk of Claxis scattered like frightened rabbits. Pranfar's patrolmen lasted a little longer; keen for action were they, but unused to determined opposition. Morca crashed into them like a steel tidal wave, mowing down every man in his path. His fellows charged after with relish, even Vorselus, whose blood was up and warm for battle against the foes who had dogged him so long. The combat was short. The enemy died, a few fleeing, more surrendering, cravenly begging for mercy. One especial fool briefly sought to contest his sword against the claws of Treenya. As it came out, the black tiger could have instructed the man in the essential elements of strategy, only he did not survive the lesson.

"That is how we do it," cried Morca with lusty satisfaction, as the she-cat daintily washed her moistened paws. "I would almost rather lop off these heads than chase down a stinking Rhexellite. Attend to our wounded. Sack this miserable town. Take what we need, send back their horses to our foot troops, and let us get going."

Claxis paid in over-measure for its contrariness, Morca having heard the full story of Vorselus' sorrows there. Then the avengers were off, driving toward the west day and night, delaying seldom for sleep, through the forest along the great road, in due time across the wide prairie. The majestic mountains that ringed the Valley of the Gods loomed ahead, grew to scrape the sky. The road inclined, mounted the steep slopes, wound toward the high crests. They rested their horses in the foothills, then clattered on, making for the next obstacle, the narrow pass under the tallest peaks. They reached this point before noon of that day.

144

Before them stood a barrier of mailed men, swords and shields at the ready. "These be true warriors," Morca observed, "of the Imperial army. They will not give way so easily in a fight. They hold over us numbers and position. Such men, however, have always been selected as born patriots. Let me speak ere we lay into them." So Lord Morca rode forth between the lines, doffing his helmet so that all could mark his face, and he gustily bellowed, "Soldiers of Dyrezan, I be Morca the bold returned to you from far places, here to rescue our sacred home. Do not shed blood for the glory of the tyrant who welters in the lives of our people. Join us, that we may more quickly destroy him."

And those men ranked across the road, with their officers, burst into spontaneous cheers, downed their weapons and surged forward thundering, "Morca, Lord Morca returns to lead us! They said he was dead, but they lied! We'll make them eat their lies!" So they became one force, a mailed fist riding and tramping through the pass, to behold at whiles the lovely circular valley below, and the beckoning jot of shadow among the clouds that was truly glorious Dyrezan.

"Never thought I to be granted this vision again," sighed Vorselus. "Home, and the possibility of a future once more; can these things be mine?"

"We're not in yet," warned Phillipan. "Our worst enemies wait on us, a league and more above the valley floor. It will be a wonder to me if we make it that far."

XVI. THE RETURN TO THE CITY

Eventually the little army spurred down the far side of the mountains, entering the valley unaccosted. More freshly mounted riders caught up with them, swelling their ranks. A handful of soldiers stationed about or passing through the fertile farmlands joined them, while a few others, liege-men of Kardowan or his associates, fled. Lord Morca halted the advance briefly, that he might send out messengers to the towns, proclaiming his cause, inviting the peasants to rise in his favor. That many of them did. Quite a number were old soldiers who had campaigned with him in years bygone. They accepted his version of events without question.

Among these volunteers who flocked to Morca's standard was Sragan, the hospitable farmer who had succored Vorselus in an hour of need. The wizard accosted him gravely, said, "I promised rewards for your kindness, good man, yet still I have nothing to call my own. Accept, for now, my good wishes and comradeship, and my fond esteem, that you willingly venture with us upon our noble enterprise."

Replied Sragan with boyish good cheer, "I wouldn't miss this for the world. I march with Lord Morca! My old days of glory live again."

No one they met could tell aught of developments in the city, save that war raged there, with remarkably differing reports issuing oft times by murky rumor. It could only be hoped that hope still remained.

At last came the day of very serious business. Morca and his men hugged the earth on the small knoll overlooking the Lower Terminal, magical gateway to otherwise unapproachable Dyrezan. They conversed while they watched a lone messenger advancing unarmed to the manned stockade. "Morca said, "If, after all this time, our friends still hold the upper, then all we must do to guarantee egress is to seize this post. What kind of men are these? Should they change sides so readily as these others, then we have it in a flash." The distant man stopped before the gate, motioned with his arms. There was commotion along the ramparts. Bows were raised. Arrows rained. The man dropped.

Phillipan growled, "Now we know whose side they're on."

Morca cursed savagely. "The craven curs!" he cried. "We will show them no mercy."

Observed Phillipan, "There isn't much of that going around these days. I'll slay them with joy, once I get at them, but how? The fort appears well staffed. While we bang our heads at the gate they'll feather us with arrows and impale us with spears. We can't squander here the men we'll need in the city."

Lord Nantrech, coming up from the foot troops below the mound, on overhearing this agreed, saying, "How be it, Morca? There is a time to rely on cleverness."

"This be that time," Morca replied. He studied long the terrain about the fort, said at last, "Come all with me, back to our camp, that I may explain to you my plan."

Plan they did, and prepare. Commands were given and received, bodies of men formed up. At this time Lord Morca must put Treenya by, as feline wiles offered no advantage in positional warfare, and despite her insistent squalling he would not risk a single black hair of her great head without logical necessity. She obeyed, with tail-swishing lack of enthusiasm.

Late that afternoon commenced the assault on the fort. It began with an advance along the road of the peasant volunteers, who proceeded in loose order with much shouting and brandishing of old military weapons and farm implements. The magician Theodises accompanied them, laying an oily brown fog before the gate that spoiled the defenders' aim. Axes bit into the gate. In an instant more men packed the wall, and the peasants started to fall. They recoiled in confusion, to rally out of range and come on again.

Meanwhile, as the gloom of dusk obscured vision, a new attack began around the corner of the adjoining wall. More peasants, stiffened by the professional troops gathered on the march, advanced noisily at the charge, those in the forefront bearing hastily fabricated scaling ladders. The ladders were raised against the lightly defended wall, but by the time the first men clambered up the defenders were ready. Here Lords Nantrech and Harmon threw fireballs at the foe above to bedazzle them and burn. Kardowan's men were shaken, but they held firm, stabbing down with spears at the climbers, dropping weights of lead on them, and toppling their ladders with forked poles. Casualties increased. Before long the attack degenerated into chaos.

Out of the falling night, from a distance, a horn blew, three blasts that galvanized the two parties of attackers to renewed effort. This it was they had waited for. The signal; Lord Morca's men were inside the walls!

Under cover of terrain Morca had led the main party, his small but fierce eastern legion and the remaining magicians, around to the back of the fort, there to wait in secret and in silence while the initial assaults drew the attention and efforts of the defenders. Gradually the ranks along the back wall thinned, until reduced to a few solitary sentinels. Vorselus employed a subtle yet cunning trick to reach out to those men from the dark, beaming his will and that of his fellows across the nighted open space to mesmerize those unwary commoners atop the wall. Quietly, without show or fanfare, they strained their minds against those others, whispering into their brains, suggesting that they fail in their appointed task. The sentinels faltered, stooped, rubbed their eyes . . . dropped their weapons. Morca gave the order in conversational tone. His men dashed forward, battle cries forbidden, reached the wall, threw up ladders in plenty. Scarcely were those instruments laid in place than his warriors charged up them almost at a run, heedless of safety, scrambling over the wall and stabbing the somnolent sentinels, and when Morca had joined them he blew his horn three times.

After that the battle became a massacre. Morca's team raced along the walls or dived into the courtyard, their only orders to kill all before them. The defenders panicked, surging this way or that, breaking into disorganized knots of useless resistance. The peasants, facing less opposition, broke down the gate, and the assailants on that side of the fort stormed inside, screaming and slaying. Afterward Vorselus thought he remembered piteous pleas for quarter, but he paid no attention then, nor did he recall any of his comrades doing so. Hard times and cruel experience demanded their fee; war against the vile Rhexellites, long suffering in wild lands, and hatred of the evil usurper conditioned good and reasonable men against conventional notions of mercy. The upshot was that within minutes the defenders had been annihilated.

Lord Morca found occasion to lovingly chide Treenya, of all his host, for her disobedience. Scarcely had the rear wall been breached than she contrived to climb a rickety ladder in pursuit of her master, and once inside threw herself with ferocious gusto into the fray. A clipped ear and a gashed flank she suffered, but those who inflicted these slight wounds succumbed in shrieking terror to her slashing claws and remorseless fangs.

Morca dictated that his dead be reverently buried, the others cast out for the buzzards. Lord Nantrech cried, "A noble achievement, my friend, yet we dare not hold back now. The Lower Terminal is ours, which opens one gate, but who holds the next?"

Groused Lord Harmon, "If it be guarded by hostile swords, we may as well be camping in ruined Tsathgon as on the doorstep of home."

With a trace of the glum in his voice Morca replied, "That has nagged me exceedingly. I chose to spare it no consideration until we won this far, yet here it is, still a sore point, and the gravest weakness in our scheme. By report, now weeks old, our friends hold the Upper Terminal. Who can prove that accurate this night? Without my full complement of magical materials I am at a loss to scan the skies for information."

"All we wizards share seats in that donkey cart," sighed Nantrech. "There is but one way. A hero voluntary must ascend to Dyrezan. He will tell us the good news, or by his permanent silence confirm our worst fears."

"I go," declared Morca.

"That you do not," cried Vorselus. Quick he was to remember at all times that Lord Morca embodied the sole solution to the more arcane complications of his life, and he thrilled with fear whenever Morca risked his life, which the man preferred to do on a regular basis. This, however, was too much. "We must not throw away our trump on a reckless gamble," Vorselus explained, in terms he believed his comrades would appreciate.

They did, clamoring for their commander's safety. Said Phillipan, "I'll go. My life is trivial in the scheme of these times."

"Nothing of the sort," Vorselus persisted. "Mighty warriors we must husband for the gigantic battles ahead." He considered Phillipan, or that portion of him known as Philip, to be his responsibility until all big matters be concluded. Vorselus went on, "I you can risk. Your sword arms are worth their measures in gold; mine, merely serviceable. Until I regain my materials, I am little more than an eager soldier, and those you have to replace me, if the worst comes. I shall rise to the Upper Terminal on the instant, nor do I brook opposition in this."

Morca nodded curtly, almost smiled for a moment, said, "I can operate the controls, I think. The mechanism is simple, I know the method, and my fellow mages can aid me. Leave your sword, Vorselus. If friends await you, I would not have them misunderstand your appearance. If enemies, then may hap an unarmed man can plead for his life. Come, let us do the deed. Further delay galls me."

As it happened, the functionaries of the magic terminal were on duty, still alive, cowering within the large bronze dome behind their machinery. Out of fear or loyalty they accepted Morca's dictates without complaint or cavil. Vorselus delivered his sword unto Phillipan—"Hold it until you may hand it back to me"—and took his place on the vast bronze floor inside the railing. Morca, after a consultation with his colleagues, took station at the controls, as did they. Under their watchful guidance the servitors of the machines activated the terminal, propelling Vorselus into the realm of nothingness through which men and goods were transported to the Sky City.

Vorselus re-emerged into the world, stepped out of the railing into the rough waiting arms of many menacing soldiers. "Justify or accuse yourself," they cried, these dirty men who resembled the worst of cutthroats. A blade, indeed, pressed his throat. Gasped he, "The wizard Vorselus, returned to Dyrezan, meaning no harm to the patriots who love Skyrax." The man who wielded the sword barked with a snigger, "Words thrown about easy these days. For whom do you stand?" Vorselus could not avoid the admission, mean it life or death: "I serve the just cause, as an enemy of the traitor Kardowan, companion to Lords Morca and Nantrech, who await my report below."

It was enough. The blade drew back. A female voice wildly screamed, "Professor!" A girl pushed through the ring of big men. It was Teresia, who threw herself into the arms of Vorselus. "You came back, Professor."

"Do not call me that," Vorselus chided into her ear. "They will not understand."

"Sorry. I've had plenty of time to think while I've been stuck here. I figured it all out. I know who you are, and how you got me into this mess." Apparently he and his other half had been prone to underestimating this girl, or both of them. She asked, "What about the other one? Did you ever dig him up?"

"He's been with me for some time, is down below now. Keep that as well to yourself, please. I am Vorselus, and only he. You are Teresia, my slave girl, nothing more."

"So you say," muttered the girl. "I've my own ideas."

"What's going on?" demanded a grizzled officer whom Vorselus recognized, despite the wear of time, as the commander Kozmak. "State your business, fellow."

"I come as Lord Morca's emissary. He lives, and Nantrech too, leading an army to reinforce the rebellion against the criminal Kardowan. Your friends stand ready below. I have but to give the word, and they come."

"Give it."

So all of the army currently available rose up to Dyrezan in four great batches, cramming the terminal chamber. All came, including the faithful peasants, most of whom never dreamed of setting foot in the land above the clouds, a place to them concretely real yet verging on the mythical. Morca assumed command on the spot and convened an immediate council of war. During this meeting Kozmak took center stage, explaining what had transpired in recent weeks.

"They hit us with everything they had," he related, "and if it weren't for this little girl, they'd have squashed us flat. Thanks to her we were ready for them. We clobbered them so thoroughly they haven't dared risk another all-out assault. We've tangled with them often since, but we've managed to hold our own. However, I've lost over two-thirds of my men in doing it. I've wondered a time or two whether this post was worth it."

"Your stand," Morca replied, clasping the man's shoulder, "made possible our quick return to the city, which amply justifies your labors, and the sacrifices of your fallen heroes. In better days to come our people will acknowledge your valor. What goes in Dyrezan?"

Here the news was grim. "A vicious stand-off," Kozmak said. "We have the numbers, they the best magic. Lord Varador, restored to health, wages unequal battle against the likes of Kardowan and Albragon. The latter has not been heard of in a while, but he is not our friend, and those of such magnitude we need,. Every attack of ours undertaken against the heart of Dyrezan has failed disastrously. It'll take fresh blood to break the deadlock."

Morca slapped his chest, replied, "I have that in plenty. Get me and mine to our hidden materials of arcane power, and you watch how Kardowan and his mangy hosts shrivel." His audience roared their approval, interspersing gallant cheers with profane oaths almost comical.

From the fortified perimeter Vorselus and Teresia gazed out over the distant towers of central Dyrezan. He was saying, "To be home is to live again. Here all things are possible."

"What of us?" asked Teresia.

Vorselus grimaced. "That depends on the 'us' you mean. First we must gain victory. After that, whatever can be sorted out, will. I know not what comes. The Gods do, and Jacob Bleek, I suppose."

"That awful name!" cried Teresia with a shudder. "It was that pesky *Black Book* of his—of yours—that screwed us up royally. Part of me says, 'Yay for Dyrezan, and may Vorselus be a sweet master—'"

"Really, girl."

"—While the other part says, 'Vorchek, you dope, get me out of this crap.'"

Vorselus laughed, not without nervousness. "Enough! You weary me. My brains are as scrambled as yours. To a lesser degree so are Phillipan's. Ah, yes, I have still to introduce you."

That he did, and Phillipan marveled at the beautiful girl of whom he had heard so much, and seen so much in the mystic well of the sorcerer Bleek. He felt, so he admitted, a gentle something in his

151

mind, a throbbing cadence of elusive memory when he spoke with her. Teresia's subsequent comments on him were straightforward: "About what I expected. The typical sort; nothing special." Far more to her taste was Treenya of the black fur and white stripes, with whom the girl, after reasonable hesitation, made a fast friend.

Come the sun Lord Morca announced, "We go forth. Lords Nantrech and Harmon hold our position. I lead the main body in an endeavor to break the ring of siege and re-establish contact with Lord Varador. Form the ranks."

He said to Vorselus and Phillipan, in the quiet moments before battle, "We have had Goddess Luck on our side too long. Kardowan did not hurl murderous magic at us from aloft while we approached, because he, most likely, truly thought us dead by now, and he was not on the watch for us. Kozmak and his few lads held the terminal against all comers, to our great advantage, when a man scarcely less brave would have abandoned the apparently useless post. Now we are here. Count no more on luck. Henceforth we wage war in earnest, minding each risk, hazarding not a single stumble. Soon the veil shall lift from Kardowan's penetrating gaze."

They stormed the enemy line, overran the barricades, swung right and left to butcher all who stood. At first Kardowan's men held on, thinking the attack a raid by inferior numbers, but when the masses of peasants surged through the gap they realized the tide had turned and fled for points unknown. Within the hour Morca had contacted elements of Varador's forces, who formed a guard for him and the other leaders and conveyed them to their headquarters deep in the lowliest district of Dyrezan. As they marched through the lanes of the city the newcomers beheld evidences of brutal combat and wanton devastation. Vast swathes of the city lay wrecked, burned, callously pillaged.

Said Harmon when he had joined them, with sadness and fury commingled as he surveyed the ruins along the Street of the Veiled Eye, "Words desert me. We did not treat Tsathgon so."

Lord Varador greeted them in his fortified chambers with joy and awe. "So it be true, as I am told, that the honored dead rise up to do battle for us."

"Not dead," replied Nantrech, "merely absent, for far too long, while our city has agonized."

"I submit my army to you," said Varador.

"And Lord Morca commands our joint hosts henceforth." To that worthy Nantrech added, "We are all in your hands, your loyal

152

soldiers, to the death."

"Then we commence our final campaign from this moment," Morca declared. "First, let us turn our homecoming to advantage. Varador, proclaim us in the streets, from the tower tops, announce our coming via the magical means you have available. Let it be known that we and the army have arrived. Avoid specifics when describing our strength. We will compensate for the gaps in our ranks with impassioned fury."

Said he to Nantrech, "We must retrieve our arcane materials. We do not dare confront Kardowan's ire without full weaponry. My house, I know, being so near the palace, is denied us for the time being, yet others may lie within our zone. Varador, bring me maps, that I may learn what we hold."

Presently this was done, and in conference the great lords and mages reached understanding of conditions beneficial and baleful. Morca snorted in disgust. "So many of our fine dwellings and repositories behind enemy lines! Even if our materials be safe, which is likely—surely all practiced adequate safeguards?—they are far away, requiring major battles to gain. That will not do. Kardowan will readily take steps to block us. See here, Vorselus: this enclave of ours extends into your street. If I get you to your home, have you anything we may utilize for military purposes?"

"I possess a selection of powerful items," came the prompt reply. "In my hands they may serve well; in yours, I cannot overestimate the possibilities."

"Very good. My companions, let us sleep like the dead this night. Tomorrow we act."

Meanwhile word spread of the Lords Nantrech and Morca in the city. The news traveled by word of mouth. It hung draped from banners stretched across the avenues. Lord Harmon employed a weird trick he knew to great effect. He sent men into a portion of park land under patriotic control to collect birds. It proved a more difficult task than expected, for as they explained, that territory had been cruelly abused by Kardowan's toughs, but they returned with a nice flock of ravens, large, wicked-eyed black birds, and these Harmon instructed with his spells, and he sent them forth into the sky, and they shot like benighted missiles across the city, alighting here and yon to speak to all within earshot. And the ravens cawed and shrieked the tidings, repeating what the magician had whispered to them in magical tongue: "Deliverance is at hand! Rise up against the evil of Kardowan. Break his chains! May the Gods protect our

153

King!"

Vorselus accompanied thirty men, led by Phillipan with Fenji by his side, to slip between the enemy posts and reach his house where, it was hoped, his items of magical powers lay still hidden. It was not far. They made it without being discovered, and at long last Vorselus beheld his domicile. The sight sickened him. The tale of Teresia, added to the knowledge gleaned from the visions of Jacob Bleek, had hardly prepared him for the destruction visited upon the place. Indeed, he guessed more had occurred since she last fled from it. Spiteful or callous hands had applied fire to all the west wing and most of the upper story. Shattered windows and staved in doors completed the sorry picture.

His magic, however, resided safe where he left it in the secret, enchantment-guarded chamber; the secret, he remembered with upwelling emotional pain, that faithful Ling-das had died to keep. Vorselus cleaned it out and back they went, with assigned men bearing loads. This time they had to fight, for a patrol discovered them, blocking them while enemy reinforcements charged in. After that it was a running battle until they reached safe haven. The rear squad fought to the last man that their fellows could live to convey their precious burdens to those who would avenge them.

"There is much meat here," Morca announced after examining the haul. "Vorselus, you collect well. I shall study these scrolls, decide on the proper course without delay. These make a fair start. With your materials—" He broke off, distracted by a racket in the street outside. "What means this?"

"I would know that as well," Vorselus muttered. He opened the outer door, which gave onto a group of soldiers gripping a corpulent prisoner in rough fashion. Vorselus came face to face with the man. Both their jaws dropped at the same instant.

"You!" cried Vorselus, his hand clutching his sword. Responded the other with cheerful, if tremulous voice, "Vorselus? Joyous I am to find you hale." The counter-response: "You will die ten times over, traitor, before I finish with you."

Other worthies hove close, amidst exclamations of surprise. The prisoner they hauled into the building, where he nervously faced them all. Intoned Nantrech coolly, "Lord Albragon, it has been too long since we met. Much I have heard of your bold exploits."

Varador bellowed, "Kardowan's pet toad, taken alive! This is a treat I craved. I am of two minds, whether to eradicate this poisoned blemish of a man now, or to reserve his execution for public display

154

after our victory. Nailing him to Xenophor's Column suits me."

"This is an ill day," said Morca, "for you, Albragon. I say hand him to the troops. I do not dirty my own hands with the extermination of a loathsome insect."

"I beg you to reconsider," said Albragon, the fat man perspiring and twisting uneasily in the grasp of his captors.

Vorselus said, "He, perhaps more than infamous Kardowan himself, is responsible for all the woes that befell me. This creature lured me into the trap that made me a refugee. I will cut him down myself." He drew forth his sword, keen to match deed to words.

"Less haste, I beseech you!" cried Albragon. Smiling his oiliest, he went on, "Before you act, my fellow citizens, ask these heroes of yours how they caught me, under what circumstances."

Prodded with questions, the leader of the captors explained, "My lords, he came running to us, I grant, with a pack of our enemies at his heels, and threw himself into our arms. He made for an easy catch."

Nantrech said, "Albragon, this odd tale buys you a few strained minutes of life, solely because it piques my curiosity. Tell all, dismal fellow, and make good your oratory."

Albragon told. He talked endlessly, earnestly, rapidly, as if dreading to pause for breath until all was said. This, in sum, was his story:

"I am now, as ever, a loyal servant of glorious Skyrax. I stand for Dyrezan, without regard for my own reward. Yes, out of foolishness I served—nay, cooperated with—Kardowan, but he was the King's choice, not mine. Like you, I was ever skeptical of his motives, but I reined my concerns to the dictates of my sovereign. Seek no blame in that.

"I sought nothing for myself. Only Kardowan grew greedy for unlimited power, unfettered by any restraint. He behaved accordingly. His actions became oppressive by degrees, then monstrous by bounds. This infernal war; so unnecessary, entirely orchestrated by him, for his sole benefit. Finally I could not stand it. I withdrew from his circle.

"No more could I do. He has the King in his palm, sealed from genuine news. Skyrax does not understand! Kardowan pressed me for aid. I pleaded indisposition. As a result, my own situation grew dangerous! Then I heard of your return, my lords. I knew what I must do. By my unwilling association with Kardowan I possessed freedom of movement. I approached the lines as if on assignment, then made a break for it. Barely did I escape. I come as a friend! I wish to serve the cause of justice."

With Albragon removed to safe keeping, the patriots communed over these developments. Said Vorselus, "It is a pack of lies he speaks from beginning to end, interspersed with minor snippets of truth. Phillipan, tell them. We saw."

Said the officer, "My friend describes the matter rightly. They were thick as thieves, Albragon and Kardowan. Our new compatriot supported the ogre so long as he expected the crown to be handed to him. They fell out over Kardowan's ambition and increasing brutishness. Now the fat one turns his coat again. Believe me, his instincts are self-serving."

"And possibly useful to us," interjected Lord Nantrech.

Lord Morca nodded. "It nauseates me to admit, but we can turn this offal to account. I cannot deny his greatness as a sorcerer. Let us employ this tarnished resource in our interests, keeping him under our thumb. I will offer him a choice without options, snapping his neck myself if he balks."

Vorselus sniffed at this, groaned out of pent frustration. Morca clapped him fondly on the shoulder, said with sympathy tinged with barely suppressed anger, "It is a pity, but this moment demands the most pragmatic wisdom of us all. We need him."

XVII. KING SKYRAX CHANGES HIS MIND

They knew something of frightful bigness impended, for of the night the outposts of Kardowan's army withdrew from their forward positions in many parts of the city, leaving the patriot forces facing silence and empty desolation. Lord Morca passed the word that all his men brace themselves for the emergency about to erupt. Then with the dawn the awesome voice of Kardowan, magnified to superhuman pitch, thundered and reverberated from the sky, threatening torture, madness, and death as the penalties for defiance. It was his legions that struck first, advancing in a solid wedge, a phalanx of grim men heralded by showers of blinding, stinging, searing magic. This, it soon became clear, heralded their all or nothing assault, the battle to end the war and grind their foes into

156

oblivion. No longer a contest of position and advantage, they came as a rampaging horde, seeking not to occupy and conquer, but to slaughter and destroy.

They hurled themselves across the demolished grand avenues, through the woebegone parks of the corpse-fouled Tethe, down the Ancient's Road into the blasted wreckage of the olden poor district where lay the heart of their opponents' hosts, coming to grips in fury at the outset, giving no quarter, hardly sparing themselves. Kardowan, it came to be known, had whipped his men into a drunken frenzy, to a fever pitch of blood-lust, terrifying them with the consequences of failure, promising them heaps of stolen wealth and avaricious mastery as reward for victory. They charged. Magical blasts shot back at them, but they came on, battling block by block into the dense network of antique stone houses and shops, stabbing, slashing, impaling.

Under the resolute command of Lord Morca the defenders weathered the storm. Their casualties mounted hideously—the butcher's bill left its red fee splashed on walls, in doorways, in the streets—but they fought on grimly, giving up ground step by step against superior numbers, yet never surrendering terrain without a fight. The formal advance degenerated into a hundred close combats, each a microcosm of the battle for Dyrezan.

As the day dragged on, one death at a time, each tick of the clock a lost life, Morca called in his men from all over the city, funneling them into the critical areas, building up ferocious strength. Vorselus took charge of the employment of his magic, which in the sure hands of his comrades (and yes, in the hands of dubious but mighty Albragon) began to decimate the attackers. Perhaps they had not expected that rain of the murderously arcane. At last, with the battle sweeping over Morca's command post in an abandoned market, leaving it consumed by flames, the frightful onslaught faltered.

"Now is the time to crush them," Vorselus advised. "We have the numbers now, and our magic matches theirs. Let us pound them until they break."

"Not hardly," replied Morca. He had led from the front, inserting himself with uncanny timing and precision into a dozen critical contests, turning them all his way. Stern strokes had riven his armor with dents and splotched it with blood, his black hair steeped in crimson where it protruded from his gashed helmet. Soot stained his sunned face. He said, "It is not my plan merely to drive them back. By their own detestably spirited efforts they wade into the mire. I

157

could expend ten thousand driving them out. Instead, we circumnavigate their masses, strike for greater prizes. Remember that our King, may the Gods protect him, is a befuddled prisoner, knowing it not perhaps, yet ever in danger. Lord Varador!"

"Ever ready, your liege," responded that battered nobleman, who had fought likewise, to the extent his worn old body would allow, and more than was meet. "What say you?"

"Locate for yourself a new base of operations. You will direct our advance in the coming day. Here are your orders."

Kardowan's army burrowed like moles that night, solidifying their lines across the contested zone, preparing to renew the battle on the morn. It did not develop as they anticipated. Abjuring movement, they braced for blow and counter-blow, a continuous war of bludgeons. Vorselus, privy to the schemes of his lord commander, realized what the mind of that clever campaigner meant to the fortunes of his side.

Teresia had accompanied Vorselus throughout that interminable and gory ordeal, ever at his side where she was as safe as anywhere else in the blood-crazed city, conveying messages for him or tending the wounded when need arose. To her he said, as blackest night began to pass, "This day look for wonders and glories that will be told in song so long as Dyrezan endures."

The grand counter-attack commenced. It got underway in the dark, as a sweeping maneuver by large elements of picked troops including Morca's heroic little band, the dwindling survivors from the Rhexellite campaign who spearheaded the thrust. They swung behind their own lines to the west, then south, beyond the interlocked battle lines, then turned to the east at a swift march. With the dawn they were driving down the Avenue of Azamodeus toward the royal center of the city. At first meeting no opposition, they shortly encountered wandering detachments of enemy hooligans, men more eager for rapine than combat. Morca and his van snapped them up by mouthfuls, obliterating them, trooping on past their mangled corpses. Treenya, as much a soldier as any man, pranced among the fleshy debris, roaring her bloody satisfaction. Presently a more serious blocking force appeared ahead. These were soldiers of the Royal Guard. Morca took matters into his own hands, mounting a horse and galloping forward alone to face them.

"Dare you draw sword against me?" he thundered after revealing his identity, bawling at them like a squad leader dressing down raw recruits. "Which one of you chooses to lay down his life for the usurper, that you may swap strokes with your just lord?" Those men across the way broke into cheers, crying out, "You are Lord Morca, whom we obey in all things. Lead us, we implore!" So they crossed over, as a body, to join their natural leader.

"Guard the rear," Morca commanded them, "against attempts to cut us off. The rest of you, follow me. We march to liberate the palace of Skyrax!"

In their rush down the Avenue of Azamodeus they approached the finest section of the city, which in their confident eagerness they desired to quickly emancipate. Unfortunately their route ran them square against the flank of Kardowan's main force. A vicious combat broke out. The officers were all for driving home against the foe, but Morca would not be turned from the grand prize. To the consternation of his men he called retreat, broke off the battle. Confusion reigned in the ranks until he ordered the side-stepping march that carried his army around the enemy, and via side streets on a course leading inexorably to the great plaza. The towers of the court of Skyrax loomed dead ahead, the huge square to the fore masked by a large assembly of enemy troops. Though accoutered as Guards, from a long way off Vorselus recognized their commander by his mutilated face, and knew those soldiers for what they were.

"That is Garok at their helm!" he cried. "These be the retainers of arch-demon Kardowan himself. They are criminals all, the backbone of his hellish reign. He counts on them to deny us the palace."

Replied Lord Morca, "Then Kardowan miscalculates. Form the ranks. Files to the left: advance at the charge!"

This battle was naught but crazed murder. Every man of both sides recognized the stakes, understood the critical nature of this fight. Glory or desperation drove each soldier to paroxysms of brutal prowess. Swords clashed; shields rang under ringing blows; spears jabbed and flew; arrows whistled at close quarters in speedy profusion. It was a welter of death and pain, a kaleidoscopic amalgamation of a thousand fleeting moments of individual hopes and torments. Vorselus flung magic until the chaotic nature of grisly melee precluded it, his efforts endangering friend as well as foe; then loosed his sword and rushed into the fray with the best of them, ignoring Teresia's pleas that he protect himself from needless harm. Perhaps madness unleashed reigned at large that day, but Vorselus, when he found time to think, felt himself not alone in the irresistible tide of craving to deal mortal punishment. This he did, until a big brute's smashing sword blow against his shield numbed his arm and hurled him to the pavement stunned, the massive stroke reverberating throughout his body into his brain. The battle raged over him, surged past, became like a dark dream.

He saw, as a befuddled spectator, something of Lord Morca's duel with ugly Garok. The great sorcerer was wholly capable of besting his scarred opponent with arcane skill, but that was not his way in the thick of a fight. Morca swung his sword like a club, wielded his shield like a battering ram, relentlessly hammering Kardowan's chief henchmen. That one snarled, "Back, or the King dies!" which only increased the fury of the onslaught. A fresh stroke of singing steel sent his sword flying into the air, a hand still grasping it. Garok faltered, went down to one knee, his one whole arm upraised for mercy. His ugly face twisted in anguish, he begged for life. Morca's sword stabbed the wretch to the heart, grating on the flagstones at his back.

The defense collapsed. Kardowan's survivors scrambled pell-mell in every direction, the remorseless avengers at their heels. A few of the fugitives broke wildly for the palace. Bellowed Morca, "Cut those rascals down. Eternal shame on us if they reach the palace steps!" They did not. A pack of remorseless pursuers, soldiers blood mad, led by a ravening, hissing beast of a monster black cat, encompassed them and dragged them down, massacring them before the stone stairs that mounted to the great doors.

Treenya proudly rejoined Lord Morca as he issued a stream of orders to any squads within earshot. Vorselus, groggy but on his feet again, stumbled after the units dispatched to enter the grand edifice, verify the safety of the King and guarantee his continued health. They passed the doors, dashed through halls, searched for stray enemies, overawed and questioned the palace servants. The King lived! Skyrax waited safe in his chambers, accompanied only by a handful of royal officials, plus the few court magicians who had wisely withdrawn from the fight before it commenced. Vorselus, with his fellows, made for the stated location, but at that door a big hand grabbed him by the shoulder and stopped him with a jarring yank that rattled his teeth.

Cautioned Morca, "Not yet, my friend. The King has heard sinister tidings of you. Let me seek audience with our lord, and in the doing seek to restore your reputation with him. I dare say that the evidence of my own senses shall suffice to absolve you."

So Morca entered the chamber alone, leaving his people and

Vorselus without the door, and from there Vorselus heard all. The King greeted his long time counselor with heart-felt warmth, first expressing genuine puzzlement that he lived, for he had been told otherwise by his more recent minister. Morca, stained and scarred by battle, bowed to his sovereign and coolly reported, "Sire, there is much of error in that which you have been told and, I fear, calculated error, the product of deliberate mischief. Grant me leave to correct the record." Morca launched into a fulsome and exacting disquisition on the events of those tumultuous months, explaining and justifying his own actions, revealing the enormities of Kardowan to which, until this moment, the King had still been curiously blind. Also Vorselus, among many others, Morca absolved of blame for mythical crimes. When he had done Skyrax responded in a casual, chatty fashion, saying:

"Well, I suppose there is much for which good Kardowan must answer. Perhaps he inadvertently exceeded his authority. That is not proper, no indeed. I will have words with him, that I will. Dear Lord Morca, you must see to it. Find Kardowan, bring him to me, that he may resolve to my satisfaction these disputed matters. Maybe it will prove necessary for me to chastise him."

Vorselus wished to shout a reply, but of course he checked himself. Teresia came up with the Princess Lora, whispering girlishly. Lora said quietly, "Good Vorselus, happy I am to find you safe, and my friend Teresia, who risked all for us. There should be a song for heroines as well as heroes. Does my father love you again?"

"It appears," said Vorselus dryly, "that I am once more a citizen of good standing in fair Dyrezan."

"Which is merely your right, well-earned and owed. Teresia tells me of your exotic and perilous adventures since last I saw you. Surely the King shall show appreciation for your services."

Morca emerged from his audience, declared, "By the King's command, Lord Nantrech and I again serve our master, while Kardowan is formally deposed from office. Our sovereign imposes cumbersome complications. You heard?"

Vorselus nodded with wry face, said, "All, my lord."

"Quite." Aside, Morca said to him, "I tell you that I have already condemned Kardowan as a treasonous wrong-doer. He will not soil the King further with insolent lies. The usurper must die. I intend to arrange it on the sly. That outcome, however, depends on circumstances. The contest hangs still in the balance. We have work to do. Let us return to war, now with the entire blessing of King

161

Skyrax."

Events crowded upon one another that day and the next. At Morca's behest Skyrax issued a stream of mandates, requiring that Kardowan produce himself for interrogation; that the army of Kardowan lay down its arms; that the Royal Guards accept orders, as formerly, only from Lord Morca; that the court magicians and the various instruments of state place themselves at the beck of Morca and Nantrech.

This transfer of power proceeded with remarkable smoothness and speed, largely because Kardowan's military engine suffered an unexpected—nay, shocking—collapse when the news of the King's liberation spread throughout the city. The Guards necessarily deserted him at once, never having gladly submitted to his whims or the dictates of his hand-picked officers. Some of the latter fell into line, many others abandoning their troops to join their master, having carried out his sternest commands with too much relish. They were temporarily safe from retribution. A few more, choosing to flee too late, met justice at the hands of their men. Those were messy affairs, but final.

Many more deserted him, the commoners impressed into his service with threats, others who had clutched at his star during the period of his ascendancy. With his numbers drastically diminished, Kardowan's remaining legions of renegades withdrew sullenly from their posts across Dyrezan, surrendering the wrecked districts over which they had fought so hard and so meanly, harried all the way by the victors. His soldiers filtered back into the best section of the city, where the great ones kept their homes, anchoring that still extensive stronghold on the forbidding castle of Kardowan. There he prepared to accept siege.

This was known, for the rebel lord continued to issue pronouncements via magic that blanketed the city with his ostensible estimate of the situation. "A coterie of murderers and plunderers," his voice explained, "have invaded our glorious city from without and, having feloniously seized the person of the King, force him to act as their helpless instrument. Their leaders, the false Nantrech and Morca, assuming the names of the celebrated dead, come to poison and pollute. Swords and spears of the upstarts shall not avail against my invincible arts. Be bold and brave, my people, for I will restore the sanctity of Dyrezan."

Foolish bravado perhaps, but the fellow had nothing to lose by spouting so hotly, and Vorselus wondered if it were all vain rhetoric.

162

He spoke thus at an informal conclave called by Lord Nantrech in the receiving hall of the palace to discuss the state of affairs. Everyone of note was there, if only to hear and indulge in the grandeur of that moment of history.

Vorselus said, "Kardowan is a rat in a trap, but that trap is a well-fortified castle, defended by the determination of those other vermin who rightly expect no mercy from our justice, and therefore will not give themselves—or their lord, the chief bulwark of their strength—up to us. Also, he wields the most monstrous magic, which he may now employ, in a constricted area, solely for his own defense. He cannot count on winning the upcoming fight, but he may expect not to lose it, in these circumstances. It is a knotty problem. I do not look forward to this next clash with eagerness."

Phillipan warmly responded, "He's beaten and he knows it. I'll lead the charge against his walls myself."

Teresia, seated behind Vorselus with her boon companion the Princess, leaned over his shoulder, whispered, "That's right, isn't it? We've got it made."

Said Lora, "If by that you mean, that surely our brave warriors no longer fear defeat at his hands, then yes. All we have to do is enter the beast's cage and roust him out."

"Do not look for that blessed event with such ease," replied Vorselus. "Kardowan's cage constitutes the strongest fortifications in the city. In elder times the structure served as a royal prison. I presume our enemy laid in a well-stocked larger prior to the recent festivities. He might hold out indefinitely."

The lords of Dyrezan inclined to this same view. Said Varador, "Our men draw the net tight about his perimeter, but from that our foes refuse to budge. Not an hour ago a shower of burning rain fell on a company that advanced too far forward. Now I have more dead men, to no purpose."

Said Nantrech, "We should do nothing by halves. Also, look not to a contest of physical strength. Judicious art must win the day."

"That is the proper deduction," Morca replied gravely. "I spent all last night preparing myself for the coming bout. We must blast Kardowan with the concentrated energies of the Gods, channeled through the collective abilities of every man among us skilled in the mystic arts."

Said Harmon, "Perhaps this our less than favored guest may confer his opinion."

Morca nodded. "With this you agree, Albragon?"

That one stirred uncomfortably in his seat. Associated with these men out of necessity, yet held apart from them due to their suspicions, Albragon's lot was a miserable one, fraught with the peril faced by a friendless man who dreads a single misstep. His brow glistened as he said, "You war against the very devil in Kardowan, wise, cunning, and merciless. Think of the blood on his hands. He will stop at nothing.

"Great in all the ways of magic, he has specialized in the arts that kill. On his own ground his skills must devastate. No one of us— perhaps not even you, mighty Morca—can stand before him. A concerted effort, possibly, may bring him down. You spoke of the Gods, Morca. I implore that we invoke Them for our protection before we dare enter his den."

"We shall see," growled Lord Morca, "when it comes to it, who is the better man. I say it is settled: we strike. Marshal the army for fateful endeavors. Beg King Skyrax to encourage the men with royal praise. Gather together all the liberated materials of the magicians at our command. Stoke the enchanted fires, whisper the words, steep the potions that generate the mysteries of terror and death . . . and yes, pray to the blessed Gods, all of Them, fair or foul, that victory be ours. To Their king, especially, we must pray. Let Xenophor smile on us when next we march, even He, to whom all worldly deeds are naught but dust. Let us go forth to bring Kardowan down."

So it was decided.

On the evening before the final assault Vorselus spoke thus to Morca, saying, "My lord, think of your own safety, and what it means to your comrades and fellow citizens, and to myself and my friends in particular. I, your devoted friend Phillipan, and my girl Teresia suffer from a nagging curse imposed by personalities of another age, a curse which I am unable to lift with my own pitiful powers. No doubt remains in my mind that you are the answer to our dilemma. The solution is yours to seek and to command. I beseech you, give us this chance. For once, allow others to risk life and limb in your name."

Replied Morca, "Vorselus, you are my brother in arms, and Dyrezan is indebted to you for much more than your sword can bestow. Phillipan is indeed my friend, and a fine officer, worthy of favor. This girl, I suppose, means something to you; she is surely the darling of the Princess, which must ever carry weight. All that I grant. Do not ask me, however, to shirk duty by one whit. Tomorrow means glory or death for us all. I shall not rest until the black scorpions of the deepest hells snap at the slimy soul of Kardowan. Tomorrow he dies, or I die. Great Xenophor Himself inscribed that truth in fiery letters on tablets of iron at the beginning of time. Thus He wrote at the first moment of eternity, and shall it remain ever so, until a thousand eternities pass. Therefore forbear, I say. Know without question that, should I survive, all my arts will be bent to your purpose." Vorselus humbly thanked him, but took leave with a heavy heart.

XVIII. MORCA VS. KARDOWAN

The lords of Dyrezan, the warriors and the magicians, did everything they could to ensure that their fighting hosts could break the enemy line. Lord Morca said it could be done, and it was done, under cover of darkness in the hours before dawn. A barrage of magic spells blasted and blinded the soldiers of Kardowan where they crouched in their trenches within the ugly ruins of the river park, and through that gap surged the avenging army. Scarcely had they commenced the advance when the arcane retorts of mighty wizardry struck back, felling men in droves. The sinister harvest continued without let up, death heaping upon death, movement hindered by the grotesque obstacles of shattered, burned, and bloodied bodies underfoot. The defenders at the point of breakthrough held out long enough for the rest of their compatriots to withdraw behind the formidable dark gray walls of Kardowan's castle. Morca's legions tramped through the lawns and gardens of that benighted citadel, taking up stations as first light breathed on the highest battlements.

Brave Phillipan volunteered to lead the first wave of attackers—the forlorn hope—against the massive, heavily defended gate, trusting to momentum to see them through without delay. Vorselus groped his way through the gloom, through the billows of acrid smoke and poisoned air to warn his friend against rashness. "Valorous fellow, you have nothing left to prove," said he. "Preserve your life, and that other, without regret, for you have established your bravery before man and the Gods." And Teresia, who somehow, impossibly, had won through with her master, cried, "Phillipan, come

165

back with us, that we may all live, we three and more." But Phillipan, his blood afire, heeded them not, save to say, "We shall sing together of great feats and happy days to come, when the ogre is dead," and then he left them, to stand at the head of his men, and to lead them with a rousing shout against that gate.

They advanced with shields held high against the rain of arrows and spears, with men between their files laboring to haul forward engines of war, battering rams with blunt granite heads propelled on armored transports rolling ever faster on iron-shod wheels. Straight up the ornamental path to the gate they marched and dragged and pushed, picking up speed, bracing themselves against the shattering impact. Then a sinister laugh from above assailed their ears, and murderous power smote them. An avalanche fell from the skies, an earthquake rocked the air; nothing seen, nothing heard other than a quiet rumbling from nowhere, only men went down suddenly as if an invisible mountain had toppled onto them. The engines smashed to pieces, splintered and crushed flat, and likewise the hardy warriors of Dyrezan died in quick but tragic manner. Amidst the wreckage and charnel debris one man still stood: Phillipan, alone beneath the gate, brandishing his sword, his features contorted by hatred and amazement.

Vorselus, who guessed the source of that insidious laugh, heard now from a distance the sneering of the reptilian voice that followed, those familiar genteel tones curiously altered by the evil that saturated them. "Welcome, noble guest," mocked Lord Kardowan from his perch atop the high wall over the gate, "welcome Phillipan, who wishes to call on me. I appreciate the honor, but you come early for the entertainment. While I complete the plans for my invited guests, amuse yourself with this taste of my hospitality." And Kardowan spoke a word, said it simply, without drama, yet it sounded like the howlings of ten thousand fiends. And Phillipan cried out, and he jerked weirdly, and he began to dance, the spasmodic motions of muscles controlled by a source other than his own will. And blue light radiated from his tautly twisting frame, flashing and crackling, and he screamed once. No more was heard from him, for on the instant his armor fell away, revealing his bare skin; then his skin sloughed off, exposing the wet lumps and cords of viscera beneath; then he unraveled hideously, spinning and staggering mindlessly until nothing but the white bones obscenely pranced. They dropped in a heap, terminating the nightmarish performance.

"By the Gods," shrieked Vorselus, "it cannot be! Not now, not like this, not in this insanity. Kardowan, I swear you will pay dearly for your spite."

"So he will, Vorselus," Lord Morca roared harshly, anger shaking him, "and it will happen all the sooner if you get back and continue with your making of magic. Stir the fires of your hate and of your cruelest sorcery. Join me in fueling the arcane fury necessary to smash that gate."

Kardowan called, "I hear you, Morca. Why do not you come forward, that we may test ourselves with lancets of skill unknown to these lesser creatures?"

Morca replied, "Soon, my lord, very soon. I add to the ledger one more crime for which you must pay." He instructed Vorselus on what they must do, retired to gather the other mages for the effort.

Kardowan disappeared from the battlements, but his influence remained to fight against the power beamed at his fortress. This Vorselus knew, for despite his concentrated efforts, and those of Lord Morca, and Lord Albragon, and Lord Nantrech, and Lord Harmon, and a dozen more worthy mages, he felt resistance of force, a countervailing emanation that slowed the process which should have been instantaneous. For a dreadful, brain-pounding period nothing happened. Then the very walls of the castle shuddered, a peculiar rippling effect. Kardowan's fighting men aloft reeled, some dropping from sight. The big gate creaked loudly as if struck, though the battering rams lay abandoned and broken. The gate creaked again. Came a noise of ripping, cracking wood, a harsh, metallic grating as of misused joints, and the gate sagged on its hinges. It did not fall. A near miraculous power held it upright, like the arms of an unseen colossus holding it desperately in place. The hinges gave—sparks sputtered from the iron—they snapped apart, but still the giant door stood. Nothing but absolute will sustained it.

"Fall, blast you," groaned Morca, grimacing with actual pain. Vorselus felt sick and worn, at the end of his strength. "Fall!" shouted Morca, and Nantrech echoed him, the elderly mage sinking to his knees as if stricken, and suddenly the contrary force departed and the door fell, collapsing inward, crashing to the ground in a cloud of dust and flying splinters. With the entrance laid bare an enormous cheer rose from the crouching warriors tight-packed on the lawn. They leaped to their feet without awaiting orders and rushed the opening.

The defenders by this time were hopelessly outnumbered, and without stout walls of strong stone to protect their bodies they had no chance. They fought, with swords and spears, teeth and fingernails, fought because they must die, and few men submit meekly when hope is gone; fought on, until hacking steel finished them. Blood showered the gloomy courtyard. Treenya the tiger raced in with the attackers, claws like razors tearing open the enemies of her master, spraying their life juices. The outcome was sure, yet strange allies belatedly arose to support the handful who gained the keep. Out of the long shadows from beneath the walls and behind stairwells crept black, shambling figures with glaring red eyes flashing white talons from thick multiple arms, denizens of dark spheres called up by Kardowan to rend his enemies. They waded into the assaulting ranks, emitting repellent odors, squealing their hateful glee, swiping fiercely with horny pincers, and when those remarkably long and dexterous arms sliced the air, a man went down headless, or with trunk raggedly ripped, or limbs lopped. Men screamed in terror or roared with rage, but regardless they hacked and stabbed or grappled with the hideous things. Terrible those were, but it was too late, much too late, for the warriors of Morca to admit defeat.

They destroyed the monsters, chopping them at last into fragments that, for a spell, still quivered with unholy life. Treenya shredded the last one, worrying its remaining writhing fragment until it ceased to struggle and its unearthly stench overcame her lust for combat. The courtyard cleared of defenders, the walls vacant of humanity save for those victors who hoisted the royal banner of Skyrax to flap in the morning breeze, Morca commanded, "Search the manor, slaying anyone who opposes us. Break into the keep, wipe it clean of these filth, but do not attempt Kardowan yourselves. Discover his location and report."

Said Vorselus, "My lord, his power is broken. We can take him as a man. Let blades perform this task."

"No more, my friend; unhand me. I have spoken. Kardowan belongs to me."

Even Lord Nantrech tried to remonstrate with him. "Remember the pronouncement of Skyrax, that Kardowan be presented before him. Though little to our liking, we must obey."

Morca smiled. "I shall present him to our King, chunks of him in a sack, diced for dog's meat."

A soldier called from an upper window of the keep, that tower of angular stone, saying, "He lurks above us, my lords. Kardowan lies in the highest chamber, still defiant. I fear it is his secret room of magic."

168

"I dare say," muttered Lord Morca. "You there, I acknowledge. Retire to the courtyard. I come quickly." Without further word or gesture to his companions great Morca dashed into the keep, to vanish into its mysterious interior.

"After him!" cried Vorselus. He leaped over bodies, through the smashed door, pounded up the winding stairs, following the sound of rapid feet on the steps above. He heard others come after, heeded them not. He had little time to marvel at this portion of Kardowan's abode, though with leisure he might have seen much in the artistic adornments, the mysterious devices, to feed his aesthetic or professional interest. He thought only of the stairs leading up, past one floor, then another, then opening into a broad hall from which several doors beckoned. That one to the right still swung from being rammed by a ruthlessly charging body. Vorselus passed through, saw Morca ascending, with measured tread now, one final flight.

Morca disappeared into the chamber at the top. From within a faint red glow throbbed and flickered. A harsh voice screeched, "It is the finish! I shall live, Morca, to dedicate your bones to the Dark Ones. They will relish the taste of your succulent soul."

Vorselus reached the door. Soldiers crowded behind him. None chose or dared to enter. The chamber was octagonal, with high peaked ceiling painted with lurid images of indescribably ugly fanged horrors, walls of plated iron, festooned with scrolls and vessels on shelves, with a marble table in the center, greenish in hue, at least appearing so in the weird yellow glare of the urn that flamed and smoked upon it. Morca and Kardowan faced one another across that table. Its owner asked acidly, "Whom do I fight, an illustrious champion or a contemptible mob?"

Lord Morca discarded his sword and replied, "You deal only with me, traitor."

"Traitor?" Kardowan barked. He laughed, his sharp eyes bright, his high bald pate gleaming in the strange light. "Dyrezan is mine by right, by conquest, by desire. I do not authorize you to wrest it from me. Since you violate my commands, you die."

And on the stroke of the last word Kardowan attacked. He commenced the battle of mind and magic, his eyes spewing carmine beams from the force of his mighty conjuration. What that was Vorselus could not guess—what man alive could plumb the secrets of Kardowan?—but Morca staggered back, thrashing his arms and hoarsely groaning as he recoiled. Pain, or magically induced fear; one could judge solely from outward appearance. Huddling his massive arms to his body, Morca wrenched himself erect. The big man trembled, then steadied.

He motioned with two fingers, spoke a word which Vorselus recalled hearing among the Rhexellite sorcerers. He grinned, realizing that Morca had studied well, all the while masterminding his military campaign. Kardowan, much the smaller man, though just as deadly, shrieked and went to the wall as if blown by great gales. His skull cracked against iron plate. He sank to a crouch, gasping.

"That one is new to me," he croaked. "Very good. You offer me a legitimate contest, my lord. I approve." He staggered to his feet, began to mumble a fresh formulation.

A gray, bat-winged thing materialized, flew at Morca's face. Flailing nails scarred his cheek, gnashing teeth nipped at his eyes, until his large hands closed upon the unnatural creature, squeezing it to pulp. Another came at him, lunged for his eyes, to be knocked down by a hammer fist and stomped under gore-encrusted boots.

Kardowan panted, "It is little I asked, that I hold power over this domain. What is it to you, noble man, whether you serve my ability rather than the weakness of Skyrax? There would have been a place for you in my kingdom. Still there can be, if you seek not a death of agony at my hands."

Morca choked back, "Without the ancient tradition of Skyrax, we would ever be a clutch of warring wizards, all like you, grasping and killing for momentary gain, until the next thief of power raised his filthy head to renew the bloodshed. There must be peace at the heart of empire, or that empire dies. Dyrezan is eternal; therefore, history condemns you, and I condemn you."

"Not while the furnace of the Gods burns in my breast."

"Then I dowse that ill-used fire." Morca sliced air with his hand, hurling a sparking, gelatinous mass Kardowan's way. It splashed against him, enfolded him, ate into his white flesh. He bellowed in mortification, perhaps fear. He rallied somehow, scraping away the searing, clinging substance, held out both hands with fingers splayed and spat an incantation. Green rays shot from the ceiling, focusing on Morca's broad back, charring his armor molten and crushing him to the table, his teeth rapping on stone. His wrist swept against the flaring urn, overturning it. The sickly yellow glow faltered as the urn disgorged its bubbling, lumpy contents. Curious vermin, rather like spiders with far too many legs, crawled from the seething mess. Morca, recovering, smashed at them with the flat of his hand.

"Die, villain!" he cried, spewing between bloodied teeth a spell in a language wholly unknown to Vorselus, one not allied to any of the antique scripts that the lesser mage had studied. Weird lights flashed and blazed in that chamber. As if on command Kardowan stood oddly upright; which is to say, that he jerked fully erect as a puppet would propelled by strings, with his knees locked, his shoulders angled against the rules of anatomy, his thin arms bent as if to snap their joints. He opened his mouth wide and gave vent to a dreadful scream. Then, even more disturbingly, that terrible wizard began to plead, to beg mercy of his tormentor. Horrible sounds emanated from his spare frame. Invisible power rent, tore, ate at him. He sagged limply, like a man without bones.

"It is done!" he moaned. A dark radiance flared from him, and then Kardowan fell in a heap, to lie motionless on the stone floor. There seemed little enough of him now, crumpled like that.

The onlookers thrust into the room, crowded around victor and vanquished. Vorselus went to Morca, who likewise had fallen, helped him to his feet that he might lean against the table. That lord presented a tragic sight: bloody, marred, uncharacteristically pale, shivering from unnatural weakness. His breath rasped irregularly through flaccid lips.

An officer cried, "Commander, this one lives. The evil one holds to life!"

"Impossible," snapped Morca. He half fell across the table to observe what lay on the other side. Indeed, he espied faint signs of vaguely persistent animation in that gruesome pile. "Incredible," said Morca. "That spell should have killed a herd of Kardowans. Such power resides in that brain! I must esteem the wizard, while detesting the man."

Lord Nantrech arrived, pushing through the throng to take in the scene, learned all quickly by adroit questioning. Said he, "Our King, the benevolent Skyrax, has decreed. This one must be delivered unto him."

"On my responsibility," declared Morca, "on my head, I decree otherwise. I order that Kardowan be taken to the city ramparts, and from there his carcass be hurled into the void as just and necessary punishment."

"But our King—"

"Our beloved King relies on his faithful liege-men to protect him from murderous scoundrels. This charge of fealty I undertake as a duty. I see to it at once."

"As you insist, dear friend and conqueror," replied Nantrech, "so it will be done. The King will hold me accountable. I accept this woeful task—you men, remove the body, convey it hence!—I accept, while you recover your strained health. Lord Morca, I intend no insult by pointing out that you are good for nothing at the moment. Shake off the bale of magical combat. Regain your notable strength, for Skyrax may call you immediately to great deeds."

So Nantrech took charge, and he and the soldiers left that despoiled chamber with their wretched and insensible burden. Vorselus remained behind to conduct the faltering Lord Morca down the many steps to the pavement reeking of carnage below. Despite the awful vista the sun shone brightly now, emerging from behind rapidly fleeing black clouds, on this new day in Dyrezan.

Morca muttered to his wizardly helpmate, "It is over, Vorselus. Ours has been a glorious association, one filled with amazement and hardship and stirring mystery. I have not forgotten, friend, the strangest mystery of them all. Shortly my King will call, and I will attend to him and his concerns as I did before. First, however, I must pay a debt of honor. I seek rest, then my books, that I may study on your behalf. You are plagued by a two-fold mind. The time comes to break that spell, to release you, and to send the other, that Vorchek, back to his own age, never to disturb you further."

XIX. THE AWAKENING OF VORCHEK

Could it be doubted that the great Lord Morca, sorcerer supreme, he who bested the mighty Kardowan in combat arcane, would fail not to resolve the peculiar dilemma of Vorselus? Vorselus doubted, to be sure, but he had grown gloomy from travail and the long sojourn with his alternate self, to the point that he began to accept the intimations of a permanent condition. That the solution lay beyond his own ordinary powers he granted early on, yet this Morca was a wonderful man, even by the exalted standards of grandiose Dyrezan. No secrets were denied him, no sources of the high arts. He possessed insightful scrolls at hand to unroll, revealing their awesome secrets; chiseled tablets of elder mystery to peruse, laden with primordial lore; inscribed amulets tucked between corroded fingers in shunned tombs which, with his august connections, he

172

might purloin. In the fullness of time all these things Morca did, and he assembled relevant data, gleaned curious answers, gathered to himself the dreadfully costly materials required, and came the night he did the deed.

They met in the special chamber in the house of Lord Morca, only the three of them, Morca, Vorselus, and Teresia, who was quite obviously also a party to the proceedings, and whom the master magician accepted as a favor to his fellow mage. One other should have attended, but he had passed beyond mortal cares into the misty lands of the dead, laid in a hero's grave in a marble vault topped by an eagle's statue with lowered head and sad, drooping wings. He could not be there, which fact, and many memories, tore bitterly at the heart of Vorselus and at the mind he shared, as if that eagle assailed him with its claws to upbraid him for the loss of two, when the loss of one was sufficiently terrible.

Lord Morca donned for this task a unique robe, a filmy lavender-colored affair overlying his muscular frame, rather incongruous for the man, yet vital, for it was woven of exotic silks impregnated with rare spells. The fabric of his dress lent extra power to his finely honed skills. His unusual golden headdress, something quite unfashionable that peaked above his scalp and descended over his ears, he had likewise imbued with magic force, that gleaming helmet wrapping his keen brain in cosmic potency drawn down from ethereal spheres.

His private room of magic possessed a curious property of malleability, in that it could assume different shapes as he chose. For this rite he made of it (Vorselus could never grasp the how of it) a lengthy triangle, with Vorselus and Teresia at the far apexes, sitting on cushioned benches, while Morca stood before a trestle table loaded with odd accouterments at the end of the long angle. Behind and above him on the sooty wall of enameled brick glowered a frightful painted visage illuminated with surprising brightness by the blue flaring of the single dim table lamp. It was a terrible face, an amorphous greenish mass sporting a myriad of searching yellow eyes. They glared across the room at the two subjects with fiendishly life-like intensity.

Morca said, "I begin. Vorselus, I salute you for your service and devotion to justice throughout your long ordeal. Should I fail, inadvertently blasting you into the dark kingdom, know that your memory shall live."

Teresia whispered to Vorselus, "I thought you said he was the real deal."

Said he, "Hush, child." Her manner of speech, so affected by that obtrusive other personality, disturbed him. "We stand or fall on the merits of Lord Morca. That is the meaning of the prophecy told by none other than Jacob Bleek himself, whose *Black Book* and its oblique contents instigated our difficulties."

"You mean your meddling with it." "Not I. I have told you—" "You're just trying to dodge—"

"Silence." Morca's command carried enough gravity to bring them back to a sense of respect for the moment. He said, "In this hour I call on the Gods, no less, I seek of their King Xenophor, before whom all sentience grovels, for a boon."

And he spoke strange words torn from dim eras of history, recited the incantations wrested from unhallowed chronicles of the dead, and as he rapidly spoke he moved, quickly and economically, lifting beakers, mixing steaming contents, stirring them into a frothing cauldron, spicing the smoking solution with dashes of poisonous herbs and gritty powders of metals, mummy's dust and shreds of flesh best unsourced. That broth contained an effusion of chemicals never before composed by human intellect, not in all the long tale of man's existence and man's straining toward the extremities of arcane possibility. So Morca had characterized his scheme beforehand, and Vorselus had no firm cause for doubt. He wondered if the wizard Bleek, in some lost channel of the eons, had anticipated or reproduced this ritual. Perhaps he, but if so, then only he. Possibly, on the skirts of some unfathomed abyss outside eternity, he watched now, nodding and laughing.

Teresia suddenly cried out in terror, "What are you doing to me?" Vorselus said nothing, yet he must clamp his jaws firmly lest he cry out, for he felt too the swelling wave of sickness, the insidious pull from nether regions. On the instant the dimly seen room disappeared.

Vorselus, disembodied, without true physical sensation, nevertheless sensed himself falling into darkness that burned with its chill. Down, down, down he tumbled, a fall into foreverness, a plunge that spanned the alpha and omega of time. It did not end; it could never end, for there were not ages enough to the universe to encompass that fall. And it was dark and cold, the cold of lightless fires that frigidly scorched.

It was Professor Anton Vorchek who grew aware of the pulsating greenish glow at the impossible bottom of that limitless well of night. He remembered, as from a dream, what had gone before, groggily recognized himself for who he was, and vaguely for where, to the extent that he conceived a "where." He did not see or hear himself, but he knew of his existence. Nearby glimmered a pale, pink star that kept with him as he fell, he from that twinkling mote deriving impressions of familiar consciousness. It lived, that star, the essence of a human being, the spiritual fragment of Theresa Delaney, bound to him by the spells of Lord Morca. They journeyed together toward their destination.

For an instant this realization cheered Professor Vorchek. Then doubts crept into his non-corporeal mind, the wisp of entity that was he. What meant this thing that lay below, the green immensity? Not below now, but ahead, sprawling amorphously before and beyond. It roiled and seethed; lights glittered within it. No, not lights, but eyes, yellow eyes in their thousands, millions, billions; he imagined an eye for every soul that had ever lived or would, an eye for each atom created from bemused nothingness at the beginning of all. Every eye watched him as he drew near.

A voice spoke. Not a voice—no words, no logic of grammar— yet he understood, and with a body of flesh he would have shivered. It said, "Return as thou wilt, dust, or embrace Me. Accept the mockery of My illusions, become one without care or hope within My essence. Choose this, and struggle no more."

In thought Vorchek cried, "No."

"So be it. It matters not, until the end of being it matters not. Then, for a pitiful period, your meaningless dance goes on." That thing—the greenish, ever watchful cosmos of intellectual ice— vanished. It slipped sideways, somehow, and was gone. Came darkness again, unbounded darkness forever.

So it seemed for cycles of eternity, until a speck of faint light appeared ahead. It expanded, until Vorchek recognized in that tiny mote the entirety of the universe that he knew, the one into which he, his unique persona, had been naturally born. It grew until he made out galaxies with their myriad stars, black clouds of fulminating gas drifting in the vast spaces between. He saw this from afar, but it came quickly closer, as if viewed down a widening tunnel.

The pink star remained with him, as if tightly linked. He saw something more, away to his side in the surrounding night: a feeble flickering of hazy gray radiance, fitfully sparking at intervals. Vorchek imagined that it tried to make itself seen, weakly to pace itself to his motion. He did not wish to ponder the meaning of the thing, but something about it held him, tugged at his soul. What was it? Did he detect the rudiments, the half-effaced dregs of mentality in that patch of weakly glowing mist?

Suddenly he realized the truth, and without vocal apparatus Professor Vorchek managed to scream, "Philip, Philip, hear me! I see you. Hang on, boy, stay with me, hold yourself together in my presence until my flight be done!"

The material universe exploded around him. He dived past, around, and through blazing suns, white, yellow, blue, red, shrieking along at incredible speed, at a velocity that made the speed of light seem a snail's pace. One galaxy, another, still another; there one he thought he recognized from astronomical photographs; yet he approached it not, but swung away toward another of lesser size, unfamiliar but relatively near. It grew big—it dazzled him as it filled his vision!—he sailed straight into it. Individual stars again flashed by. One loomed dead ahead, a trivial yellow star like countless others. It came at him with breath-taking speed. A pale crescent of a world in white and blue thrust itself between him and that star. All went black once more.

The return of sensation came to him first as a back-hand slap of pain. So his snapping, awakening nerves informed him, although only seconds passed before he understood the feelings for what they were, the characteristic signs of normal, if strained physicality. He felt pressure on his face, on his hands, his chest, the soles of his feet, pressure weighing lightly across his body. His body: he was clothed, with his feet to a floor, his upper torso, hands pressed to the table. He felt himself in relation to the universe. He pushed himself up in his seat, struggled to grasp his surroundings. This table—this room—all had changed. The impressive figure of Lord Morca before him had vanished, and with him that strange milieu that had become familiar. This weird, exotic place; it required a forced expenditure of mental ability to recognize it as his basement laboratory. He, master of this small domain, who knew himself as Professor Anton Vorchek. The dominating element of the wizard Vorselus had been banished from his mind.

On the table in the gloomy room lay the book of Jacob Bleek and the Cross of Xenophor. The cross glowed faintly. Vorchek reached out to touch it. It felt oddly warm, like a living thing. As he watched the glow died, the warmth departing under his fingers. He drew back his hand.

A little cough caught his attention, drew his eyes to focus on the girl. She raised her head—that golden blonde head of hers—revealed the welcome, healthy face of Theresa Delaney. She shook her head, glanced at him. Her eyes narrowed.

"You boob," she said. That was her customary voice. all right. "I'll never let you drag me into one of these nutty schemes of yours again. This takes the cake, even by your goofy standards. Next time you get a bright idea, count me out. I'm not sufficiently suicidal—"

Vorchek remembered something. "Hold that thought," he commanded, rose quickly and strode around the table to examine the third member of the team, the still supine Philip Matthews. Vorchek remembered everything. Fear chilled his heart. He gripped a rubbery wrist, felt for a pulse, to his enormous relief found one. He rolled the fellow onto his back atop the table, massaged face and temples, slapped from him hints of life. "Snap out of it, boy. Hear me. Come back to us."

Within minutes Philip had revived to his attendant's satisfaction, complaining, "I feel like I've been drugged. I slept through the whole thing. What happened?" That, as it turned out, was the whole story from his point of view. Philip remembered nothing at all. He slept, he woke, and as soon as it was politely possible, they sent him packing, to drive himself back to town alone, never the wiser. Vorchek had no more use for him.

Still later, the professor and his pretty assistant conversed at leisure. Vorchek paced up and down, round about his den, puffing his pipe and fingering documents and books as he talked. Theresa lounged on the sofa, smoking her cigarette and sipping her drink (a tall one), with the graceful black feline Claudia snuggled against her thigh. She listened and, occasionally, interrupted.

Vorchek said, "In sum, not an altogether unprofitable session. I very definitely increase the scope of my knowledge. I achieved certain goals, with a minimal expense of time. Here comes the dawn. The entire experiment consumed mere hours, a trivial temporal cost for a wealth of data. All involved are hale and hearty, completely recovered from the employment of the arcane formula. I have established that Jacob Bleek's ancient *Black Book* does open pathways into hitherto unknown realms, and have done so economically and safely. When I think of that, my dear, I consider it quite an achievement. I am proud of my efforts, and you should feel proud as well."

"I suppose you mean proud of you," Theresa retorted, with just a tinge of heat in her languid tones. "Professor, I've held it back long enough. The way I parse it, you screwed up everything. Totally by accident you got us into a fine pickle. Oh, forget niceties, you got us into a deadly mess, is what you did. I'd tell you to crack Bleek's book again to find out what went wrong, only I'm afraid you'd do just that, and try to make it right, and this time get me offed for sure."

"You seem remarkably fit."

"No thanks to you! What happened to all that garbage about safely observing? You dunked us body and soul into that pukey world, got our brains mixed up with those of somebody else, and almost got us killed ten times over. Or is it a hundred times? When I think of the horrors that happened to me—" Theresa sat bolt upright, shuddering at the recollection. "Enslaved, abused by perverts, hunted by thugs, and generally treated like dirt most of the time: there's your success. What if I'd died over there?"

"Ask Mr. Matthews."

""He was real lucky," Theresa sulked, "and so are you, otherwise you'd have his death to explain. You'd count on me to back you up. What could I say?"

"Something meet and to the point, I am sure," Vorchek soothed. He grinned lamely, sat beside her, knocked out his pipe in the ashtray. "Fair enough, Miss Delaney. You win. I confess to certain unexpected developments. I go so far as to admit that the experiment undertook, of its own accord, to carve its own sinuous channel like a river in flood, without controlling input from myself."

"Hallelujah."

"Also, I note with deep regret, it proved impossible, employing that particular spell, to retrieve corporeal artifacts which would objectively establish the reality of our journey. Mr. Matthews, I suspect, has drawn a permanent blank, so we do not even have a disinterested witness to verify our stories. The recollections of the experience are wholly subjective."

"Like a bad dream."

"But it was an adventure," he pointed out. "We may be the sole denizens of our age vouchsafed such a unique experience. In return for a night of quiescence, we have been granted a mighty span of life replete with wonders and marvels, great feats and grand surprises. That alone—never mind the fascinating knowledge—should commend the effort to you."

"It doesn't," she replied. Theresa stubbed out her cigarette, gulped the last of her drink, hopped to her feet. Claudia grumbled at the loss of her human pillow. "Maybe it will tomorrow. Right now

178

I'm worn out, bushed, just happy to be alive."

"Tired? But you have done nothing."

"Well, Teresia did—remember her?—and I lived every bit of it, and it practically busted me. I'm heading home, going to sleep the day away. Don't you dare call me." And that, presently, was that. Professor Vorchek puffed alight another full pipe as he watched her speed away in her sporty coupe. Her thoughtlessly churlish views distressed him, but he guessed she would get over it. Miss Delaney was a remarkably versatile girl, with a pleasingly elastic nature. She would be there for him, when he called.

He returned to his den, removed the book from where he had secreted it in a drawer, sat down in his easy chair and lovingly thumbed through it. Claudia joined him, dark as ebony like another kindred feline of long ago, assumed possession of his lap. The *Black Book* history called it, this tome of the mysterious Jacob Bleek. That suggested darkness, benighted secrets, the unfathomable. That was wrong, thought Vorchek. The book revealed rather than hid, explained rather than obscured. It contained a wealth of intellectual value. So far he had but dabbled with its possibilities.

"And Bleek was wrong," Vorchek declared. "Yes, he himself, despite a limitless intellect. His weary soul views the universe large and sad, through eyes obscured by oppressive ennui. Our advent into that world meant more than an eddy of hapless fate. We intruded into a particular place and time, one in which our actions counted. Every trivial event, every stray conception introduced by our mental presence mattered, had an effect on the outcome. Something more than empty chance was at work there."

He genially mused, "Vorselus was a decent fellow, one whom I could quite admire; a product of his times, to be sure, but are not we all? As a comrade—one with whom I need not split a brain—he could prove invaluable. Also, I feel I owe him something for the trouble I caused him. Our modern methods should fascinate the man. Too, he can tell me much. There remains still the location of wondrous Dyrezan to discover. We might excavate there together, if I managed the affair properly. I have the book, with all its unplumbed secrets, and the cross, still steeped in its supernatural, perhaps godly power. Truly, I must determine a way—the appropriate means, mind you!—of getting Vorselus here." And before long Professor Vorchek commenced to study in earnest, seeking that specific olden formula of Jacob Bleek which could once more make happen the impossible.

179

Facts in the case of Jeffery Scott Sims:

A degreed anthropologist, wilderness enthusiast, and photographer who makes his home in Arizona, Jeffery Scott Sims is a writer of fantastic and weird fiction. He is the creator of popular characters such as Professor Anton Vorchek, investigator of strange mysteries; Sterk Fontaine, self-serving dabbler in the supernatural; Jacob Bleek, the obsessively questing medieval wizard; and the combative and colorful heroes of ancient Dyrezan.

His publications include the collections *Science and Sorcery*, *Science and Sorcery II, Science and Sorcery III, Eerie Arizona;* and the novel *The Journey of Jacob* Bleek, plus well over a hundred short stories of the bizarre and the macabre. A number of these tales are set in the exotic and mysterious wilds of Arizona, or in imaginary lands of far times and places, ranging from forgotten eras to the distant future.

The author maintains a literary web site, *The Weird Writings of Jeffery Scott Sims*, which in addition to providing useful information on his works also offers an ever growing collection of entertaining essays devoted to unique or unusual topics related to the weird tale. This material may be freely accessed at

http://simsweird.infinityfreeapp.com/index.html